THE
DECEPTION

FIONA PALMER

ABOUT THE AUTHOR

Fiona has been writing rural stories for Penguin and Hachette for years and is now indulging in her love of YA. She is a full-time writer, farm-hand, speedway racer and mum of two fabulous teenagers, from rural Western Australia.

www.fionapalmer.com
@fiona_palmer

The Recruit
The Mission
The Deception
The Crescendo

The Family Farm
Heart of Gold
The Road Home
The Sunburnt Country
The Outback Heart
The Sunnyvale Girls
The Saddler Boys
The Family Secret

Secrets Between Friends
Sisters and Brothers

ACKNOWLEDGEMENTS

I couldn't do this without Jim, thank you for always answering my questions and helping my creativity along. Also to my friends and family who read my work, thank you. To my writing buddies, especially Rachael Johns, thanks for helping and understanding. A huge thank you to Cathryn Hein for being the reason these stories are available in print. Thanks to Claire De Medici for being such a fab editor for this series. Big thanks to my family Darryl, Mackenzie and Blake for their understanding. My mum for being my biggest fan, both mum and dad read my work. And as always, thanks to the readers who make all this possible. Thank you.

For Jim Jim

CHAPTER 1

BANG!

Jaz jerked awake like she'd been slapped. Sweat coated her body, making her long black hair cling to her face and neck. Sucking in air, she waited for her heart to stop racing. A vein pulsed in her neck like a death march, just like it had the last few mornings. Yet another nightmare. The same one.

Jaz is fighting for her life, struggling with the bullet wound in her leg and fear racking her body as a man aims a gun at her best friend Taylor.

Tommy. The man who had seemed so nice when she'd met him. But now he is laughing, the sound scratchy and sinister. Jaz raises the gun she found in the gravel. There's no time left; even in the dark Jaz can tell by his breathing and his movement that he's going to kill Taylor. On instinct she fires. The big man pauses before his gun arm drops. His body crashes to its knees before toppling by her feet with a thud. Dead. She has killed him.

The only problem is, this isn't a random dream. It's a memory and it's replaying repeatedly in her mind, night after night. Each nightmare brings back new details: the echo of the gun, the thump as the bullet hit and tore through human flesh, the whistle of air that left his lips as he fell to the ground, and the metallic tang of the blood soaking the ground. She was a killer. And Jasmine Thomas wasn't even eighteen.

With a groan Jaz tried to sit up in bed, but pain shot down her leg. Another reminder of the truth; she only had to see the raw circle of skin around the bullet wound and reality slapped her wide awake.

And the worst thing? She had school today.

School seemed so inconsequential compared to what she'd just been through. So much for school preparing you for the rest of your life; self-defence and killing someone hadn't been covered in Human Biology or English.

Jaz fought off the nausea that came with her dreams as she tried to get dressed, covering her legs with tights. Which wasn't easy, with one leg out of action. But each day was getting better. Day three after the shooting and she could put a little bit of pressure on it. Jaz slung her schoolbag on her shoulder and grabbed the crutches before heading downstairs.

'Jaz, Taylor's here!' yelled her mum. Tasha stood behind the marble benchtop in the kitchen, skolling her coffee. 'Oh, there you are,' she said, spotting her. 'Do you mind taking Simon with you? I want to get to work early.' Tasha held out a chopping board with two pieces of toast.

Jaz grabbed them. 'Thanks Mum. Yeah, he can come with us.'

Tash came around and held Jaz's face in her hands, studying the split lip and bruising on her face. 'You should have put some make-up over that, sweetheart.'

Jaz pulled her face away. 'I forgot. It's okay, Mum.' They shared the same blue eyes, cheek structure and lean body shape, but that's where the similarities ended. Her mum had dyed blonde hair and fair skin, Jaz had midnight-black hair with skin that looked forever tanned. Not that she was complaining in the looks department, but she did stand out from the rest of the family. As if on cue, her half-brother got up from the dining table, completely ready for school to the point of perfection. He wore glasses like his father but hid them in his bag until class. Simon was also fair but had slightly greener eyes. He was three years younger.

'You still look like crap, sis. That'll teach you for not using your safety gear,' said Simon matter-of-factly.

'Thanks for your input, Si, I feel so much better,' she said with a sigh. If only it were that simple.

'Do you regret getting a skateboard now?' he said with a smirk.

'No. No pain no gain.' Jaz tried to smile, but it probably came off as a grimace. It was hard work lying to her loved ones while suffering pain, not to mention the guilt – she had, after all, killed one man, and probably another. Oh yes, her facial injuries were not from her skateboard. Instead they were inflicted by the first man, who'd caught her escaping the warehouse. He'd grabbed her, they'd fought and she'd knocked his gun away; then, more fighting, a punch to her face, and she'd dug into the gravel trying to escape when she'd found a brick. Jaz grimaced as she remembered all too clearly what she'd done next. The crunching sound echoed through her mind, churning her stomach.

'You okay, Jaz? Are you sure you're up to school? I'm worried you might still be concussed.' Tasha's eyes were piercing.

Jaz shook off her memories, hiding her fear, revulsion and sickness. Swallowing hard she smiled. 'I'm fine, just need breakfast.' Jaz took a big bite of her toast as if to prove it. It took everything she had to gulp it down.

A horn tooted.

'We're late. See you, Mum. Let's go, Si.' With her crutches she hobbled outside as quickly as she could, throwing the rest of the toast behind a big leafy plant in the garden while no one was looking.

Simon opened the car door for her. 'Thanks bro.' He smiled and climbed into the back. Arriving at Saint Christian's in the back of Taylor's blue Mustang was a social climb for Simon. Taylor had legendary status at school, which was funny because Jaz was at the other end of the scale and yet they were best friends. How it worked, she wasn't sure.

'Hey, Jaz. How's the leg?' Taylor had his sunnies on and an arm leaning out the window, just oozing sex appeal. His hand rested on the gear stick, waiting for her reply before they moved.

'It's getting better.' It was the truth, she could put pressure on it now. But it was such a relief to be beside Taylor because he knew the truth. After all, he'd been there too. You could say they jointly killed that man, both firing at the same time. Neither of them had hung around long enough to deliberate over whose bullet did the job, but she had checked for a pulse. Nothing. He was dead. If he had survived he would have come after them and they'd both be in danger – still, it didn't make Jaz feel any better or safer.

'Good.' Tay didn't smile. He hadn't smiled much since that night. Neither had Jaz.

They didn't talk in the car, too caught up in their own thoughts and not wanting to discuss things with Simon in earshot.

'Thanks for the ride, Tay,' said Simon when they reached school. He ran to catch up with classmates.

They remained in the car, staring at their school and the rush of kids.

'How are you sleeping?' asked Tay eventually.

'Not so good. You?'

Tay hardly shook his head, Jaz nearly missed it. 'What do we do, Jaz?'

She shrugged. 'I don't know. I'm just sorry I brought you into this.'

The leather seat crackled as he turned to face her. 'Jaz, is this really what you want to do? Risk your life?' His voice dropped to a whisper. 'Kill people?'

She couldn't raise a smile. The look on her best friend's face made her clench her teeth. 'It seemed so much more exciting and heroic when I first learned about what Ryan did,' she eventually whispered. 'And I was flattered when he said he wanted to recruit me. I did think it over a lot before I joined the Agency, Tay. I want to make a difference. I want a job that saves lives.' Tay shot her a look. 'Yes, even if it means killing others to do so. I could tell you about the loss of lives, kids hooked on drugs, mothers killed in cold blood over poppy fields in Pakistan.' Jaz squeezed her hands remembering the story Ryan told, of kids shot and pushed into a mass grave, all so they wouldn't be able to tell. Her voice grew stronger as she spoke. 'And what about that year nine kid last year who died from a drug overdose? This is my chance to do something about it. I'm sick of lying in my comfy bed watching death and destruction from afar and wishing I could do something about it. Don't you, Tay? Don't you want to do something worthwhile?'

'Of course,' he said gruffly. 'But I was thinking when I was much older, after being trained by the SAS or the Army. Not while I'm still eighteen. I knew it was possible in my future that I would fire a gun at someone, but … I just didn't think the blood would be on my hands so soon.' Taylor rubbed his thumb across his palm. 'I wake up still seeing your blood all over my hands, Jaz. Do you know how raw I've scrubbed them, and yet every morning it's back there.'

Jaz reached over, grasping his hands in hers. 'But I'm okay and I'm right here. I'm not going anywhere.'

'I can't believe Ryan got you into this mess,' he said angrily.

Not that long ago Ryan Fletcher had appeared in her local boxing gym, The Ring. His dark mysterious eyes had drawn her in until she was immersed into his life of lying and spying. He'd asked her to join his secret agency to fight the war against drugs, guns and bad guys. Jaz had said yes and hence started her own life of lies. Not to mention how deep her feelings had grown for Ryan, not that they were the reason she joined up. From her parents to her best friend Anna, she had to lie. It didn't sit right, and she knew it probably never would. Like a tumour in the pit of her stomach, it seemed to fester and grow with each mistruth. The only thing that eased that pain was knowing she was fighting for the greater good, to save those unable to save themselves. And to think Jaz had always wanted to do something important with her life, to make a difference. Well, she'd certainly got that chance with her new mission with Marcus.

Jaz pulled her hands back. 'It's not Ryan's fault, Tay. I'm just supposed to be learning the ropes and watching Marcus's father from afar. I took too many risks, which ended up involving you, and I'm sorry for that. None of this was supposed to happen.'

He lifted up his sunnies; motionless blue eyes held hers. 'Would you have ever told me about this? If you hadn't needed my help that night, would I ever have known?'

Her teeth were clamped so tightly her jaw began to ache. 'I wasn't allowed to tell you. It's a part of the job. I really wanted to, Tay. It's been killing me, keeping this all to myself.'

'So, that's a no?'

Jaz nodded. 'I did tell you bits, what I thought I could,' she added, but realistically she knew it wouldn't help. If Tay had been the one going on missions and keeping her in the dark, she'd feel just as disappointed and angry. 'If you were in my shoes, would you tell me? If Ryan had recruited you and swore you to keep it quiet, would you have told me?'

He pulled the keys out of the ignition and squeezed them in his hand until it went white. 'I guess not. So, Marcus is your mission, not your boyfriend.' He turned to face her. 'How does that work?' he said raising his eyebrows.

It was the million-dollar question that Jaz was still trying to figure out. 'It just does. He's a nice guy, that's what's so hard.' Jaz had questions of her own. 'Hey, um, when you came back to Ryan's the next day, what did he say? Anything?'

'Just that he had to leave and you still hadn't woken up yet. He wanted me to keep an eye on you, told me how to redo your dressing, then said to lock up, hide his key and that he'd try to catch up with us today. I think he wanted to be there when you woke up but he mumbled something about needing to meet with someone.' He shrugged.

His answer just created more questions. She already wanted to ask him what would happen now? Should she stay in contact with Marcus? Should she lie low? All this churned through her head and yet she still had to go to school. 'I don't want to be here today,' she mumbled.

'That makes two of us, but I'd rather be here than alone.' Taylor got out and ran around to help Jaz. Slowly they both headed through the big metal gates to school. Anna, their other best friend, was waiting for them by their usual seat.

'I hate lying to Anna,' mumbled Tay.

'I know.' The words caught in her throat.

'Hey, how's the pulled muscle?' said Anna when she saw them. Her long strawberry-blonde hair was braided down her back and her freckles moved as her large smile erupted. The white shirt and black school tie made Anna look as smart as she was, and her extra-long red-and-black tartan skirt screamed studious.

'You know, I'll live. Just another day in my life.' Jaz turned away to hide her cringe. 'And Simon already gave me a lecture on skateboarding, so you can save that.'

Anna opened then closed her mouth. 'I wasn't,' she said, but her cheeks flushed. 'How're you?' Anna touched Tay's arm. He'd been staring blankly towards the school.

He jumped a little. 'Yeah, fine. Hey, I'll catch up later at lunch.' Then he walked away, not even joining his mates. Even with his head down and his shoulders slightly hunched, he still looked strong and athletic. Taylor's steps were heavy as he merged with the crowd of school kids, his popular greetings and fist pumps missing from his normal morning routine.

'What's up with him? You know, he didn't return any of my texts over the weekend.'

Anna reached for Jaz's arm worriedly. Jaz flinched. 'Ouch. Watch the gravel rash.'

'Oh, sorry.' Anna dropped her hand but leaned in closer. 'Hey, you don't think something's up with Tay's dad, do you?'

That was a better theory than the truth, so Jaz went with it. 'Probably. I don't think he's taking it too well. His dad's always been this great cop, and to find out he's being blackmailed? You know Tay; it would be killing him not being able to help his dad.'

'I know. I think he just needs us around more. I've told Ricky that I can't see him as much as we used to, that you guys need me. He seemed okay about it.'

'Nice of him.'

'Yeah, he's cool. If he wants to see me he'll just have to sit with us at lunch and realise that Taylor won't bite. Don't know why he feels so scared.'

More like threatened, thought Jaz as the siren rang signalling the beginning of the day. As they made their way to class, Jaz tried to avoid any knocks on her leg in the crowded hallways. 'So, did you see Marcus over the weekend? Did he come and see you after your stack?'

'I didn't tell him. Didn't want to worry him or make myself look like a dick for face-planting in the first place,' she lied.

Marcus. What was she going to do about Marcus? He was the guy she was dating but only because he was her mission. His father was suspected of dealing drugs, and Jaz had been sent in to gather information. What was awful was that she liked Marcus. A cute, nice, sweet eighteen year old who, she suspected, knew nothing of his father's extra-curricular activities. And if Ryan wasn't around she'd seriously be happy dating Marcus, but she had to remember that he was just a mission, that this whole scenario was planned and that there was nothing real about it. Yet her time with Marcus felt genuine. Her head was so confused; nothing seemed easy.

Marcus had been texting her, but what should she reply? What could she possibly say after she'd killed the two guys who worked at his father's warehouse? The same two guys Marcus had introduced to her on their recent visit. Worse was what she found at that warehouse. She'd found the truth: Marcus's dad, Carl Sinclair, was dealing drugs. How could she look

Carl in the face again? Come to think of it, was her mission even over? Would they make her go back?

'What about Ryan? Seen him?'

Jaz sighed and felt as if she'd lost the last of her energy. Anna always seemed to know what was on Jaz's mind. Or maybe she just knew that Jaz had deep feelings for Ryan. Feelings she thought he returned.

After she was shot he'd told her that he cared; at least, she's sure she remembered that but with the pain could she have been delusional? When she'd woken the next day he'd gone. Jaz had been thinking about it ever since.

'No, he's off on another job.' Jaz said 'job' with meaning and Anna nodded understandingly.

'I see. So, no love from either one.'

At that moment a loud crash sounded down the corridor, causing Jaz to slam back against the lockers. Who would be firing a gun at school, she tried to rationalise while her heart was in her throat. Her eyes darted up and down the corridor.

'Jaz?' said Anna, who hadn't moved at all.

Why was she not ducking? Come to think of it, why was no one running around screaming? Taking in the scene before her, Jaz realised that it wasn't a fired weapon but a dropped folder on the cement floor that had made the noise.

'You okay?'

'Yeah, just lost my balance,' said Jaz, hiding the truth of her fearful reaction. She was on tenterhooks. Did Tay feel the same? The nightmare of that night was not done with her yet. Just how long would she have to wait until it was forgotten? On the bright side, she was no longer having the nightmares about the man she witnessed die in Pakistan. One horror had surpassed another.

Nonetheless, today at school, her reaction had caused a few students to glance her way, not hiding their disdain. Well, no more than usual.

The worst of the bad vibes came from her nemesis, Minka Schubach. Laughing with her crowd – the rich, pretty and arrogant – Minka narrowed her eyes at Jaz. As Minka noticed the crutches and Jaz's facial bruises, a smile grew on her plump red lips. Minka was probably planning some retort for later, which normally would have made Jaz angry, but now she felt nothing. Now that she had seen and met people far more frightening and dangerous, Jaz finally realised that the bullying in school, the social standings and crap that went with it, was nothing. It was just five miniscule years of your life compared to what was outside. After what Jaz had seen, nothing Minka could do would ever hurt her ever again.

CHAPTER 2

SHE SPOTTED TAYLOR waiting for her on the school steps. His whole body screamed out his internal struggle: shoulders hunched, vacant gaze, even his hair wasn't styled. It was as if the real Taylor had taken a vacation, leaving a deadpan clone in his place. She missed her happy-go-lucky best friend and felt guilty for contributing to his current state.

'Hey,' she said, sitting beside him in an unladylike cascade of legs and crutches. Kids ran past, calliing out to friends, oblivious. Jaz put her arm around Tay and hugged him close. 'How're you going?'

He turned to her, blank eyes searching her face. His lips moved but nothing came out. Instead, he shrugged.

It was hard enough for Jaz to deal with the things that were torturing her mind; what made it worse was knowing that Taylor was going through the same thing and she couldn't do a damn thing to help him. What could she say? *Sorry we killed a guy. It was self-defence. She'll be right, mate.* Jaz rested her head on his shoulder. Maybe there were no words to fix this.

'I'm here,' said Anna in song. She stepped down and stood in front of them. 'You guys okay?'

They both faked smiles and nodded. 'Yep, glad school's over,' said Tay.

Anna's eyes narrowed but she didn't press them. 'So, what shall we do? Wanna fire some rounds at the range,' she said eagerly.

The range was Taylor's favourite place. He loved spending time firing ammunition at targets until his aim was perfect.

'No,' said Tay quickly before clearing his throat. 'Um, no I was actually thinking of heading to The Ring. See if Ryan was about. I want to know if he's got any info on my dad.'

Jaz thought his recovery was well done. She knew damn well why he didn't want to go to the range. Probably the same reason Jaz had freaked when she heard that noise and assumed it was a gunshot. They were both still on edge. 'Cool. Sounds like a plan. I wanted to head there too, to see Pax,' said Jaz.

'Well, let's get moving, skater girl.' Anna held out her hand to help Jaz up and walked beside her as they made their way to Tay's Mustang. Anna was still trying to convince her parents she needed a car. They were a little old-school, so if they did let her get one it would probably be something small and safe. Jaz had only just got her own, but with her sore leg she couldn't drive her beautiful black Jeep Wrangler.

'Hey, is that your stalker guy?' said Anna quietly, without drawing any attention to where she was looking.

Jaz looked past Anna to see the man in dark glasses on the opposite side of the road. He was smoking, leaning back against a black SUV. It was him, all right. Her stomach tightened. 'Damn, I should have noticed.' Jaz should have been the one to identify the threat, not Anna. After all, this is what she did best, what she had trained for – and she was the one who had spotted him in the beginning and worked out he was following Taylor.

Tay tensed beside her. It's not every day you were followed by a man from a gang who was blackmailing your father, who was high up in the police force, for information. Jaz let out a nervous giggle. Her friends looked at her strangely. 'Sorry. I think I'm going a little crazy.' And she laughed again. Life *was* a little crazy. Taylor must have felt the same, because he joined in. It was a laugh-or-cry feeling and now was not the time to cry. But the release was just the same.

Anna watched them both. 'You two go smoke something while I wasn't looking?' she asked as they got in the car.

'No, maybe just tired. We've had some late nights,' said Jaz as she managed to control her outburst.

'Riiiiight.' Anna leaned back and put her seatbelt on as Taylor started the car.

He smiled, and Jaz could see that some of the tension had left him.

'Just had to let out some of the crazy,' he added, before flooring it out of the school car park.

Neither of them bothered to look in the mirrors for the guy in the black SUV. They knew he'd be following and there was nothing they could do about it. Ryan had suggested they just pretend they didn't know he was there and that soon they would use that to their advantage. How, Jaz wasn't too sure. But knowing Ryan, he'd have a plan. He always did.

They left their posh school area and drove past multi-million-dollar houses towards the cheaper side of the suburb. It was a less salubrious area, a place where you didn't go out after dark alone. Jaz had made that mistake once and been attacked by a gang – if it hadn't been for Ryan, she probably wouldn't be here today. Automatically Jaz glanced at the small scar on her arm, made by a knife and stitched up by Ryan. Her first war wound. Strangely, like a badge of honour it gave her strength, as if to remind her she made it out alive, and of her own determination and might.

'Do you think he'll be here?' asked Anna.

'I hope so. He said he'd try to see us today,' said Tay as he pulled up next to The Ring.

Jaz got out, careful not to trip over the cracked, uneven street. Weeds grew through the gaps, adding to the unmaintained look of the area. The Ring was her second home, had been since she was two. It was a large shed-like building, the sign was faded and the white door was peeling. The front of the business had big glass windows and she could see bodies moving inside.

'Looks like Bags is busy,' said Anna as she opened the door.

The smell of sweat and leather greeted them. Inside, a tall bulky guy with short hair and plenty of muscle was taking a class of six. Bags looked like a bouncer or a man you'd run from, when really he was a sweet guy who loved writing prose. He was part of The Ring family, along with Tick and Niles; they were always working out or running classes.

'Now uppercuts,' said Bags to his group who were paired off and taking turns to hit into pads. 'Hey, guys.' He gave them a big wave and came over to hug Jaz and Anna. 'What's up with you, Jaz?' I'm away for a few days and this happens?' he teased.

'She thought she could skateboard,' said Anna, rolling her eyes.

Bags laughed, his pecs moving under his singlet with each chuckle. 'You let a skateboard bring you down? Gee, Jaz.' He shook his head as he stepped back to his class, giving them a smile before he turned his attention. 'Right, now change to left cross, right jab, left elbow.'

Jaz scanned the rest of the gym. No one was near the mats or the boxing ring, nor the speedballs. Maybe Ryan had left her a note in the change room again?

'Do you think he's been here?' asked Tay.

'I'll see if Pax is home,' said Anna and headed to the office. Tay followed while Jaz made her way to the change room. It was a big communal room with toilets and showers. Jaz had her own private shower cubicle at the end with a lock, which other girls could use, but not many did. Those who came for a lesson preferred to go home to shower.

She opened the door of her cubicle and checked the back for a note. Nothing. Her body sagged against the wall. She hated this feeling, missing Ryan. Not being able to see him.

'Thinking of taking a shower?'

Jaz jumped at the voice and turned around. 'No. Do I need to?'

Tay was grinning at her. 'Sometimes you can be an open book, Jaz. Ryan's here, he's in the office with Pax.' He went to turn but paused. 'Oh, you might want to hide that delight on your face,' he teased.

Jaz reached out and hit his arm, but he was right. She had been grinning like a fool. Ryan had that effect on her. And she was finding it hard to take steady steps to the office and not sprint in there like she was in a three-legged race.

Tay opened the office door for her. The office was shielded from the gym by a two-way mirror, which allowed Pax to keep an eye on the gym, and it came in handy when they needed to talk spy stuff.

Jaz smelled Ryan before she saw him. There was something strong and masculine about his scent, mixed in with woody earthy tones. Luckily she had crutches to hold herself up. Pax sat in one chair, Ryan in the other, and Anna was sitting on the computer desk next to Ryan and admiring the view.

Anna shot her a huge grin, which screamed, *Look who I'm next to!*

Taylor grunted behind her.

'Jaz.' Pax got up and embraced her. He wore a white T-shirt with a blue patterned button-up shirt over the top, which hung open either side of his belly. He had teamed this with worn denim shorts and brown sandals.

It was like being wrapped up by a loving grandfather. His squishy belly and the smell of coffee and icing sugar was what she expected with each hug. 'How are you, love?' he asked gently, but the question was loaded with greater meaning. Jaz had only just found out that Pax had worked alongside Ryan at the Agency for years, and for years before Ryan was even recruited. He'd kept that secret her whole life, only now did she know he made all the documents the agents needed. Until recently she had thought Pax had been all about his gym, when in fact he'd been in the Agency for most of his life. It made her wonder if she really knew anyone anymore.

She gazed into his warm lined face, his glassed perched on his head, as his eyes narrowed.

'I'll live,' she said.

Pax groaned and shook his head. 'You're not a cat, Jaz. Don't think you've got nine lives to use up.'

'I know.' She could see the worry in his eyes and hated being the one who put it there.

'Well, seeing as you lot have arrived, shall we go pick up some afternoon tea?' said Pax, rubbing his hands together.

Anna laughed. 'Why not? I'm starved. Seeing as Jaz can't carry much I'll come and help you. Coming, Tay?'

Taylor glanced at Ryan, who only just now moved his chair so he could see the both of them. Her breath caught in her throat. Ryan was sexy. Short clipped hair, tanned muscles and dark eyes that held many secrets. But it wasn't just that, it was the way he carried himself. His shoulders were never slouched, instead erect and straight as if he was always on alert. Which was understandable in his job where he couldn't really trust anyone and was constantly aware of his surroundings. Even here, with them, he seemed on edge.

Ryan gave Taylor a nod.

'Sure, I'll come,' said Taylor, reading Ryan's message loud and clear. 'Cappuccinos all around, then?' he added.

While Anna was writing down everyone's order, Jaz reached across and squeezed Tay's hand. She knew he was dying to talk to Ryan about that night and about his dad but now wasn't the time. He understood that, even if it was killing him to wait.

'All right, are you driving?' said Pax as they headed out of the office.

'Depends,' said Tay. 'Are you paying?'

After they left, Ryan got up and closed the door. 'Let's go into the house. We won't be interrupted there.'

Jaz gulped. Since everyone had gone and left them alone, her heart rate had increased. Some of it was slight panic at being alone with this gorgeous man, and some of it was fear of what he had to say. Was she about to get a lecture about her thoughtless escapade? Was he disappointed in her? Did he have news about the men they'd fought? Was she in trouble? Well, the last one was probably a given. Trouble seemed to just find Jaz whether she liked it or not.

Ryan still hadn't even glanced in her direction, as if pretending she wasn't in the room with him. Had she disappointed him? Had he expected more from her? Jaz wished she'd thought it through properly before she went to the warehouse, but it had seemed harmless at the time. She was still trying to figure out how a 'quick look' had turned into murder.

Ryan led the way into Pax's house, which adjoined the gym by a solid wood door. He wore a snug army green T-shirt and relaxed-fit stonewash jeans, along with his black commando boots. Ready for action. Jaz pulled her eyes away from the tight fit of his T-shirt and limped past.

Pax's house wasn't anything special. From the outside it looked like it was falling down, much like the gym, and on the inside it was old and outdated. Pax still had the original beige lino, which had worn through to brown on the heavy traffic areas. They sat in the kitchen with its yellow tiles and old table with mismatched chairs. Anyone would think Pax was poor, but that couldn't be further from the truth. He had shares in Anna's grandad's huge computer business, which her father now ran, and Pax had plenty of money of his own. Jaz's distaste for materialistic things had probably been honed growing up around Pax. She felt more at home in his comfy small abode then she did in her own massive multi-million dollar home.

'So,' said Ryan after he sat down.

Jaz took a seat, dropping her crutches to the floor. 'So,' she replied, not sure where to start. Funny, considering she'd had a heap of questions just moments ago.

'How's the wound? Keeping an eye on it?' He lifted his head, his strong jaw set firm, as his eyes finally met hers.

A tingle ran down her spine. Being the object of his attention was now unnerving her. Jaz picked at her fingers, unable to hold his gaze. For a moment she wished things could go back to when they'd first met and would spar together and joke. Now that she'd stepped into his world, his job, things had become more serious. She felt like she'd grown up, that the things she'd seen had aged her by at least five years. Which would put her at Ryan's age.

'It's much better. I can put some weight on my leg now.'

He nodded as if all was as it should be. 'I've informed the Agency about what you found at the warehouse. They are pleased, not about the casualties or that you put yourself at such risk, but they want you to see this through and continue at the Sinclair house,' said Ryan.

Jaz sat back as if he'd shouted. His sudden jump right into information overload took her a moment to catch up. But when she did, Marcus's face came to mind. 'They want me to go back? After I ... did that?' She couldn't bring herself to say *killed Tommy*. It made it all too real; it made Tommy a person, a life. Jaz felt lightheaded and hoped it was from lack of food.

Ryan leaned closer, his hands reaching out, but then stopped just short of her fingers. His familiar scent washed over her, snapping her from her thoughts on Tommy.

'Jaz, I know it seems like you'd be walking into a lion's cage, but trust me. They don't know anything. To them you're still just Marcus's girlfriend.'

'But what about my leg and face? What if they put it together?' How could she face Carl again, or Marcus? How would she react if they talked about the murder?

'They won't. Why would they think a teenage girl would be involved in a shooting at their warehouse? You have to keep up appearances, Jaz. This is the best time to be at their place. This would have rattled them, they could be reaching out to suppliers or making mistakes while they're scared. We really need you on the inside.'

Even when Ryan was serious he was handsome. 'Did you find out if both the … um … guys died?' Jaz swallowed. Sweat was gathering on the back of her neck.

'Only one did. The other is in hospital with serious facial injuries. They're calling it a robbery.'

'Did the cops search their warehouse? Find the drugs they'd shipped out that night? Have they got any leads? '

Ryan shook his head. 'No, nothing. But we need to keep you in place until we can get this next shipment and find out where it's coming from.' His chest rose as he breathed in deeply. 'Can you do it?'

Could she do it? It seemed like a stupid thing to do, like walking into belly of the beast. It would be her biggest test yet. But she didn't want to let anyone down and she didn't want to walk away just because it was getting hard. No matter how terrified she felt she found herself nodding her head. 'Yes, I can do it.'

'Good. Great.' He almost smiled. 'Are you still in contact with Marcus?'

'Yep.' Jaz pulled out her phone and sent Marcus a message saying she'd just found her phone again and could they catch up. 'I've told everyone I stacked it off the skateboard, if you're wondering,' she said, glancing at Ryan.

Ryan cocked an eyebrow. 'Skateboarding?'

'Marcus is teaching me a few tricks, so it fits.' Jaz shrugged. She put her phone down on the table and wondered how long until she'd hear from Marcus. Was his household in chaos after Tommy's death? Would they go to his funeral? Would he want Jaz to go? What if he'd had a family? Kids? She needed to think of something else and right now! 'Have you heard anything about Taylor's dad? Anything we can do there?'

'No, just keep ignoring this guy for now. I have other work to do but when I get a moment, we'll try to follow this guy home. See where he goes and who he meets.'

'Okay.'

'How is Taylor handling all this?'

'About the same as me, I think. A little freaked out. How do you get past this?' she whispered. Jaz felt weak and soft. And she hated it.

Ryan dragged his lip through his teeth before he spoke. 'It's not easy,

Jaz. There's no miracle cure to nightmares or jumping at every sound.' His dark eyes were full of compassion.

Jaz felt herself relax. It was as if he could read her thoughts. He knew what she was going through.

'I was in your position too, remember. I've been through what you're dealing with and I wish I could help.' He cleared his throat. 'You don't know how much I wanted to save you from all this, Jaz. And from what happened in Pakistan, watching me take a life.' He squeezed his eyes shut as if he'd been the one witnessing the blood pool from the man's cut throat as the life fled from his eyes. 'Once you've seen and done things like that you can't take it back, nor erase it. I'm angry that I brought you into this mess, especially so soon. I feel like I've stolen your youth.'

Jaz's mouth fell open. Ryan's jaw was clenched so tight it was almost pulsing along with the grinding of his teeth. That's when she noticed the darkness around his eyes and the shadow of stubble. He wasn't travelling so well either.

'It's not your fault, Ryan. You weren't to know.' The killing in Pakistan wasn't supposed to happen either, just bad luck on both counts. A simple retrieval mission gone wrong. 'We both knew this was going to happen eventually.' She could see the burden weighing heavily on his mind, and she wished there was a way to make him feel better.

He remained silent and broody.

'How did you get through it?' she asked eventually. 'The first time?'

He relaxed his jaw as he sighed. 'Badly. I lost sleep, got to the point I didn't want to sleep but that just set me back. But I realised the nightmares wouldn't kill me and I'd get past that stage. So, I jumped back into work. I wouldn't let it defeat me. There were people who needed me, I focused on that. I focused on stopping these bastards.'

Jaz was drawing shapes on the table with her finger but Ryan's words sunk in. She knew that there were paramedics and police officers who witnessed gruesome things every day yet they continued because they were needed. Jaz had to think about the bigger picture. The people she was saving in the long run.

'Are you regretting your choice, Jaz?' said Ryan. He slid his finger along the table until it met with hers. 'You can get out now if you want to. Many an agent has and no one would hold it against you if you did.'

He was giving her an out. But did Jaz want it? Sure, it would be nice to go back to the oblivious, easy life she had before, but could she go back to normal after that? Jaz didn't think she could get that back and the truth was, she didn't want to go back. She'd come so far. Nothing had given her as much purpose in life than working for the Agency and helping Ryan.

Jaz sat up in her chair, drew her hand away from his and set her steely gaze on him.

'I don't regret anything.'

CHAPTER 3

MARCUS GOT BACK to Jaz just as Anna, Pax and Taylor returned with the coffee and pastries.

'Here you are, except we're down one because Pax couldn't wait,' said Anna with a grin. She handed out the cups and they all sat around the table. 'Is that Marcus?' she asked while Jaz was reading his message.

'Yep, he's just saying sorry he hasn't been in contact much because stuff's been happening at home. He wants to catch up.' A flutter of nerves bounced around her chest. She resisted the urge to glance at Ryan. Beside her Taylor shifted uncomfortably in his seat. 'Thanks for this,' she said, drinking her coffee in hot gulps, hoping Anna was done with questions on Marcus.

The table fell quiet under the weight of the secrets everyone was trying to keep. Anna didn't know about the attack at the warehouse or of Taylor's involvement, or that Marcus was Jaz's mission rather than her real boyfriend; and Pax didn't know just how much Anna knew about the Agency or his involvement, or indeed that she had been in his secret room and done some unofficial work on his behalf. Oh, what a world.

'So, are you going to see him this arvo?' asked Anna. Persistent as ever. 'Yep.'

'How are you going to get there?' Anna gestured to her crutches.

'I can drop you off on my way home, if you like,' said Ryan softly.

All this did was spike Anna's curiosity. Her eyes widened and Jaz knew her mind would be trying to process this scenario. Ryan, the guy Jaz had feelings for, taking her to Marcus, the guy she was dating. Anna's nose twitched, moving her cute freckles. She must be ready to burst and no doubt this would warrant a call to Jaz later.

'Sure, thanks.' Jaz gave Ryan a small smile before texting Marcus.

'Everyone seems so glum lately. I think we need to do something exciting. Maybe we should plan your eighteenth, Jaz! It's only two weeks away. You in, Tay?' asked Anna.

Taylor, who'd been rather quiet, nodded. 'Sure, maybe you're right. Let's have a party. I'll help you, Anna.' He smiled at Jaz. 'Don't worry, we'll throw you something you'll love.'

Jaz wasn't so sure about that, but she was just happy to see Taylor smile. They talked randomly about what she would like for her birthday – Dice for her car? A neon helmet for her skateboard? – but when she tried to think of something she really wanted, nothing came to mind besides Ryan and maybe having her own gun. Then she wouldn't need to rely on other people. If she'd had her own gun she wouldn't have needed to call Taylor and he wouldn't be suffering right now. Her guilt weighed heavily. At least she now understood how Ryan felt.

Ryan glanced at his watch. 'I need to head off. Jaz, you ready for that ride?'

'Okay.' Jaz grabbed a pastry from the box on the table. 'Tay, I'll call you later.' Since he'd been attacked in his own house, knocked unconscious as a warning to his dad, both girls were keeping a close watch on him.

Jaz shoved the apricot-filled treat into her mouth and then reached for her crutches. Pax was staring at her leg in a way that made Jaz to panic and check her wound hadn't bled through. She was still wearing her school uniform and her black tights hid the bandage. She shot him a reassuring smile. 'I'm fine, Pax. It will be better when my bruises fade. Looks worse than it is.'

'I'm sure you love them. Like a badge of honour, you wear them with pride,' said Anna with a wink. 'And it freaks the kids out at school.'

Jaz laughed. 'That's true.' She did love how they backed away from her in the corridors. 'See you later.'

Ryan got the door for her and together they made their way out to the front of the gym where his black SUV was parked. Without a word he opened the passenger door, held her crutches while she got in then handed them back. Before he started the car, he reached across her and opened the glove box.

'This is for you.'

Jaz took the phone he held out, her fingers brushing against his. He was so close she only had to lean forward to kiss his lips. Before she could even contemplate doing it, he sat back in his seat and started the car.

'If you need me, call me on that. It's untraceable.'

'Okay. Thanks.' Now she just had to keep it on her without anyone finding it. Easier said than done.

'Hopefully you won't be calling me on it,' he almost growled.

Jaz shot him a smile. 'We'll see,' she teased.

His hands clenched the steering wheel like they were choking something. She loved getting under Ryan's skin. Especially because he was someone not easily rattled. They sat in silence for the drive even though the air was thick unsaid thoughts.

'Are you ready?' he said as he pulled up at the bus stop closest to Marcus's house.

Always precautions; always careful. 'Yep. Just like acting, right?' Jaz got out quickly, hurting her leg in the process. She cursed as she hobbled to the curb. The tint on Ryan's windows was dark but she could feel his eyes watching her. She gave him a nod before making her way up the road towards her boyfriend's house.

The only thing that helped calm her jangled nerves was the crash of the waves across the road. The salty sea breeze filled her lungs as she counted her steps. Four hundred and eighty-four crutch-wielding steps later she reached the Sinclair house. It was a big two-storey place that overlooked the ocean and the many sunsets. Worth a pretty penny, no doubt.

With a shaking finger, she rang the doorbell then took two deep breaths to steady herself. Please don't let it be Carl, she prayed.

As the door cracked open, Jaz felt relief as Marcus stood there in his school uniform. His tie was gone, the top button on his white shirt undone and his hair was out, almost brushing along his shoulders.

'Hey,' she said.

Marcus was an attractive guy, and she couldn't help but smile at the way his dark green eyes lit up when he saw her.

'What happened to you!' he said as he took in her bruises and then the crutches. 'Oh geez. Come in.'

'Thanks.' Jaz moved past him and headed into the lounge room. Marcus sat beside her on the couch, his hand caressing her face. The concern in his eyes made her melt, until she remembered how she'd got the injuries in the first place.

'Jaz?'

'Don't worry, it looks worse than it is,' she said with a smile. With a big sigh, she repeated her well-rehearsed lie. 'It's stupid really, and I'm a little embarrassed to even tell you. That's why I haven't been around, I felt silly.'

'No! You don't need to feel that way around me. Come on, tell me.' He grabbed her hands with a gentle squeeze.

'I was trying to do an olly on my skateboard.'

'Oh.' His eyebrows shot up along with the corner of his lips.

'Yeah. *Oh.* Well, I said more than that when I stacked it. I came down funny and did my hammy before face planting. I'm so glad no one was around to see it. But still, it doesn't help my wounded pride.' Jaz pulled a face while Marcus tried not to laugh.

He reached around her and pulled her up against his chest. 'I'm sorry, babe. Don't worry, I've been there and done that. At least you were giving it a go.' He rested his chin on her head as she lay against him.

Jaz felt herself relax into him. His warmth. His tenderness. 'I missed this.' Her hand rested against his tight abs; there were nothing like Ryan's, but still, for his age, Marcus was pretty damn toned, mostly from his skateboarding. If she were a normal girl, in a normal situation, she'd be a happy one. But this was all make-believe. This was her job. Some days she wished it were real because it felt like it could be real. She liked Marcus a lot and she cared what happened to him, but she had to put her mission first.

'Me too.' Marcus cleared his throat. 'I could have used a few hugs over the weekend.'

Jaz frowned and was glad he couldn't see her face. 'Why's that?' she said casually.

'You know my dad's warehouse? Well, there was a break-in and ...' Marcus paused and took a breath. 'The intruders shot Tommy.' Jaz felt the rise and fall of his chest. 'He, um, died. And Rich ended up in hospital.'

Knowing she couldn't hide from this, Jaz sat up, hoping her face was full of shock. 'What? When?' Her leg was squished against his, the pressure on her bullet wound stung but she pushed it aside.

'Saturday night.'

'Oh my gosh. What happened? Did they steal anything? Did the cops catch them?'

'Rich managed to call Dad. His face was bashed in. Suffered some concussion. He's coming out of hospital today, I think. One eye socket is fractured but he'll still be able to see. The cops don't know who did it. Rich fought with them, said the guy was lean but strong and had got in through the toilet window. Dad thinks they could have been junkies looking for cash. But they think there was more than one.'

'I can't believe it. How do they know there were more?' Jaz sat back a bit, hoping Marcus couldn't hear how fast her heart was thumping. She could hear it rattling out, *It was me! It was me!*

'Well, Dad said Tommy was shot twice. In the back and front.'

Her hand went to her mouth as her stomach rolled.

'Unless he was shot, then turned around and was shot again. They're waiting for the report to find out for sure. But there were no guns found. Police are calling it a break-and-enter gone wrong.'

Jaz tried to nod but the tension in her muscles was so tight they were like a rubber bands. She just sat there, frozen and couldn't think of anything to say that wouldn't give herself away. Carl must have arrived before calling the police and ambulance, because Tommy's gun didn't get a mention.

'Tommy's funeral is on Friday. Mum and Dad are still in shock. Tommy's been with us for years. Dad's been really messed up.' Marcus let his breath hiss out between his teeth. 'He hasn't been himself these past few days.'

This was interesting. 'What do you mean? Your dad seems like a strong guy,' she said, gently but encouragingly.

'I understand he's stressed out about his warehouse and Tommy, but it doesn't mean he can bite everyone's head off. He snapped at me yesterday because I answered the phone, and he's shutting himself away in his office and growls if Mum or I open the door even to tell him dinner's ready.'

Jaz smiled sympathetically, all the while thinking of her 'boyfriend's' dad. Clearly Carl was stressed big time. He'd lost his main man who over-saw the movement of the drugs out of the sea containers. He was prob-ably also desperate to know if anyone had found out what really went on in his warehouse, which was a front for his wife's art business. Jaz sighed. How long had Carl been with Rich before he called the ambulance? Had he gone through the warehouse first, checking it was clean of every-thing incriminating?

'I wouldn't take it to heart,' she said to Marcus. 'Death affects us all differently. For all we know it could even be bringing back all the pain and sadness of your sister's death. I'm sure your dad just needs some time.'

'Yeah, I never thought of that.' Marcus pulled her back into his arms. Jaz tried not to yelp as her weight rolled onto her wound. 'What would I do without you, Jaz. I'm glad you're here.'

'Me too.'

His hands caressed her face moments before his lips found hers. Gently at first, before it became hungry and needful. Jaz understood how getting lost in the moment helped the problems fade away. Ryan had certainly helped her survive her first experience with violent death while in Pakistan. Mind you that had ended badly but those few moments in his arms had been what she'd needed.

Marcus's hand slipped from her cheek, finding its way to her breast. Jaz arched into him, into his warmth and the distraction she'd been craving. His tongue brushed along her teeth as she sunk her hand into his long hair. But with all this going on, Jaz still couldn't clear her mind. She was think-ing of Carl, of Tommy and of Ryan. Always Ryan. His strong muscled body and the fire in his deep dark eyes had a way of reaching every corner of her mind, no matter how hard she tried to fight it.

Marcus shifted closer, leaning over her until she was lying back on the couch. He eased his body on top of her until she felt him hard against her. She closed her eyes and groaned, revelling in the feeling of being wanted. Marcus rolled to the side and her eyes shot open as she yelped.

'Oh, sorry, are you okay?' he asked, holding himself up, his eyes green depths of concern.

Once the pain had subsided enough for Jaz to speak, she nodded and smiled. 'Yeah, sorry. I'm still really sore.' She sat up, brushing her hair back. 'I feel like an idiot.'

Marcus chuckled and pulled her back against him. 'Don't be. That was awesome, before I hurt you. I'm sorry.' He kissed her forehead.

God, Jaz felt awful. If he knew the truth he'd probably hate her.

After a few minutes – well, for as long as Jaz could handle the throbbing ache in her leg – she suggested they get something to drink.

'Sure. Coke?' he offered.

'Yes, please.' She watched him from the couch as he walked to the open kitchen. 'So, have you done any more drawings?' she asked.

'Maybe,' he said with a grin before his head disappeared behind the fridge door.

The front entry opened and slammed shut. Jaz sat up just as quickly as Marcus shut the fridge.

'Dad?' he said cautiously.

Carl threw his briefcase on the countertop. 'I'm going into my office and I don't want to be disturbed, okay?' Carl's eyes had dark circles beneath them but he was still dressed impeccably in his suit pants, tie and shirt. He spotted the two cans of Coke Marcus was holding and froze, realising they weren't alone. Forcing a smile he turned towards Jaz.

'Hi Jaz,' he said before clearing his throat. 'Um, you kids have a nice time. Just keep it down, yeah?' Carl said pointedly to Marcus.

'We will.' As Carl walked off to his office Marcus's shoulders dropped as he came back to the couch. 'See what I mean.' He handed Jaz her Coke. 'He's just not his normal self.'

'I noticed.' Jaz didn't like the frown mark along his forehead. He was too cute to carry that. 'So, do you think I can see the pictures you've done?'

A smile spread along his lips. 'You really want to?'

'Of course. You know I love your drawings. I wish you had more confidence in your own work.' Jaz frowned. She knew his doubt came from his dad's disapproval.

'Wanna come …' He paused, looking at her crutches. 'Um, you wait here, I'll go get them.' He winked and moved off the couch.

Jaz didn't waste any time. She got up quickly, ignoring the niggling pain and stepped to the kitchen as Marcus disappeared around the corner, past his dad's office and up the stairs to his room.

Jaz was after one thing only: Carl's briefcase, which he'd left on the kitchen bench. Her heart began to race. She only had a few seconds. Since the moment Carl had flung it there, she'd been thinking of ways to check it out. Was anything important lurking inside? Had Carl left it behind because he'd been distracted by them or did he not keep anything special in it? Maybe he didn't think his family would find it important, but Jaz wasn't family. Any little thing could be crucial.

Marcus's footsteps were heading up the steps as she flipped open the leather case. She prayed Carl had his door shut tightly so that if he opened it she would hear.

Jaz had seconds.

She slid out the papers inside, her eyes running over the contents as quickly as possible. Invoices, customs documentation and forms, but nothing she thought helped. Unless he had a man in customs? Jaz quickly sought out the name on the paperwork. Daniel McNally. And filed it away in her memory, she didn't have time to get her phone out and take photo's. That would be too many seconds she didn't have.

Next she checked out the business cards he had slotted on the inside of the leather case. 'Jameson Figlomeni, Figlomeni Enterprises. AFMA member.' There was a phone number and an address in Hillarys.

There were none for De Luca Industries, but maybe she was a bit naive to think Carl would cart that around on him. But what good would that do – she already knew Carl was tied up with De Luca. She'd seen them together first hand after following Carl. De Luca was a known drug trafficker, just no one had the proof to do anything about it yet.

Heavy footsteps dropped against the steps. Marcus was on his way back. The pounding of her heart and the fear of being caught made her giddy with adrenaline. So much that her hand was shaking badly as she tried to slide the paperwork back in. It was almost impossible to stay calm knowing Marcus would be walking towards her and she was still trying to close up his dad's case. But if her training had taught her anything, it was how to stay cool under pressure. She could do this.

'I think you'll like these,' said Marcus from right behind her. His Converse shoes barely made a sound against the marble floor.

Swallowing her fear, Jaz flipped the cover on the case hoping her body hid the act, picked up her can of Coke and forced a smile. She turned slowly. 'Why? Are they of me?' she said, hoping the words didn't rush out to highlight the nervousness that she felt. She sipped her Coke to hide her discomfort.

Jaz turned to offer up the table space so they could spread out his drawings, and while doing so she slid Carl's case further behind her and with any luck, further from Marcus's mind.

He laid out three white pages with lead pencil sketches on them.

'Oh wow.' Jaz leaned over to see one of her. The way he'd captured her hair, so free and beautiful, was amazing. 'It looks so real.' Her lips were drawn plump and the detail was crazy. 'You have such a talent, Marcus. I just wish your dad could see it.'

Marcus placed his hand low on her back and he leaned over to kiss her neck. Automatically Jaz tilted her head, giving him easier access to her skin.

'So do I.'

When he finished kissing her Jaz pulled the other two drawings closer. One was of the ocean outside his bedroom window and the third … the third caused her heart to skip.

Every night in her dreams that face haunted her. Tommy.

'What's wrong?' said Marcus.

Jaz cleared her throat. 'Nothing, it's just sad,' she managed to whisper. It was hard to speak when her body was frozen in terror. That night she'd shot Tommy she hadn't seen his face in the dark, but in her nightmares it was clearly visible. Seeing his face now was like living her bad dreams. 'Did he have a family?' she asked.

'He has a daughter he doesn't see. I think the mother has sole custody. Other than that, I don't really know. He lived alone, talked about his favourite football team and loved betting on the dogs. I feel bad that I didn't really know him much outside of work.'

The lump in Jaz's throat seemed to grow with each fleeting second. She needed to get away from the picture of Tommy. The way Marcus had drawn him, he seemed so full of life. His eyes glistened, and the creases on his face were happy lines, as if he'd recently been laughing. If Jaz stared at it any longer she would lose it. Already she was fighting back the tears. 'I just need to use the bathroom,' she said, tucking her crutches firmly under her arms. 'Be right back.'

The click of her crutches against the solid floor echoed around the house but Jaz pressed on faster, past Carl's closed door towards the toilet. Once inside she bent over and sucked in deep breaths. After ten big ones she righted herself, only to see her reflection in the mirror. Who was that girl she saw? She didn't look like a killer. Instead, she looked like a scared teenager with red-rimmed eyes and a grim line for a mouth. Jaz clutched the end of the sink and leaned closer to the mirror, as if hoping to see into her soul through her blue eyes. Could Marcus see her inner torment? Was she doing a good enough job of hiding it all? Was she strong enough to keep fighting the feelings that plagued her?

Her reflection could answer none of her questions.

Turning on the tap, Jaz washed her face with the cool water. She used the plush hand towel to pat her face dry before squaring up her shoulders, pasting on a smile and leaving the sanctuary of the bathroom. All that she knew was that she had to keep going. At night in her bed was when she was allowed to fall apart. Until then, she had a job to do.

CHAPTER 4

JAZ ASKED MARCUS to take her home ten minutes later, saying she had a serious headache, which she blamed on her skateboard stack. Marcus, being so nice, immediately understood.

After she waved him goodbye she didn't go to her room and lie down. Instead, she went into the house in search of pen and paper while putting her phone to her ear.

'Hi Tay. Are you busy? Can you pick me up and take me to the cemetery please?'

She only had five minutes to wait, so she quickly wrote a short message for the Agency, listing the two names she thought should be investigated. The agency wanted her to leave messages in code using a simple format with the book they had given her, only these names wouldn't be in the book so she was doing away with any message. They would understand with just the two names and know they were worth looking into.

With the note tucked in her hand, she hobbled back outside to wait for Taylor. The rumble of his Mustang could be heard long before he turned into the driveway.

'Need a ride,' he said with a smile.

'You'll get sick of me soon. Hopefully as soon as I can put some weight on my leg I'll get back driving,' she said, after fitting herself and her metal legs inside the car.

'I don't mind.' Tay looked relaxed with his shirt sleeves rolled up. How he managed to make a plain white school shirt look cool was something she'd never be able to duplicate. He wore his dark sunnies and she wondered if his smile reached his eyes. 'How did it go with Marcus? Did he say anything?'

Now she understood why he was so keen to come pick her up. 'Where's Anna?'

His lips stretched into a thin line. 'She's with Pax at The Ring. I managed to convince her to stay and that I'd be back. She's taking this protection thing a little seriously.'

'She cares about you. We all do.'

Tay stopped at a red light before he turned to her, lifting his glasses. 'How bad was it? Are we safe?'

Jaz let his words sink in. Are we safe? From others or from ourselves, she wondered. 'I think so. Rich, the other guy, is okay but I don't think he can make me out. Seems to think I'm a guy, so that's good, I guess. Carl isn't taking it well, all the extra attention at the warehouse and worrying what the cops might find out. He's really crabby and Marcus is tiptoeing around him.'

'Man, it's all so weird. I really like Marcus.' Tay let out a breath.

'I know. I really like him too. I guess you can't help who your family is, hey?'

'Yeah. I guess it's no different to finding out your dad is leaking information to the bad guys,' said Tay.

Jaz reached over and gripped his shoulder. 'Hang on, you're dad's only doing that to protect you. I'm sure he's working hard to find a way out. Imagine the pressure he's under? He's not a bad cop, Tay, you know that.'

Tay eventually nodded and fell silent for a few minutes. 'What about the bullets? Did they find them at the warehouse?'

'I don't know. They know there was two of us due to the shots in … um, Tommy.' Jaz shivered saying his name. She just couldn't connect the nice Tommy she'd met to the one she'd ended up killing.

'But they have nothing on me?' said Tay, his voice straining.

Jaz shook her head. They sat in silence until they reached the cemetery. 'I'll keep my ears open and I'll let you know everything they find. Hopefully nothing can trace back to us.'

'What if they find something, Jaz? Maybe someone saw my car?'

'Unless they can put your car at that warehouse, then you were just driving past minding your own business. Besides, once they see you're a cop's son and just eighteen, they'll dismiss it.'

Who would think an eighteen year old capable of murder? Sure, there were some bad dangerous kids in gangs, but once they saw squeaky-clean Taylor they wouldn't believe it. Even Jaz was struggling with the notion and she was a witness to both their crimes.

Taylor turned off the motor and they got out, heading to her sister's grave. Her sister had only been a baby when she'd died but he agency used her grave as a message drop off point, a place she could visit on occasion without causing suspicion. The note was still safely in her hand and she hoped her sweaty palms wouldn't ruin it. The first thing she did when they got there was to put the note inside the flower she'd left there last time.

'What did you just do?' Tay asked, his brow creased.

'Why? What did it look like?' She was curious. If Tay could tell, could others?

'I don't know. You were fiddling with the flower, but knowing you, you were up to something.'

Jaz put her arm around Tay and leaned in close. 'I was leaving a note for the Agency,' she whispered.

Taylor nodded. 'Do you regret it, Jaz? Do you feel like you're different now?' His words were sad and softly spoken..

But Jaz was so packed full of emotion. It was accumulating like a pressure valve. Since the shooting, since Pakistan, since going back into the Sinclair house, she was holding in everything. In the safety of Tay's arms the cracks began to widen. A tear slipped down her cheek as she stared at the grassy ground. 'I don't know what I should feel or think anymore, Tay,' she said as she began to tremble. 'I look in the mirror and I see myself but I don't see me, if you know what I mean? Something has changed. Inside I'm not the same.' She bit her lip, trying to keep a grip on her tears. 'I don't know how to deal with the fear, or the nightmares or the fact that I'm lying to Anna and now I've brought you into this. The guilt is sometimes worse than the fear.'

Lifting her head, she found understanding in Taylor's blue eyes, which were glassy and red-rimmed.

Tay wiped away her tears with his fingers while blinking back his own.

'I've never seen you so upset, Jaz. I don't like it,' he said before his tears escaped. 'But never doubt for a second who you are, because Anna and I don't. We know you. You are fearless, strong and our best friend. You fight for the underdog and we love that about you.' Tay kissed her forehead and then enfolded her tightly in his arms in a hug that gripped them both. Her crutches dug into her sides but she hardly registered them. 'I know a little of what you're going through,' he whispered against her ear. 'We'll get through it together. You're not alone, ever.'

'And neither are you, Tay,' she said between hiccups.

They stayed like that, clinging to each other as silent tears eased some of their burdens. Her arms were beginning to ache for holding him so hard.

Suddenly someone cleared their throat behind them. Jaz lifted her head from Tay's shoulder and wiped away her tears, only to see Ryan standing there awkwardly.

'Ryan, what are you doing here?' she said, quickly stepping out of Tay's embrace. She felt like she'd been caught out, for being with Tay and for being weak. Ryan had seen enough of her weaknesses already.

Taylor didn't turn around, just stayed facing the grave and wiping his face slyly.

'I came to see you. Are you both okay?'

Ryan's deep gravelly voice caressed her, his concern nearly starting a fresh batch of tears. 'Yeah, we're all right.' She glanced around the cemetery before returning to Ryan and his muscled arms. 'How did you know we were here?' she asked. His eyes went to the flower on Becky's grave. He had eyes everywhere.

'Can we talk?' he asked, causing Taylor to finally turn around. 'Taylor, I'll take Jaz home, if that's all right with you?'

Tay turned to Jaz. She nodded. 'I'll call you later.' He reached for her hand, gave it a squeeze and they shared a smile. This moment had been a release for them both.

'Later.' Taylor gave Ryan a brief wave before walking off through the cemetery. Jaz watched him leave, not yet ready to face Ryan's questions.

'Are you two …' His words fell away into emptiness.

'Helping each other deal with what we've been through? Yeah, we are,' she said rather harshly. Her emotions were still simmering underneath the surface, not yet back in her tightly locked box. But her anger dissipated a few seconds later when she felt the heat from Ryan's body directly behind her. She had to use all her strength not to lean back into his chest. To seek out the comfort she knew she could find there.

'I'm glad you have someone to help you through it.' His gentle words floated over her right shoulder.

Neither of them moved even though Jaz was acutely aware of how close he was. She closed her eyes and just enjoyed his scent that calmed her like a relaxing bubble bath. 'How did you know we were here?' she eventually asked.

'We have eyes everywhere, Jaz. Not just agents but people who go about their daily jobs and collect information for us.'

'So, someone at the cemetery works for the Agency?' she said, finally turning to him. In the late afternoon, Ryan looked sexier than usual, and more dangerous. His brief nod was his only reply. Jaz so badly wanted to glance around her. How many people worked at the cemetery and which one reported back when she left messages? How the Agency worked was amazing. 'So. What did you want to talk about?'

'Come, let's walk back to my car,' he said, reaching for her arm.

His touch was temporary, his fingers dropping away once they started towards the pathway.

'What was it like at Marcus's?' he asked.

Yes, work. It always was. 'Fine. No one was out to charge me for murder,' she tried to joke but it came out flat. 'I did come across two names in Carl's briefcase that might be of interest.'

'His briefcase?' His tone was one of warning.

'It's okay, I was careful. I wasn't caught.' Jaz went on to tell him about the customs forms and her theory on Carl having someone on the inside. 'I also found a business card for Jameson Figlomeni.'

Ryan stopped her. 'Are you sure on that name?' he asked a little too gruffly.

'Yes. Why?'

'No reason,' he said and began walking again.

Jaz felt a spark of fury begin to burn in the pit of her stomach because she knew Ryan was holding something back. 'Do you know that name? Have you been watching him? Why won't you tell me?'

'The less you know the better,' was all he said. 'Come on, I have someone who wants to meet you.'

Jaz gritted her teeth and almost stamped her foot in frustration. She hated not knowing all the details. 'One day I hope you can trust me enough to tell me.'

Ryan strode to his car, his pace steady while he replied. 'Jaz, it's not about trust, it's about keeping you alive.'

Ryan drove as all the streetlights began to come on in the dying afternoon light. He pulled up outside a church fifteen minutes later. She raised an eyebrow but didn't mutter a word, even though she was curious as to who would want to meet her and why in a church. Was it a priest? Was he going to save her soul? Would he try to get her to repent her sins, because murder was a bloody big one and a few Hail Mary's probably wasn't going to cut it.

'Now, this is a pretty big deal. The Commander is an amazing guy, he's our senior rank and also one who has personally helped me. Jaz, this guy doesn't just meet people for the hell of it. He's heard about what you've done, the info you've got us, and he's intrigued.'

The smile on Ryan's face was full of pride and Jaz felt her body glow with warmth. 'So, this is a good thing?'

'Yes. It's an honour, Jaz. The Commander received the *Légion d'Honneur d'Afrique* medal from the French Foreign Legion in Djibouti, and was also honoured by our own Queen.'

'Like as in the Queen of England Queen?' His smile confirmed it. 'Really? Wow, that's amazing,' said Jaz in disbelief.

'Yep. His Queen's Honour is held on the secrets list in Whitehall in London. He's seen so many things, Jaz, and what he's taught me on various missions has saved my life more than once.'

Jaz took a moment for this to sink in. 'So *d'Honneur d'Africa* from the French … you guys really must get around.' Her brow scrunched with the thought.

'We're not just a small Perth agency thing, Jaz. It's a worldwide connection we have, working with other countries on international missions. It's been going on for years.'

Goosebumps prickled along her skin. Jaz felt just a little bit important and it made her feel proud to be a part of this organisation. People like Ryan worked hard, offered up their life, gave up their family, all to save others. Now she was training to be one of them. 'Have you received any awards or medals?'

'I have. One from a foreign country last year for leading a platoon on a live operation.'

He wasn't gloating but Jaz could hear the pride in his voice and she felt so proud of him.

'And you're the first person I've told about it,' he said with a smile.

'Wow. That's very cool, Ryan. And it's a little sad that you don't get recognised for all that you do. Except for a medal you can't ever show anyone.'

'None of us do it for the awards, Jaz.' He was spot on; it was exactly how she felt. 'Come on, let's get in there.'

Ryan led Jaz into the large brick church through huge arched doors. She'd never been inside a church but an eerie feeling came over her, like she was somewhere very special. It might have been the high-swept ceilings, beautiful leadlight windows and the many burning candles.

They walked on a red patterned carpet down the centre of the rows of hard-looking pews. Arched windows on the far walls matched the massive arches held up by big white pillars. There were six people scattered about, some with their heads bowed. Ryan led her to a pew off to the right, which was behind a large pillar and near a door. It's where she would have picked to sit too.

As they sat down she glanced around. 'Is he here?' she whispered.

'He'll be watching. He'll join us in a minute.' Ryan leaned forward on his knees and stared at the huge colourful mosaic on the end wall..

Jaz chewed her lip and jiggled her leg. Ryan shot her a look. 'What?'

He glanced at her leg and she stopped immediately but then found she was tapping her fingers.

'There's nothing to be nervous about,' he said with a hint of a grin.

'I'm not nervous,' said Jaz. 'It's being in here. It's new to me.'

'You don't do Bible studies at your fancy school?' he teased.

Jaz wanted to stick her tongue out at him. 'No, I got out of them.' Skipped class more like it.

Ryan's face came over all serious and she realised they had company. He didn't say a word as he reached past Jaz and shook the man's hand.

He was dressed in a khaki-coloured shirt with lapels on the shoulders and pockets on the front, and wore a leather belt and jeans. He seemed like anyone else except for his upright posture that gave away his strength. And his steel grey eyes and stern jaw were those of a leader.

The Commander looked to be in his late forties, with a few lines on his face and some scars. Others would dismiss them as nothing but straight-away Jaz wondered what kind of combat led to them, and whether his body was as scarred as Ryan's. She also knew that if Ryan trusted him, then so did she. Sitting beside him gave her the similar feeling of protection and safety that she only ever got from Ryan.

'It's good to see you again, Ryan. Hello, Jaz,' he said in an authorita-tive voice but with a smile, and Jaz instantly liked him. She was no fool, though. In his eyes and in the grip of his strong fingers she saw a dangerous man, a man who had seen many deaths. What scared Jaz more was that she was able to recognise this.

'Sir,' she said.

'Call me Ian.' His eyes never sat still, always checking, always on alert.

Then they rested on her briefly. She wondered what he thought of the girl in a school uniform sitting beside him.

'Finally we meet. I've heard some great things about you. It's not often we bring someone in who doesn't need all the training like the others. You've already proved your strength and your bravado.' He chuckled at this. 'Although Ryan thinks you were a bit reckless, I'm willing to put it down as determination. I think we're going to see amazing things from you, Jaz.'

Ryan shifted beside her, his leg momentarily touching hers. 'Thanks, I think,' she replied.

'But there is much yet to learn. While your leg is healing, Ryan has some more training for you planned and then there's the issue of what you've uncovered with Carl.' Ian, without pausing, glanced about casually. 'This mission will be all yours.'

Jaz gulped as those steel-coloured eyes locked on to hers. 'What do you mean?'

'Exactly that. You know all the details, so you are to give it a name, work out the details of the sea-container sale, put people in place to watch, follow the drugs, and decide on when to give the order. It is your operation and you are in charge.'

She was having trouble understanding exactly what he was saying. Surely he meant Ryan, not her? Flicking to Ryan she waited for an answer but he just nodded seriously.

'I'll follow your lead, Jaz,' said Ryan.

Jaz's mouth fell open. 'Are you serious?'

'Deadly serious,' replied Ian. 'It's a developed system that is our best for instant training. It will give you the confidence to do it and to do it well.'

This was not happening. 'But I'm not even eighteen. What if I stuff it up?' Had Ian breathed in too much of the incense burning by the front door? Or taken one too many hits to the head? Jaz glanced to Ryan for reassurance that Ian was totally sane.

'I was just nineteen when I led my first mission, Jaz. It's like a great big hurdle; once you overcome that, everything else is easy.'

Jaz felt like sliding off her pew onto the floor in a fainted mess. This was ten times worse than the feeling she got before cramming for a big exam. With this, so much was riding on the outcome. It wasn't just a grade, this could affect people's lives, even cause deaths. A curse rumbled up her throat. 'Fuuu …' And then she remembered where she was. 'Far out.'

'Nice save,' teased Ryan.

His words were light but the pressure of his arm against her body gave her calm. She knew he was doing it to show his support, that he was there for her. But did he realise just how much she depended on it? How much she craved his touch and just how much belief it gave her in herself? It was as if she could do anything as long as she knew Ryan was in her corner. Even stop a million-dollar drug trade without inflicting any casualties. As the seconds ticked by, thoughts were coming together and plans were formulating as if Jaz were writing her own scene in a book. Her confidence grew with each idea. She could do this, couldn't she?

'If you have any questions or problems you have Ryan, so don't feel like you are doing this alone. But on the day, all will be under your command.'

'Mine?' Jaz pointed to herself, just to make double sure. 'And you'll be there?'

'Yes, if need be. You let Ryan know how many operatives you'll need to see your plan through and we will be there.' Ian smiled as if he'd just set a date for a picnic.

If only.

'Right. Cool.' Jaz didn't know what else to say. Later millions of questions would probably swamp her, but right now she couldn't think of one.

'I'd best be off. Until next time, Jaz.' Ian shot her a smile and for a moment he reminded her of Taylor's dad. The same gentle smile mixed with an air of significance.

'Thanks. Bye.' She had no idea why she was thanking him after what he'd just told her. Ian disappeared from the church. Jaz turned to Ryan who was watching her intently.

'What just happened?'

CHAPTER 5

Jaz clipped her seat belt into place.

'Where to?' asked Ryan. 'Home?'

'No. Can you take me to Taylor's please?'

Ryan blinked twice. 'You're going to tell him everything, aren't you,' he said with a sigh.

'Yep. You may be able to keep it all to yourself but I've always had Tay and Anna in my corner. Nothing goes any further than them, I can assure you. Besides, since I brought Tay into this mess I like having him to discuss it with. It's one less person to lie to.'

Ryan started his car and drove through the streets with his lights on. The sun had gone but the sky was still lit from its last rays. 'You have me,' said Ryan softly.

'Pfft. Really?' Ryan was away on his missions most of the time doing God knows what, God knows where and with God knows who. Jaz couldn't contact him unless it was important. At least with Tay, he was always around and she could text him whenever she needed or cry on his shoulder. 'Sorry Ryan, but I can't depend on you.'

'Oh.' His tone was flat and hurt.

Jaz bit her lip. 'Wow, sorry that came out wrong. I mean you aren't always around when I need someone to talk to. You have important stuff going on and I understand that and I can't keep running to you with all my small problems.' She was really making a dog's breakfast of this. She was sounding a little neurotic and it annoyed her. 'With Tay in the loop I can go to him instead of bothering you with trivial things.' And maybe she'd learn to survive without the constant yearning to be with Ryan. Every time she got close to him he pulled away.

'You could never bother me, Jaz. And did you ever think I might like you coming to me? Besides, I also think these "trivial" things you talk of end up being mammoth things.' He shot her a look, the corner of his mouth curled in a smile. As the streetlights flashed past they illuminated his dark eyes.

Jaz laughed. He had a point. 'You think I'm too reckless?'

Ryan stopped at a red light and turned to her, his chin jutted out seriously. 'I just worry about you, Jasmine.'

His deep and husky words sucked the oxygen out of the car. The way he said her name had her gasping for air. Her heart throbbed in her chest as she tried to remain calm under his gaze but it was impossible. Every part of her was in chaos, from shivers to hot melting centres. She felt like she should say something, anything, but she was trapped in his sights like a deer in the headlights. But before she could analyse this moment further a horn tooted behind them, and Ryan turned his attention back to the road. She wanted to ask him what it was between them. Because it was something, she felt it with every fibre and she was sure he did too. Was he really keeping her at a distance for her safety? Or for the sake of the Agency's rules? Or was it something else? The need to reach out and touch him was so strong she gripped her seat.

Ryan cleared his throat. 'So, over the next week or two you are going to do some more training. Pax will help with a few things, mainly testing your awareness skills. You'll also need to start thinking about how this operation is going to go down, and start planning it. How long until that sea-container sale?'

'It's in a few weeks.' Jaz shifted her crutches. They were always in the way or resting somewhere uncomfortable. Maybe she was just moving them to hide the nervous jitters that skipped through her body at the thought of her new task. Jaz had led a normal, rather unexciting life until Ryan came along. Now each day held some kind of excitement, nerves or danger. She felt like she was on a rollercoaster, one she didn't want to get off.

'Good. Plenty of time. Also, once your leg is better we'll tail that guy following Tay and see if we can question him a little.'

Jaz raised an eyebrow at the word *question*. Her interpretation of Ryan's question meant using a fist or a gun. 'So, sometime next week?'

'Yep. You should be walking on that leg in the next few days but I need you fighting fit in case things get out of hand. Never go into a situation with a weakness. On saying that, you should get a large bandage and wrap it around your … um, chest so you are protected from hits.'

'You mean strap my boobs up?' Ryan squirmed in his seat and gripped the wheel. Jaz smiled. Teasing him was such fun. 'Really?'

'Yep. Our female operatives all do this and the guys go into battle with a groin protector.'

'Oh.' But she could see the benefits. A kick to the family jewels was a successful way to drop someone, and being prepared for that could save your life. 'I'll remember that,' she added. Wearing a bandage would also hide her gender, making her harder to recognise. It made her wonder if Rich had noticed the bumps on her chest when they were wrestling. An unwelcome shiver ran the length of her body. Damn.

Ryan pulled up at Tay's house. Jaz didn't move. It just didn't feel time to leave him. Maybe it never would. Every minute spend with Ryan was never enough.

'So, I'll drop round The Ring when I can. Pax is going to take the reins in between. Just focus on getting your leg healed and then we can help Tay.'

'Okay. He'll be glad to hear you have something planned. All this waiting is driving him insane. And knowing he's always being followed and the pressure his dad is under.'

'Tell him to hang in there. The moment you can kick me without wincing, we'll be good to go.' Ryan got out and ran around to get her door.

He held out his hand. Jaz reached for it, clutching his strong arm as she pulled herself out of the car carefully. She didn't want to let him go but she had to get her crutches. Good things never last, she thought with a sigh. He smelled so fine she just wanted to crawl under his shirt and wear him. Probably not a good look.

'Hey.' Ryan reached for her shoulder, warmth spreading from beneath his hand. 'I meant it before. If you ever need someone to talk to, about anything, no matter how trivial, I'll always be around … somewhere.'

Jaz smiled and was about to say 'Thanks' when his hand moved up to her face. His thumb brushed across her cheek and before she could nuzzle into it, he'd moved away.

'See ya, Jaz.' Ryan jumped back into his car and drove off, leaving Jaz alone in the street outside Tay's house. A piece of her always went with him, hopefully ensuring he always came back.

Jaz waited until his car had disappeared before she clicked up the driveway to Tay's back door, banging on it with the bottom of her crutch. 'Open up, Stewart!'

Anna opened the door. 'Welcome to our home,' she said with a warm smile and a wave of her arm.

'Hey, didn't think I'd find you here. Is everything all right?' Jaz stepped into the house and felt the prickle at the back of her neck. Even though it was a while ago, she still relived the moment Tay was held at gunpoint in his own home. She'd suffered a serious knock to the head from the same assailant. They were so going to catch the bastards who were toying with the Stewarts.

'No, everything's fine. Tay just asked if I could help him with his Trig homework. We're in his room, come on.'

'Hi Jaz,' said a voice from the kitchen.

Jaz paused. 'Oh hey, Mr Stewart. What are you up to?' It wasn't often that he was home from work this early, which made Jaz suddenly worry that something was wrong. Had the Shesha Serpents threatened him again? Was Mr Stewart home early to protect Tay?

'I had a meeting today that finished early, so I'm home to make dinner. I'm going to cook my famous steak, chips and eggs, if you're interested in staying?' Mr Stewart cocked his thick eyebrows skyward. They were the same colour as his sandy blond hair, which was going grey at the sides near his sideburns. He looked a little on the thin side, which Jaz put down to stress and not eating well. The lines at the corner of his eyes made him appear tired. But his smile was just like Taylor's and you couldn't help but see the handsome similarities between father and son. Maybe now was a time to press him for some information? But Jaz dismissed the idea straightaway. She could not do that to Tay. It felt wrong and she didn't like the idea of mixing her work with her 'normal' life.

'Thanks Mr Stewart. I will if that's okay.' Jaz paused to text her mum and let her know. 'You staying?' she asked Anna.

'Yep, of course. Mum's making her meatloaf.' Anna pulled a face like she was going to throw up. 'Totally not going home to that.'

Mr Stewart laughed at Anna as he pulled some meat out of the freezer. 'Great. I'm glad you're both staying. We love having you around. It's good for Tay and it's good for this house to have some laughter again.'

The sad smile on his face tugged at her heart. She knew he must miss his wife every moment of the day. It wasn't that many years ago that she passed away from cancer.

'Let us know if you need a hand,' said Anna. 'We'll just be with Tay.'

'I should be right. Unless you see lots of smoke,' chuckled Mr Stewart.

Anna opened Tay's door for her so she could swing her crutches straight in.

'Hey,' said Tay, jumping up from his bed.

To his credit, there were work books strewn across the bed but Jaz was dubious about him needing Anna's help. Tay wasn't exactly struggling at school.

'So, how's the study going?' said Jaz giving him a sly wink. Tay's jaw flexed but he didn't blush.

Tay checked his door was closed tightly as he whispered, 'Painfully. I'm glad you're here. I've been dying to know what Ryan said.'

They all sat huddled on the bed.

'He said as soon as I'm all better we're going to follow your tag and see where he goes. Hopefully get some information,' said Jaz.

'I want to come,' said Anna.

Jaz frowned.

'I'm going too,' Tay determinedly. 'It's my family they're threatening, so there's no way I'm being left behind either.'

'Ryan won't like it on either count.' Jaz chewed her lip. 'Maybe I could text you where we end up, but you'd have to stay back.' She gave him her sternest expression.

'We will,' said Anna nodding vigorously.

'Anna, I don't think it's a good idea—' began Tay, but he was cut off.

'You will *not* leave me out of this. I don't care if it's dangerous. You are my best friend, no one messes with my friends. Besides, I know how to fire a gun,' Anna said, matter of fact.

'Um, no one need take a gun,' said Jaz. Shit, Ryan would kill her if he found out what these two were planning. 'I'll only text you where we are *if* you promise to wait outside in the car. Let us handle it.'

'Why do you get to go?' asked Anna suddenly.

Jaz realised her mistake. 'Um, only cos I know how Ryan works and I'll be his eyes and back-up.' Anna squinted and Jaz waited for her to call her out on her lie.

'I guess you do know how to fight. Damn, I wish I had some special skills,' said Anna, dropping her head forward causing her hair to fall around her face like curtains.

Tay leaned against Anna, bumping her shoulder. 'Hey, you do. What you can do with a computer leaves us for dead. Just look at how you saved Ryan's arse by figuring out Pax's secret computer stuff.' Tay's words put a smile on her face.

'Yeah, I am pretty speckie, hey?' Anna joked but didn't smile. She gazed at them with big round eyes.

Jaz felt the guilt at lying to Anna gurgle in her stomach. Her friend knew they were keeping something from her but she didn't pester them, which only made Jaz feel worse. She reached over and held Anna's hand.

That night they sat around the table eating together like a family, and by the way Mr Stewart and Taylor smiled and laughed, Jaz knew it had meant the world to them. Something they hadn't had in a while. They told jokes in between Mr Stewart's crazy cop stories from his early days. Tay hung on every word even though he'd probably heard them all before. It was more than likely the first time either of them had relaxed in a while, knowing Tay and the house were being watched.

Afterwards Tay drove them both home, which seemed silly because they lived close by but her bad leg made the decision easy. Mr Stewart hugged them goodbye and came out to the street to watch them leave. But Jaz knew he was checking the area, scoping out any undesirables.

As Jaz headed up to her room she thought back to six months ago when life seemed boring, when she was oblivious to the ugly side of life and still innocent when it came to death. Gosh, how times had changed.

With Ryan's words echoing around in her mind, Jaz got down on the floor and did a set of push-ups and crunches. She needed to be ready to go as soon as possible. There were people to hunt.

The next day after school, Pax was waiting in his little red car to take Jaz to The Ring while Anna went to the library and Tay to basketball training. It was the little bit of freedom from her friends she needed to get some work done with Pax. Although she wasn't quite sure what work it would be exactly.

Pax parked out the front of the gym, which was weird because he always went around the back.

'Okay, Jaz. I want you to walk into the gym and by the time I get back in there I want you to tell me all the things you notice that are different.' Pax pushed up his glasses and grinned.

'You're having fun with this, aren't you?' she said with a smile.

'It's not often I get to be involved like this. Go on, I'll meet you inside.' Pax drove off and parked around the back while Jaz headed inside the white door.

Bags was working out on the speedball, sweat running down his skin like a shower. Usually a tell-tale sign that the characters in his book weren't doing what he wanted. But instead of asking him about it, Jaz focused on the rest of the gym interior.

She made a mental note of things that had been moved, removed or just seemed out of place.

'Righto, how did you go? List them,' said Pax who'd come in through the office, puffing slightly. He had a clipboard and a pen.

'Mohammad Ali's photo isn't straight; there's a strange bag by the window and a note stuck to the change-room door; the back corner light isn't working.' Jaz's eyes darted about as she listed all the things she could spot. She rattled off nine details in total while Pax's pen moved across the page.

'How did I go?' she said quietly.

'Great. Amazing, actually.' Pax smiled as if she'd just won a marathon. 'You got them all except the tape over the lock on the office door.'

'Ah, yep. Am I allowed to move around? If I'd been closer I might have seen it.'

'No,' said Pax with a shake of his head. 'You might only get this far into a room, so you need to practise spotting things from a distance with just a glance. Ryan said every little detail could tell you something about what's happened in the room. A stray bag could have something significant in it or belong to someone new. A moved picture could mean someone has searched the room already, scratches or stuff around locks could mean a break-in … You get the gist. Now we'll try this again but in the office.'

Jaz followed him feeling nervous, like she was taking a test that she wanted a hundred percent on. Pax waddled to the office in his jandals, shorts, patterned shirt and clipboard.

'Now I'm going to lift this tea towel.' Jaz frowned at the dirty green towel on the computer desk. 'And you have two seconds to memorise all that you see before I cover it up again. Ready?' said Pax.

The towel came off and Jaz started from one side and worked her way across, trying to take a mental picture of what she'd seen before Pax threw it over again.

'Well?'

Jaz closed her eyes to help her focus and began to list things. 'Stapler, red pen, blue pen, three paper clips, AC/DC CD, glasses case, scissors, a post-it note with "Get lunch" on it.' Jaz opened her eyes. 'And the gym keys.'

Pax's eyebrows shot up. He didn't say anything but pulled the tea towel off for her to check.

'Ah bugger, it was four paper clips,' said Jaz.

'Shit,' said Pax, who normally wasn't one to swear. 'How did you get all of them and what was written on the post-it note? I've been trying this all day and I'm the one who put it all there and I still couldn't remember.' He shook his head.

Jaz shrugged. 'I don't know. Too many spy movies,' she teased. 'I guess I already know how important it is to remember things from Ryan and how crucial the small details are, like what's written on notes. I've had practice at Marcus's house too, Pax. Every time I step foot in there I'm looking at everything. Don't feel too bad.' She gave him a hug and breathed in deeply. 'Is that pastry I smell?' Jaz sniffed again but closer to Pax. 'It is! Pax! You know you're not supposed to eat them. What if you have another heart attack?' said Jaz, throwing her hands on her hips.

Pax turned a shade of pink. 'I have been good, but what is life if I can't have at least one now and then.' He frowned.

It was hard to stay cross with his kind eyes seeking sympathy. 'As long as it's only one a week.' Pax's eyes shot to the left and she knew it wasn't. 'Pax, people are counting on you. If you get sick again, who's going to take over?'

'Jaz, don't fret. I'm as tough as old boot leather.' He slapped his round belly.

'I used to think that, Pax, until I found you slumped on the floor half dead. I can't go through that again.' She reached out and held him tight. 'Please, look after yourself or else Anna and I will put a detail on your arse and watch everything that goes into your mouth.' Jaz had a better thought. 'Maybe you should start training Anna for Agency work. Especially if you're going to eat yourself into an early grave.' Jaz was cross and she wanted to scare him because he'd scared the hell out of her by nearly dying.

'Train me for what?'

Jaz and Pax turned around to find Anna standing behind them. All colour drained from Pax's face.

'Anyone wanna tell me what's going on?'

CHAPTER 6

'It's nothing,' said Pax quickly.

'He's been eating pastries,' said Jaz, hoping to shift the conversation.

Anna's mouth dropped open. 'Pax!'

He shot Jaz a traitorous glance.

Anna closed the office door, even though it was only Bags in the gym pounding the speedball. 'But that wasn't what you were talking about, was it? That's it. I think it's time the truth came out, don't you?' Pax's face was grim and his eye twitched slightly. 'I want you to teach me what you do. I want to be involved. I want to help, I *know* I can help.' Anna stood her ground, looking foreboding even in her school uniform.

Jaz tried to hide her smile. She was so proud of Anna. Her words were clear and strong.

'I ... um, don't know what you're talking about.' Pax's voice raised in pitch just as a line of sweat broke out on his brow.

'You can't fob me off, Pax. I know what you keep in your locked room and I know you're doing some important stuff.' Anna stepped closer, her eyes narrowed.

'How do you know—'

'Who do you think finished Ryan's special passport?' said Anna.

Pax pushed up his glasses and swung around to Jaz accusingly. 'I told you not to bring her into it!' It was as close to a growl as Pax had ever come.

'It wasn't Jaz,' said Anna. 'I found your room long before that. You have some amazing gear in there and I want to use it.'

Anna didn't mention the fake IDs she'd made them, which was

probably a good thing right now. Pax was growing redder by the second and Jaz worried he might be having another heart attack. 'Pax, are you okay?' She gripped his shoulder and he released his held breath with a rush, his colour returning. 'How about we take this into the kitchen and have a strong coffee. It's time we all talked.'

No one disagreed, so they shuffled into his house. Anna and Pax sat opposite each other at the table while Jaz made the coffee. It wasn't until they each had their cup that Anna broke the silence.

'Can you tell me what exactly it is that you do, Pax? Please.'

Pax took a big skol of his coffee, wincing from the hotness, before he replied. 'Do I have a choice? By the sounds of it you know too much already.' Anna waited patiently, her face set seriously. 'All right. I work for the government in a special secret branch. The MTG Agency, to give it a name, but we just call it the Agency.' He sighed, defeated. 'I was recruited due to my computer skills to help make the necessary documents needed for the operatives – or agents – to carry out their missions.'

'Missions? Like the one Ryan had to go on to Pakistan?' said Anna.

He winced at the knowledge she had gained, everything he'd been trying to keep from her. Jaz felt sorry for him, but they were no longer little girls.

'Yes,' replied Pax. 'Often I have to make a whole new identity for someone. I travel a lot, keep up to date with the latest technology and do special drops for documents. Years ago things were a lot simpler, but with the way technology changes it's hard to keep on top of it, for an old man like me.'

Anna leaned forward, her coffee forgotten and her brow set in concentration. 'So then, teach me. I'm ready, my mind is sharp. I want this, Pax. I want the challenge.'

But he was already shaking his head. 'I can't have you involved, Anna. It's dangerous work. It's bad enough that Jaz is involved.'

Jaz nearly choked on her coffee.

Anna's eyes popped. 'Jaz. *What?*'

Jaz smiled as if she'd just been caught eating the last chocolate biscuit. 'Sorry Anna. I really wanted to tell you but I couldn't. Guess I don't have to now, thanks Pax.' Her shock was soon replaced by relief. Her friend now knew and she hadn't betrayed Ryan or the Agency.

Pax spluttered. 'Damn.'

'Bloody hell, how many other secrets are there that I don't know about? Does Tay know?'

'He found out by accident. I couldn't tell either of you, no matter how much I wanted to. You understand, don't you, Anna? Please don't hate me.' Jaz watched her friend closely. She knew every freckle on Anna's face, she knew each smile and could read her every mood. Life without Anna just wouldn't be worth living.

Anna sighed, her shoulders dropped. 'I knew something was up with you and Tay. Neither of you has been the same lately.' Her piercing green eyes held Jaz's. 'So, what is it? Are you with this Agency too? Just like Ryan?'

Jaz nodded. 'He recruited me. I agreed to join after our school ball.' She had to tell her the truth, all of it now. Jaz wanted no stone left unturned. She'd lied for long enough to her best friend.

'Oh, wow.' Anna watched the both of them. She thought for a moment. 'Well, that's it then. I definitely want in. There's no way I'm not going to have my friends back. Pax? Please?'

Pax sunk his face into his hands and groaned. 'I wish Ryan had never stepped foot inside The Ring. I curse that day.'

'Please, Pax,' pleaded Jaz. 'The day Ryan offered me a job at the Agency was the day I felt like I'd finally found my purpose in life. Don't take that away from Anna. You know she can do it with her eyes closed. I need someone out there I can trust, and you could use the help. Especially if you keep eating crap.' She rolled her eyes.

'I can't believe you've been ignoring the doctor's warnings,' added Anna. 'Are you taking your medication?'

He sat up. 'Of course. I'm not that stupid. It's hard to change bad habits. I'm trying. You two are worse than a nagging wife.'

'We love you,' said Anna sweetly. 'So. Do you think the Agency will let me learn the ropes?'

Pax pushed his cup away from him. 'I guess there's nothing I can say to persuade you otherwise?'

Anna shook her head. 'No. Pax, let me into your world. Let me do something great.' She cocked her head to the side and smiled. 'Funny how so much makes sense now.'

Jaz chuckled, remembering how she'd thought the same after finding out about Pax.

'I'll need to check with the Agency first. It comes down to them.' Pax scratched his head. His posture was defeated, clearly he wasn't happy about any of this.

'Well, don't sell me short,' said Anna.

'He won't. Will you, Pax?' Jaz reached for his hand. The contrast of his aging skin against hers made him seem so fragile. She leaned in and put her hand on his chest. 'Do you feel that, Pax? That some of the weight has gone from your chest now there's one less person to lie to.'

And for the first time since Anna had caught him out, Pax actually smiled. He covered her hand, patting it. They both shared that feeling of relief. Jaz had only been lying a short time and it had nearly killed her. She couldn't imagine what a lifetime had done to Pax.

'Okay. I'll make contact tomorrow.'

Anna reached across and put her hand on his too. 'Thanks Pax. You won't regret it.'

'Hmm, that's debatable,' he said, as they all sat back in their chairs.

'So, how did Tay find out, then?' asked Anna.

Oh dear. Where did Jaz start? She decided the beginning was the best. She told her about Marcus and his dad and the night she called Taylor to help.

'Oh my *God*. That's a bullet wound!' Anna almost shrieked as she pointed to Jaz's leg. Then her tone changed. 'Can I see it? Does it look as cool as Ryan's?'

Jaz lost it laughing while Pax rolled his eyes. 'How about I leave you two to chat while I check on Bags and set up another test for you, Jaz. I'll be about ten minutes.'

'Okay.'

After Pax left, Jaz showed Anna her wound. It was still a little raw and sore but no longer bleeding or weeping.

'You've only just met Ryan and yet you have this *and* that knife wound.'

'In his defence, the knife attack wasn't Agency related.'

'I know,' said Anna. 'It just seems to add to it all. But what about Tay?

How are you both coping with … you know? That.' She grimaced. *That* was a better word than *death*.

'Not well. We took a life, Anna. It's haunting us both. Tay is going to be so relieved that you know. He really needs you. We both do. Thank you for understanding all of this.' Anna could have been pissed at them for lying to her and keeping secrets, and she would have had every right to be, but it showed just how thick their bonds were that she didn't turn her back on them. Instead she was jumping in with them. Like the Musketeers, one for all and all for one. Her fencing coach would be proud.

'Jaz,' called Pax from the gym.

'Right, I better go and practise some more. Well talk later, yeah?' said Jaz as she got up.

Anna nodded. 'I'm not going anywhere. I have so many more questions, you know.'

'Yeah, well, I'm not going anywhere either.'

Anna came and hugged her tight. It was everything Jaz needed.

After Pax ran her through some more memory drills she changed into her workout clothes. She needed to get her blood pumping; plus the gym needed to be cleaned. Pax didn't want her to do it but Jaz wasn't an invalid and the work was all exercise anyway. Every bit would count.

She was at the speedball, dripping with sweat, when her phone chimed an hour later. It was Marcus, seeing how she was. His concern brought a smile to her lips. She had The Ring to herself, Pax and Anna had no doubt snuck off to his special room for some geek speak. After replying to Marcus, she went and stuck her head into Pax's special room. It was weird the door not being locked anymore.

'Having fun, kids?' Both had their heads together by the big screen. 'I'm ready to head home.'

'I'll take you both. How did you get here, Anna?' Pax asked.

'Ricky dropped me off after the library. But I don't want to go home yet, this is all so interesting.'

'It may be,' he said. 'But it will still be here tomorrow.'

Anna grinned. 'I'll come here straight after school with Jaz.'

Pax was shaking his head as they got up to leave. 'No, Jaz has other plans.'

'I do?'

He waited until he'd locked the door. 'Yes. Ryan will pick you up from school, he's teaching you some hand signals with one of the other recruits.'

'Oh, that sounds like fun,' said Anna as she almost skipped outside towards the car.

'Right. Another recruit.' Jaz was a little disappointed that she had to share her time with Ryan. But the idea of learning hand signals was exciting. She'd seen Ryan use them in Pakistan with his colleague Tilly when they were in trouble. No words were needed yet they each knew exactly what the other was going to do. Jaz wanted that knowledge.

'He said to bring your study books,' Pax added.

As he drove them home, Jaz didn't ask why she'd need her books. Knowing Ryan, there was a good reason.

'Thanks Pax, see you tomorrow,' they said as they waved goodbye outside Jaz's house.

'It's funny. I always felt in my bones that Pax was different and exciting, you know. Not like my family. He just radiates something else and now, now it all makes sense. Life doesn't seem so dull anymore, hey,' said Anna as she watched the little red car disappear up the street.

'I know what you mean.'

'I also feel like I'm so much closer to Pax. His secrets are my secrets. And you too.' Anna reached out and hugged her again. 'I love you, Jaz. I'm glad there's no more secrets. There aren't, are there?'

'Not secrets, but there is more to tell.' Like Pakistan and the operation she was tasked with.

'Hello, lovely ladies,' said a voice.

They turned to see Taylor walking up the street. His walk was slow and casual, his hands deep in the pockets on his loose jeans. He'd changed out of his uniform and was wearing a casual grey T-shirt and his white Nikes.

'Tay, what are you doing on foot? Where's your Mustang?'

'Got bored at home and thought I'd see if you were back.' His eyes went straight to Anna. She launched into his arms and squeezed him tightly.

'Oh, Tay. I'm so sorry,' she said.

Tay shot Jaz a confused look. 'She *knows*, Tay.'

'Pax and Jaz told me everything. I can't believe it! But it's okay, I'm here for you now,' she whispered into Tay's neck. His eyes softened as her words sunk in. Dragging his hands out of his jeans he wrapped them around Anna.

His tension fell away as he savoured the hug and pressed his lips against her shoulder. Jaz couldn't keep the silly grin off her face. They looked so good together.

He sighed. 'Thank God. I hated not telling you.'

Anna leaned back so she could see his face. 'You were amazing to save Jaz. I'm so glad you had her back.'

Jaz cleared her throat. 'How about you take Tay home to the treehouse and talk?' she suggested. 'Somewhere quiet and private. I have to go home and help with dinner.'

Anna finally pulled away but her hand found his. 'Good plan. Come on, Tay. See ya tomorrow, Jazzy.'

'Bye Anna, see ya Tay.' Taylor shot her a massive smile, his eyes grateful. As her best friend strolled towards her house with Tay in tow, Jaz couldn't help but be thankful that she had both of them in her life. Things didn't seem so life crushing when you had dedicated friends to share your pain with. And having them by her side was what was going to get Jaz through her new life and all the changes. She could survive her nightmares with those two in her corner.

CHAPTER 7

AT SCHOOL THE next day Anna never left their sides, as if they would collapse in their own grief if she wasn't there to hold their hands. It was nice. Things were like before Anna started dating Ricky; they sat at their table at lunchtime together again, laughing and telling jokes. Jaz felt better and she knew Taylor did too. Anna was the distraction from their thoughts.

Ricky walked past and gave Anna a weak smile before dropping his head and leaving the cafeteria with a sandwich.

'You could have asked Ricky to eat with us,' said Jaz.

Anna rolled her apple around her hand, engrossed.

'I promise I'll behave,' said Tay. 'If you want him to join us.'

She shrugged. 'No, it's fine.' Anna cleared her throat. 'We've actually just gone back to being friends. I don't really want the complications of a boyfriend right now.'

Jaz and Tay shared a glance, both forcing their smiles to remain hidden. 'We're sorry, Anna. Are you sure you're okay?' So much focus had been on them lately. Jaz felt bad for not realising Anna and Ricky had broken up.

'Gosh yeah, don't worry about me. It wasn't that serious. It's not like I loved him or anything.'

Tay wrapped his arm around her shoulders. 'You still have us.' He kissed her head before letting her go.

Minka walked past, witnessed the exchange and faked a gag. Anna turned a shade of pink.

Minka sashayed away, her uniform skirt pushing the boundaries of ridiculously short. 'Some days I wish it was her dad we were investigating,' Jaz whispered softly. She'd rather Minka suffered than Marcus. While she was thinking of him, she pulled out her phone and sent him a text, explaining that she was studying with friends after school and couldn't meet up but would call him before she went to bed. They'd only just started doing that, talking to each other at night, which was nice but Jaz was worried she would come to like it too much and end up depending on his calm soft voice. It had certainly helped with her nightmares.

Once this mission with Marcus was finished she'd no longer have his calls to look forward to and would mourn the loss of a great friend. She was in no hurry to get to that point.

After school, Ryan was waiting for her, just as Pax had said. Instead of leaving her books in her locker, she packed them in her bag as requested. Today had also been a step forward when she left her crutches at home. She dragged her foot a bit when she walked and still kept most of her weight on her other side but at least she didn't have those metal legs to manoeuvre around. Walking was done at a snail's pace though, and going down the steps caused her some pain, but seeing Ryan waiting by his car made it all worth it. The man was hot. He was dressed casually in stonewash jeans with a tear by the knee. He had on a plain grey V-neck shirt with a small pocket on the right. But it was his tanned skin tight across his muscles that she noticed the most. He had amazing arms. His tall, strong body commanded attention.

'Good luck,' said Anna giving her a thumbs up and dragging Jaz's mind from her appraisal of Ryan. Tay was taking her to The Ring for her computer lessons. She'd talked of nothing else all day.

'You too.'

Ryan waved to her friends as they went past, before reaching out to take her school bag. 'How are you? No crutches, hey?'

'Yeah. It's not so bad. Still can't chase anyone yet.'

Ryan opened the back door, threw her bag inside before standing by the door for her to get in. Someone else was in the front seat!

As Ryan pushed it shut his scent saturated the air around her, making Jaz sink back into the seat like lava.

'Hi. I'm Cody. You must be Jaz?' said the warm voice from the front seat. His hand reached into the back, invading her moment of lust.

She bolted upright. 'Hi. Yep, I'm Jaz.' His hand was strong as she shook it. Cody had a mop of blond hair. He looked like a surfie, deep tan and bright blue eyes.

Ryan climbed in as Cody withdrew his hand. He didn't say anything, just started the car and drove them to a park not far away. When he pulled up in a parking space he nodded to the bench in front. 'We'll sit there. Jaz, bring your bag.' Then he got out. He seemed so formal; was it because of Cody, Jaz wondered.

At the metal bench, Ryan helped Jaz spread out her books. 'Jaz, you might want to take notes to study later.' At this, Cody pulled out a small notepad and a pencil from his back pocket.

'Now, both of you have your own ops coming up, so it's imperative that you know hand signals to control your team. There will be no speaking and no use of names.'

Jaz glanced at Cody, curious as to what his op entailed. He tucked some of his unruly hair behind his ear, which was pierced with a small black stud. How long had he been with the Agency? How old was he? Cody turned and caught her gaze. Was he wondering the exact same thing about her?

'So, let's start with the basics. A raised open hand means "stop",' he said, showing them. 'A closed fist means "go down to cover".'

Jaz quickly wrote it on her notepad along with a quick picture.

Ryan showed them the signs for listen, see, change direction, come together, move in quickly, how to show number of opposition approaching and much more. 'Don't worry if it seems like a lot, we'll put these into practice on Saturday and you'll have them sorted in no time. But if we're doing a daylight surveillance it's slightly different. You don't want to be seen waving your arms about. In the next few days, you two are going to work together to keep surveillance on someone.'

They both nodded and Jaz felt the kick of adrenaline, of excitement.

'So, if you were watching someone in a restaurant it's different because you need to be unnoticeable.' Ryan put his hands on the bench and stroked his left hand then turned it over and put one finger in his palm. Jaz bit her lip, unsure of what he'd just done. 'I just told you I have one target on my left.' Quickly they jotted this down. 'Maybe while you're sitting there you notice two guys at another table watching suspiciously, maybe they're guards, so you tell your partner "two guys on my right".' Ryan stroked his right hand then splayed two fingers on that palm. 'If you see your target making moves to leave, then you would close your fists quickly.' It looked like Ryan was just stretching his fingers. 'This would alert your man to get out so that he could follow from the front while you follow at the back.'

After Ryan had gone through all the hand signals for combat and surveillance, he tested them. He'd give them scenarios and wait for them to come up with the right command. Jaz had to concentrate because Cody was good. She felt like she was competing at school for top honours and had to go up against the best. Cody's eyes were focused and she recognised that instinct to win, the desire to be the best because she had felt it herself on many occasions.

'I'll be back,' said Ryan as he got up and walked towards the toilet block.

He'd hardly walked five metres before Cody asked his first question. 'So, how long have you been with the Agency?' he said leaning forward.

'A few months now. How about you?'

'Going on seven months.' His brow came together and his forehead creased. 'How old are you? You're still in school.' He made it sound ridiculous.

'Nearly eighteen. Why, how old are you?'

'Nineteen.'

His eyes squinted, his eyelashes were quite long. 'Have you been on any missions?' Jaz asked.

'On a couple of small ones, mainly surveillance.' He sat up as if he'd just saved the world. 'What happened to your leg?'

'I got shot.'

Cody's eyes bulged. 'No shit? Really?'

Jaz just nodded. Cody squirmed, clearly desperate to know more. 'What do you do for work?' she asked, trying to change direction.

'I work at the casino and the racetrack mainly, and a few other gigs.'

He glanced to the toilets. 'Hey, how did you get shot? And how long have you known Ryan? Did he recruit you?'

'Yep. Did he recruit you?' She countered, hoping he would forget his first question.

Cody shook his head. 'No. I was surfing with this dude called Mac on a few occasions. One day these guys were harassing a girl, I told them to leave her alone and then one threw a punch, then the others. But I sent them all home with a few bruises,' he said with a wink. 'My dad's in the Air Force, so I was carted from school to school growing up and used to get into plenty of trouble.' The twinkle in his eyes suggested he quite liked making trouble. 'Anyway, Mac had been watching and not long after that he approached me about this gig. I was amazed at how much he knew about me. Kinda scary.' He shrugged. 'Mac said he saw a great fearless leader in me, but I don't see it. Not yet anyway.'

Jaz watched him as he threaded his fingers in front of him. 'Isn't it funny how others can see things in us that we haven't even figured out yet? Nothing like this had crossed my mind before but now I think I was born for it. I'm glad Ryan thought this was for me.'

Cody's head leaned to the side as he watched her. 'You're a strange one, Jaz. You look nothing like a secret soldier,' he said with a cute smile.

'She may look sweet and innocent but she'll knock your arse to the floor if you're not careful,' said Ryan as he came to stand by the bench.

Cody looked like he was about to laugh until he saw how rigid Ryan's face was and his smile slipped from his face.

'Listen up. I want you both to write up a scenario and then you're going to hand signal it to each other. Afterwards you can check how close you came to getting the details right.'

Jaz and Cody eyeballed each other. Yep, they were both in this to win. But neither one did, both getting a few bits wrong, so it ended up a draw.

'Righto, time to go,' said Ryan.

They'd been in the park for over two hours by the time Ryan called it a day. Jaz packed up her books and notepads while some kids rolled by on skateboards. Without thinking she smiled, wishing she could use hers. If she'd never taken on the mission with Marcus, then she'd never have known the challenge of riding a skateboard.

'So, can I get your number?' asked Cody.

For a minute Jaz thought he was talking to Ryan, but his eyes were on her and his phone was in his hand ready.

Jaz glanced to Ryan, who stood with his hands pushed into his back pockets. All that did was emphasise his strong pecs. She had to drag her eyes further up to his face. 'Is that okay?' she asked, unsure of Agency regulations. Ryan's cheek pulsed as if he was grinding his teeth. 'I could call Cody if I can't get you. Be better than Tay, wouldn't it?'

'I guess so,' he said bleakly.

Jaz called out her number and Cody plugged it into his phone. When he was done, he shot her a slightly lopsided smile. He had one tooth that was a little crooked, but teamed with his smile it seemed to give him more character.

'Cool. I'll send you a text so you have mine. So, who's Tay?'

'My best friend,' said Jaz frankly. 'Oh Ryan,' she said reaching for his arm. 'I don't know if you've heard, but Anna might be joining us.' Jaz tried to lay on as much innuendo as possible.

His eyes went to her hand latched onto his arm, which she drew back quickly as if his eyes shot out laser beams.

'What do you mean?' He frowned.

'Pax let the cat out of the bag. She knows everything now and we're just waiting on the Agency's approval,' said Jaz cryptically. She didn't really want to spell it out with Cody listening in.

Ryan's brow shot up. 'Right. I see.' He pondered this for a moment before turning to the car.

Jaz and Cody followed him. At the car her phone chimed.

Call me anytime Cody X

She could feel all eyes on her, so she slipped her phone back into her pocket and climbed in.

Inside the car, Ryan turned in his seat so he could see them both. 'I want you to practise and try to remember these because Saturday we'll put them to use. It's easy enough to get your signals right when you have time to think about them, like today. But when you're in a high-stress situation you don't have that luxury. I need you both to meet me at 101 Light Street in Freo at four o'clock on Saturday. Got that?'

They both nodded, memorising the address without being told.

'Jaz, it might pay to have some heavy padding over your wound,' said Ryan. 'Just in case.'

'Her bullet wound?' fished Cody. 'How did she get that, anyway?'

Ryan started the car, his head forward, watching the traffic. 'By being reckless and going into something unprepared and without back-up. A mistake hopefully you won't repeat.' His voice was stern, not gruff.

'True? Like in a mission on her own?' Cody probed. His voice gave away his disbelief.

Ryan said no more but it didn't matter, the damage was done. Jaz was angry. She didn't like how his words made her feel. Like a child scolded. Even though she wanted to defend herself she didn't. Maybe because there was truth in what he said. Jaz realised she could have handled things a lot better at the warehouse. Next time she wouldn't let Ryan get to her. She'd keep her thoughts about him professional and do what was right. But it still pissed her off that he'd made it personal with the text he'd sent – it was that message that had sent her pigheadedly into the warehouse to prove herself, and it had changed everything. He couldn't care for her one minute, then push her aside the next, and expect her to cope rationally. She still had feelings, secret agent or not.

When Ryan pulled up at The Ring, Jaz grabbed her bag and got out without a word. She heard Cody's 'goodbye' as she slammed the door and walked into the gym without a backwards glance. She was so angry she forced herself to walk properly, not limp. Jaz welcomed the pain that ripped through her. But once inside, she went straight into the change rooms and gathered herself with shaky breaths, her anger threatening to turn to tears. None fell. She wouldn't allow it. Instead she changed and worked out on the punching bag. It made her feel ten times better. And maybe she did pretend that she was pounding Ryan's chest. It certainly was therapeutic.

That night, after she'd showered and crawled into bed in her flannel pyjama pants and singlet, she rang Marcus.

'Hey you,' she said.

'Back at ya. How was your day?' he asked, his voice soft and gentle. Jaz imagined him settling back on his bed.

'Okay. Survived school without my crutches, and Mum made wraps tonight and bought a tub of that Belgian chocolate ice-cream, so I'm lying here very full.' She'd fed her emotions, but the ice-cream hadn't given her any profound answers on how to deal with Ryan.

Marcus's light laughter relaxed her, as she nestled into her pillows and pulled up her doona.

'You did better than me. Mum and I ate takeout alone again.'

'Oh no,' she said sadly. Jaz didn't have to probe for information about Carl, Marcus gave it up freely. She was his girlfriend and he trusted her.

Her insides twisted at the thought.

If only he knew.

CHAPTER 8

On Saturday Jaz arrived at the address Ryan had given them. He was waiting out the front of a large old building, which was a couple of storeys high with arched windows encased with aged bricks. Some of the windows were blacked out, others splashed with bright colours.

'Just waiting for Cody to arrive,' said Ryan. He stood with his legs apart and his arms crossed, looking every bit a sexy soldier in grey cargo pants and a black T-shirt.

'Righto. What's this place?' she said glancing up towards the entry point. There was a sign in black with bright colours. 'Oh, paintball.'

Ryan smiled. 'How's the leg?'

'Yeah,' she said with a shrug. Now she understood why she had to bandage her leg. Getting hit in that spot would feel like getting shot again, and that wasn't something Jaz wanted to relive.

A rust-bucket red Jeep pulled in alongside Ryan's car, a surfboard wedged inside next to Cody's smiling face. 'Yo dudes,' he said coming to stand by them in his surf shorts and a singlet. He winked at Jaz. She ignored him.

'Right, let's go inside, get kitted up and then it's you two against the rest,' instructed Ryan.

'Just shoot everyone?' said Jaz.

'Pretty much. I want you to work together, sweep your way up to the top storey, clearing the rooms as you go. I'll be right behind you, watching.'

'Awesome,' said Cody. He slapped his hands together, eager to start.

Her own fingers were tingling with excitement as her competitiveness rose.

While Ryan paid for all their gear, Cody and Jaz put their heads together and whispered out some tactics.

As they pulled on their protective face covers Ryan ran over his rules, ending with, 'No talking either.'

'This should be easy. We'll knock these amateurs over,' whispered Cody after Ryan turned his back.

Jaz had been thinking the same thing, but it all seemed a little too easy, which wasn't Ryan's usual form.

They entered the playing rooms, the walls splattered with yellow, green and red. Crates and boxes covered the floors, ready to provide cover. Visibility was bright enough with the light through the windows as they stalked forward, straining their ears. Jaz could hear hushed voices and the odd click and whack as someone fired off balls and hit targets.

Jaz motioned them forward to the next doorway and they took up position either side. She had a quick glance and then told Cody through hand signals what she saw. Two on the right.

Cody replied. One left.

Jaz told him to get his target first. Her plan was that it might separate the two together.

Cody fired off some shots. The second one hit target and they heard a cry. 'Oh, damn it.'

She covered for Cody while he ran for the cover his first target was hiding by. While he was there, he covered for Jaz so she could make her way into the room and shoot the other two. And it was all going splendidly, until they headed up the stairs. The top room was dark and someone was firing at them with great aim. Jaz could feel the paintballs whizzing past. They were stuck in this room, not getting a chance to move forward; these shooters were good.

Jaz spotted a crate and signalled to Cody.

While he laid down some heavy fire, she dragged the crate upright. She gave Cody the nod and then crouched behind it, sliding it along the floor towards a pillar in the room that would give her cover. The crouched walk was killing her leg but she gritted through it as the crate was pelted with balls. Paint splashed through the gaps in the crate, small drops of yellow flecking her overalls. She heard Cody return fire, hopefully catching the shooters out and taking the pressure off. A second longer and one of those yellow balls could have found a gap in the crate, hitting her. The shooter was so good she half-wondered if Ryan had brought along some fellow agents who weren't doing much today.

Jaz made the round pillar with its peeling paint and cement cracks. With her back pressed against it, she held her gun up, ready to spin around and fire.

She knew roughly where the shooters were. It all happened so quickly, she turned, spotted the targets and fired. She got one in the arm while the other ducked for cover. But in the meantime Cody had slid in behind a box, giving him just enough cover. She couldn't help but grin when she saw him pushing the box forward as he shimmied along behind, getting closer but having protection. Nice one. She could see why he had been picked to join the Agency.

While Cody finished an assault on the last target, Jaz shot the two coming up the stairs into the room.

'Oh, man,' said one of them. The other one, a girl, screamed from the shock of being hit.

When she glanced back to Cody he was signalling that the room was clear, so they quickly headed to the doorway into the next room.

They made it to the last room with plenty more ammo to use. Jaz was disappointed it was all over. 'I want to go again,' she said to Cody as they pulled off their masks. Ryan stood nearby, his overalls free of paint splats. He was trying hard not to grin. Jaz hoped he was impressed with his students.

Cody gripped her shoulders and shook her gently. 'Totally. That was awesome. The way you used that crate to draw fire.'

'What about you with that box. Genius,' she said bursting with adrenaline.

'We had to, those two shooters were hard core, man,' said Cody. 'Better shot than I am.'

'Why thank you,' said Taylor as he walked up behind them, pulling off his mask. He was also wearing the same camouflage overalls.

'Tay!' said Jaz giving him a hug.

'Hey, he didn't do it alone,' said Anna. 'Sharp shooters times two.' She had a blue splash of paint on her arm. Her eyes were bright.

Jaz turned to Ryan. 'You got these guys?'

Ryan shrugged. 'I needed to make sure you had some stiff competition. Just as well, you mowed through the rest without too much hassle.'

'We have to do that again,' said Tay. 'I loved it.'

'I agree,' replied Jaz as they all stood by the end collection point. 'Hey Cody, these are my friends Taylor and Anna.'

'Nice to meet you all.' Cody flashed Anna his cute grin.

Taylor frowned while Anna beamed as they all started to disrobe.

'Hey, Anna,' Jaz enthused as they headed outside, 'you and Tay were awesome today.'

Anna laughed. 'Why do you sound so surprised?' She shook her head. 'But you're right, Ryan gave us a few pointers. Said we'd need it coming up against you two. For real, you guys looked like a SWAT team as you cleared the rooms.'

Cody dropped back, letting Ryan and Tay chat, and threw his arm around Jaz. 'You looked bloody hot in there, Jaz. I'd have you on my team any day,' he said with wink.

'Well, you will, next week,' she clarified with a grin.

Cody rolled his eyes. 'Smartarse. So, are you ever going to tell me about your bullet wound, or your trip to Pakistan?' he whispered.

Anna paused, flinging her arm out across Jaz's chest to stop her. 'What about Pakistan? Oh my God. Did you go on that mission?' Her face contorted in shock. Then a second later she shook her head. 'I should have bloody guessed. Explains why I had to cover for you.' Anna locked onto her eyes. 'You and I have to have a little chat later.' It wasn't an offer, more like an order.

'Yep, figured.'

Cody groaned. 'All I could find out from Mac was that you'd gone to Pakistan with Ryan. Why won't anyone tell me more?'

'Maybe one day,' teased Jaz.

'You guys wanna head to Molly's for a coffee?' said Taylor, pausing by Ryan's car.

'Sounds great,' said Anna, and then went on to tell Cody about their favourite meeting place.

'I'm in.'

'Are you guys right to head back with Jaz?' said Ryan. 'I have to head off.' He glanced at his watch.

'Yeah, they're fine with me. You got a hot date?' she said curiously.

She'd meant it as a joke but the way Ryan turned his back to open his car door made her feel uneasy.

'Right, I'll catch up with you both next week.' Ryan then got into his car and drove away.

Jaz felt that sense of loss she always got when watching him leave, and this time it was mixed with curiosity. Just who was he meeting? Something made her think it was a woman, and she didn't like it one bit.

At Molly's the coffee and company soon had her feeling better.

'My dad's been with the Forces his whole life and now trains the future Commandos and Special Air Service Regiments,' said Cody, leaning back in his chair. 'My whole life he's been filling my head with all this stuff. Physical toughness is an important attribute but it's only one component. Judgement, decisiveness, mental dexterity, leadership, innovation and humanity are all elements.' With a sigh, Cody picked up a small packet of sugar and played with it. 'He's quite old, my dad. He met my mum and they ended up with me. He's never really been a proper father and for that reason I haven't wanted to follow his footsteps into the SAS or Commandos.'

'So, what, the Agency is different?' asked Jaz softly. Anna and Tay hunched forward, listening intently.

Cody shrugged. 'Part of me believes in what they're all working for. I've been shaped for it my whole life. But this, the Agency, is more on my terms, you know? Plus I rather him not know I'm turning out like him.'

Jaz grinned. 'So, he just thinks you're a surfie bum?'

'Too right,' said Cody with a wink. 'And that's the way I like it.'

'Wow, your dad must have seen some stuff over the years,' said Taylor. 'Bet the training is intense.'

'Yeah, you could say that. More are injured in training than on actual missions. But it's like what we have to do, Jaz, for the Agency. They train us by putting us in the missions, so really it's no different.'

Jaz was seeing a different guy to the image he portrayed. Behind those blue eyes was strength and a desire for justice. 'What was it like growing up with your dad?' she asked. Something passed across his eyes and Jaz knew she'd trodden on dangerous ground.

Anna shot her a cautious look but no one said anything. They just waited.

'Some days it was great, other days he would test me. Mental stuff like going without water or sleep, and testing my resolve by pushing me to continue on when we would go hiking. If I stopped for a rest, I risked being left behind and getting lost. I'm sure it all shaped me into a strong person but I think what I needed most then was just a compassionate father. There's a reason he's a good trainer: he wants all his men to survive, so he makes sure they're tested on every level.'

'Man, I never would have known,' said Tay. 'You do the surfie look well.'

Cody smiled. 'Appearances and perception is just all a part of the game.'

Just then Jaz's phone rang, it was Marcus. She spoke to him quickly before hanging up. All eyes were on her.

'So, you going to catch up with him now?' asked Anna.

'Yep. He's booked us a table at Baciare. I have to get dressed up.'

'Nice one. Pulling out the wallet, hey. Fancy place, that. He's serious,' said Anna with a forlorn expression.

Jaz knew just what she was thinking. How serious was it going to get before Jaz could break up with him? Jaz could only hope it wasn't for much longer. She had no way of knowing what would happen after her mission.

As they finished their coffees, they made a move to the door.

'Cheers for that,' said Cody. 'Can we do paintball again? Next time me and Anna against you two.' Anna was nodding emphatically. 'Or we could go guys against girls?'

'The last one,' said Tay. 'I'm all for it.'

'Me too. Next Saturday? Same time?' said Jaz.

They all agreed. Cody left in his rusty Jeep while her friends piled into her Jeep Wrangler.

'He seems nice,' said Anna.

'Jury's still out,' said Tay as he shut his door and stared out the window.

It was a quiet trip home for all of them. Maybe they were thinking about Cody's childhood, their future missions, or maybe Jaz's date with Marcus. All three had been circling around Jaz's mind like hunting lions. No wonder she felt mentally tired. But when the time came, she'd paste on her dutiful-girlfriend smile and pretend life was rosy.

CHAPTER 9

JAZ WAS FEELING nervous.

Maybe it was the fitted blue dress with the exposed back teamed with her black high heels, or maybe it was being with Marcus and wondering how this night would turn out. Who knew? She'd picked this dress because not only did it cover her thighs, more importantly it covered the bullet wound. The high heels made her wound hurt but they also made the dress pop, so she was willing to endure the pain. In a way she put it down to training, learning to push through pain.

As she pulled up into Marcus's driveway she checked she had her fake ID and cards in her small matching black clutch.

'Welcome Jaz,' Marcus's mum said when she opened the door. 'Don't you look gorgeous?'

'Thanks Diane.' Jaz automatically checked her hair. The elegant twist high on her hair was still in place.

'Wow.' Marcus stood staring for a moment before moving to her side and dropping a sweet kiss on her cheek. He was wearing black dress pants with black leather shoes and a button-up dark blue shirt. His hair was pulled back into a knot at the nape of his neck. The whole ensemble made him look years older. 'Ready to go?'

'Sure am. Bye Diane, hope you have a good night,' said Jaz as she glanced around the house, wondering if Carl was home.

'A TV dinner and wine while watching a movie for me. It will be bliss,' Diane said with a tired smile. 'You kids enjoy your night.'

Marcus drove them to Baciare, a beautiful riverfront Italian restaurant that was booked out months in advance.

'I've always wanted to eat here. Everyone raves about it,' she said as he parked his car. Marcus came around and opened her door. He took her hand and they walked the short distance to the restaurant, past a couple making out against a red BMW. The girl wore a matching red dress and had her arms around a guy in a tailored navy suit. It looked romantic and postcard perfect, with the couple kissing in the glow from a nearby lamp and the lights reflecting off the river in the background. Would that be her after this meal, having passionate moments with Marcus by the river?

'Some people have no decorum,' whispered Marcus with a chuckle.

He pulled her hand up to his lips and kissed it before they entered the restaurant. The smell of garlic and rich sauces assaulted her nose, making her mouth water. 'Oh, I'm so hungry.'

As they waited to be shown to their table, Jaz took in the interior. The restaurant felt fancy but had a relaxed Italian feel, lots of clean lines, warmth coming from the lush red accents and exposed brick walls. Jaz felt like such a grown-up playing with the adults.

Just as Marcus leaned over the lectern to talk to the waiter, the door opened letting in the cool night and a high-pitched laugh. Moments later Jaz was nudged as a person bumped into her.

'Oh sorry,' said a lady.

Jaz turned to find the woman in the red dress from outside. She smiled apologetically as she clung to her date, the man from the car park in the deep blue suit with an open-necked shirt. There was something about the breadth of his shoulders. As her eyes roamed up, she found those dark familiar eyes. Ryan. She'd never seen him in a suit before, no wonder it took so long to recognise him.

Suddenly her heart was pounding in her chest. Jaz tried to hide her surprise while thoughts ran around her head like a group of screaming banshees. Who was this woman? Was this a real date? Had he found himself a girlfriend?

Ryan had been smiling at his date before he spotted Jaz. It fell from his face immediately. Being 'on duty', Jaz couldn't acknowledge Ryan but it didn't stop her appreciating the vision before her. He smelled divine as always.

'I have to say, I just love your dress,' said the woman. She was pretty. Long blonde hair and a curvaceous figure many would kill for, especially in that little red dress. She looked late twenties.

'Oh, thank you.' Jaz forced a smile and avoided Ryan's eyes that seemed to be assessing her dress also.

'Jaz, this way,' said Marcus, drawing her back to reality.

'Have a nice night.' Jaz tried to keep the shock from her voice. She turned, keeping her posture perfect and let Marcus guide her to their table, his hand gently on her naked back.

They were seated against the side wall, not far from the wide front windows that soaked up the river view. The moment Jaz sat in the plush red chair her eyes went back to Ryan and his mysterious woman. Ryan had his back to Jaz as he spoke to his date. Was he embarrassed? Ashamed? Caught out? Jaz wanted to let it go but her heart cried out to know if his date was something serious. Was he moving away from Jaz? Using this woman to keep them apart and focused on their work?

'You are ten times prettier than her,' said Marcus.

Jaz turned to him and smiled. 'You have to say that because I'm your girlfriend,' she said feeling a warmth spread through her at his sweet words.

'No, I just see it truthfully. She is easy on the eyes but she looks high-maintenance, whereas you are just beautiful. There's something about you, Jaz, that radiates sweetness and a down-to-earth quality. I am the luckiest man here.'

'Well, you just filled up the jar with brownie points, smooth talker,' she said with a forced smile. Jaz was calm on the outside but inside questions about Ryan and his date were still running at a rapid rate. 'Shall we order?' Jaz picked up the menu but diverted her eyes towards Ryan. He was moving across the room with his hand caressing the woman tenderly, causing Jaz's stomach to clench painfully, like an attack of food poisoning. Ryan sat at his table, right in Jaz's line of sight. He looked up and met her gaze.

Oh no. This was going to be one long dinner.

She gave him an exaggerated smile, borderline frosty. She'd been hoping to portray no interest in Ryan and act as if she were as cool as a cucumber. No doubt she'd failed miserably.

Over dinner, Jaz tried hard to forget Ryan and focus on Marcus. She'd found out that Carl was in fact away for the week on business, apparently something to do with importing art. Jaz was sceptical but noted down the date and time he was due back home, which was just in time for the sea-container sale down at the port.

'Has your dad found someone to replace Tommy?' said Jaz, choking out his name. She reached for her wine, pretending some pasta was stuck in her throat. Her body shivered as if Tommy himself were jumping on her grave.

'Are you okay?' Marcus passed her his napkin.

Jaz nodded. 'Yep, good,' she managed before one last cough.

Marcus reached for his glass of red wine. 'Dad has a new guy called Ethan. A mate of Richo's apparently.'

Any mate of Richo's spelled bad news in Jaz's book. She pumped Marcus for further details about Richo and Ethan, filing it away for later. You never knew when it could become relevant information.

In her position at the table she could see Ryan in her peripheral vision, whether she wanted to or not. And like a bug to a bright light she couldn't help but watch him. The suit totally changed him, making him look like a rich playboy. By now he'd discarded his jacket onto the back of his chair, his white shirt was open at the neck, a few buttons down. Even from here, she could see the tanned V of his chest and she craved to be closer. Visions of their night in Pakistan flooded her mind. Ryan shirtless pressed up against her, his strong hands on her breasts, so tenderly, causing such heat. It was everything she'd needed to forget the horrors of that night. Did he ever think of that night? Did he regret it? A hot wave flushed her cheeks, made even worse when Ryan's dark eyes locked on hers and watched her intently. Could he tell what she was thinking?

'Excuse me,' said Jaz, getting up quickly and awkwardly. 'I'll be back.' She needed air and cold water for her burning cheeks.

Marcus nodded. 'Want me to order dessert? Tiramisu?'

'Yes, please,' Jaz mumbled before retreating to the safety of the toilets, at the back behind a false wall.

Out of the public eye, Jaz sagged forward against the wall, resting her head on her arm as she tried to calm her wired body. Breathing in and out and trying not to picture Ryan without that shirt on.

'Jaz?'

She didn't know what startled her more, the husky sound of Ryan's voice or his warm hand that came to rest low on her bare back.

'Are you okay?'

Not with your hand on me, she thought. If she turned around to face him, it would sever the connection. She couldn't. His hand felt damn good that low on her skin. When was the last time he'd touched her like that? So personal and intimate. God she wanted him.

'I'm fine,' she said, deciding not to move.

Ryan slid his hand around to her waist, gently turning her towards him. It did nothing to slow her heartbeat. Her eyes were level with his open shirt, the one that had caused her meltdown in the first place. Looking up wasn't any easier, as his steely eyes watched her curiously.

'I'm on a job, Jaz. Her father is Jameson Figlomeni,' he whispered.

The relief burst from her like a million released butterflies, flapping their colourful wings to freedom. The woman wasn't his real girlfriend. Thank God.

Jaz let the words properly penetrate. Jameson Figlomeni. It was the name she'd pulled from Carl's briefcase. Her eyes widened with understanding and Ryan nodded.

Ryan glanced behind him quickly, and then tightened his grip on her waist. 'I'd better get back. You look amazing in that dress, by the way,' his sexy voice rumbled. 'It's making work both painful and pleasurable.' Then he let her go and walked back out to the restaurant area.

Jaz closed her mouth eventually, and blindly stepped back to her table as if she had stars in her eyes and springs strapped to her feet.

If Marcus noticed anything strange with Jaz he didn't mention it. The rest of their meal was easier to handle now that most of her questions had been answered. Jaz found Ryan watching her and something silent and private passed between them. It was weird because she knew that after his dinner he could be getting all hot and naked with Jameson's daughter. Just the thought made her stomach roll; perhaps the tiramisu was a bad choice.

After their meal, Marcus held her against his body as they walked along the riverbank under the stars. The hum from the city combined with the lapping of the water. It was during this walk that Jaz realised she might need to go all the way on her future missions, like Ryan probably was with Miss Red Dress. That the job called for whatever means necessary. Jaz wanted her first time to be with someone who mattered, someone who was real and knew her, not a mission like Marcus. If she had her first time with someone special, then she knew she could handle what was to follow. And she knew just who she wanted it to be. The only problem was getting him to understand and agree to it.

CHAPTER 10

JAZ WALKED FROM school to The Ring. With each day her leg felt stronger, probably due to her fitness. Today she wanted to change from her uniform and do yoga; well, at least see if she could do it without too much pressure on her leg.

The gym was empty, no one working out or having a PT session. But she could hear hushed, angry voices. Slowing her pace, she trod lightly towards the wall, hoping she wouldn't be seen as she closed the gap to the office door.

'She needs to know, Pax.' Ryan's voice. 'I don't like keeping this from her.'

Oh, what had she stumbled upon? Were they talking about her? His sister? Or maybe the woman in the red dress?

'I said no.' She had never heard Pax speak so forcefully.

'Hey Jaz,' said Anna, who strolled in the front door. Jaz waved her arms about, trying to get Anna to shush. 'What?' she said.

But it was too late, the voices had gone quiet and her spying time was up. 'Nothing, don't worry,' she said walking towards Anna. 'Tay not staying?' she asked as she heard the Mustang drive off.

'No, he's shooting hoops with some mates. Nice enough to drop me off first. We didn't find you, though. Did you skip last period?' Anna gave her pointed stare.

'Maybe just a little,' admitted Jaz. 'We were only spending time finishing our essays and I'd already done mine.'

'Say what?' Anna pulled a face as she tugged her hair free from her ponytail.

'Haha,' said Jaz sarcastically. She shrugged. 'Figured I better get my homework done straightaway because I never know when I might be needed, you know? Called for a night stakeout or something,' she added at a whisper. Ryan had warned her that she might be doing just that with Cody at some stage, so she was trying to stay prepared.

Anna put her arm around Jaz's shoulders and together they walked to the office. 'Some days you really surprise me, Jaz. I'm so proud.'

'Proud of what?' asked Pax as they entered the small office.

Ryan was leaning against the wall that held Pax's fake certificates; engrossed in the dirt under his fingernails. He was in running shoes, shorts and a white singlet, which looked damp from sweat. His arms shone like the gloss on a magazine. Jaz squeezed her eyes shut, trying to push the image from her mind.

In the office, the air was still thick with tension. Jaz would kill to find out what they had been talking about.

'So, what's up with you two?' she said, opening her eyes and throwing the question out there but not sure if she'd get the truth.

'Just bookwork as usual,' said Pax. 'Ready to do some more learning, Anna?'

Nicely avoided, thought Jaz.

'Of course, I'll make us a hot chocolate first.' Anna followed him into his house, leaving Ryan and Jaz alone.

'So, what was that about before? You and Pax sounded rather serious. Was it to do with me?' Jaz put her schoolbag down and sat on the corner of Pax's desk, pinning Ryan against the wall with her probing stare.

His fingers were still holding most of his attention. 'It was nothing. Just work. Speaking of which, I'd better go,' he said glancing at his watch.

He still hadn't made eye contact with her. Did he struggle lying to her? As he pushed off the wall, Jaz knew she wouldn't get anything from him until he was ready. She wished she hadn't scared him off. Hopping off the desk, she reached for his arm.

'Hey, how's it going with Jameson?' she said softly. 'Finding anything?'

He paused. 'Maybe. She doesn't live with her dad, so it's a bit harder.

Not all of us can get important intel within a week or so,' he said. The corner of his lips tugged up slightly but the true smile came from his eyes.

Her body tingled with his praise. 'If there's anything I can do, let me know.' Finally she let go of his arm. It would be ridiculous to cling to him for much longer.

'Two things,' he said. 'Ditch school on Wednesday, dress comfortably and meet me here at nine.' He started to head out of the office.

'What about the other thing?' said Jaz as she leaned out of the doorway.

Ryan was almost to the front door when he replied. 'Don't ever wear that dress again unless I'm around.'

Jaz was alone doing a blowfish impersonation, her mouth moving but no words coming out. She couldn't find one coherent thought, much less a witty reply. Ryan had totally sideswiped her again. She leaned against the doorframe, staring at the door he'd left through.

Getting out of school on Wednesday was easy when you had a friend like Anna who could set you up with a sick note. Her ability to copy people's signatures was a God-given talent and Jaz was thankful her friend was happy to be a deviant.

'Right. Are you set?' Anna held the note in her hand and was dressed for school as she checked out Jaz's outfit. Taylor had just driven Simon to school so Simon didn't know she was skipping, and Jaz would drop Anna off on her way to The Ring to meet Ryan.

'I think so,' said Jaz. She wore her black boots, boyfriend-fit jeans and a black polo shirt. Underneath she'd wrapped a large bandage around her chest, to protect herself in a fight and to help hide her sex. If they didn't know she was a girl, then she would be harder to find. 'I might wear a jumper too.' She put on a grey zip-through hoodie, laughing nervously as her fingers fumbled with the zipper.

'I don't think I've ever seen you this jumpy,' said Anna.

'Yeah, it's a bit different knowing you're going into a mission.' Jaz got it zipped up and tied her hair back into a long plait and tucked it under her hoodie.

'Well, I'll be waiting for you to get back and I want all the details.

Okay?' Anna gripped her shoulders. 'Stay safe, my friend.' After a quick hug they locked up the house and headed to school.

Anna didn't wave goodbye, just watched with a worried expression as Jaz pulled out from the school. This was the downside to Anna knowing the truth: she would worry. But not once would Anna's support waver for Jaz and what she wanted to do. That in itself was priceless and why Anna was such a great friend.

Jaz parked around the back of the gym. She didn't see Ryan's car, but she found him inside talking with Pax. Again she picked up a bad vibe between them. It better not be serious, because she loved them both and didn't want anything to disrupt their relationship.

'Jaz is here,' said Ryan, cutting off Pax's last words as she drew closer.

Pax turned and gave her a smile. Then he pulled her into a hug. There was no mixed pastry and coffee smell, which was sad because that's how she'd known Pax for so long, but at least she knew he was sticking to his diet. 'You be careful out there. Clear head at all times, okay?' After she nodded he said, 'I love you.' Then he walked off into the back of the gym.

'I didn't see your car, did you walk?' Jaz asked Ryan. She was trying not to drink in the vision of him in his fitted grey T-shirt and khaki cargo pants. He was every bit a sexy mercenary.

Ryan shut the office door. 'I have a different one. Not traceable to us.' Ryan stepped closer, then held out a knife in a leather pouch. 'Strap this to your leg. Just in case.'

When Ryan led the now-armed Jaz out to the black duel-back with tinted windows, they saw that Cody had arrived and was leaning against it.

'Ready to go?' he asked. Cody was also wearing loose-fitting jeans, boots and a black long-sleeved T-shirt. His hair was brushed flat and looked shiny and greasy. He no longer looked like Cody the surfie, more like Cody the loan shark.

'Yep. Get in.'

Jaz rode in the back, aware that this was Cody's mission and he needed to be up front. Once they were on the freeway Cody outlined where they were going and what the mission would entail. 'Three guys come every lunchtime on Wednesday to check the crop. We will detain them and burn the crop,' said Cody clearly. He went on to tell Ryan where to drive.

They turned off the freeway half an hour later and began to weave their way towards a rural area.

Cody directed Ryan to a gravel road that headed into a reserve area of native bush. 'If we park back there on the other road, we can see them head down this road. It's the only way in and out.'

Ryan did as Cody said, parking the ute and opening the bonnet so it looked like they had engine problems. Then they sat inside, looking out the back window for their targets.

Jaz was so focused on watching the gravel road that she nearly jumped through the roof when the sound of a gun clip being ejected broke the silence. She snapped her head around to find Cody checking the full clip. Of course she knew there would be guns. Except she didn't have one.

Ryan must have read her face, because he reached over to the glove box and pulled out a Star Fire 9-mm. 'Do you want to take this?' he asked.

'Yes.' Jaz reached out for it. Cody had stopped what he was doing and watched as she took the gun and automatically checked it over and confirmed the eight shots in the magazine.

'She knows her stuff,' said Cody. 'Thought you were a bit too handy with the paintball gun.' His lips creased into a smile.

Jaz said a silent prayer, thanking Taylor and his love of guns for making this so much easier.

Silence filled with tension and the occasional nonsense comment from Cody filled the next hour before they saw a ute and then a car head down the gravel road.

'That's two of the cars,' said Cody.

'Do we wait for the third?' asked Ryan.

'I'm not sure. He might not be coming, but then again he could just be running late. I'd hate to go and him catch us. But we can't wait too long because they only stop at the crop for around twenty minutes.' Cody scratched his chin.

'Your call,' said Ryan. He was twisted in his seat so he could look out the back window.

'I say we head in. Just keep an eye on our backs.'

Without a word Ryan jumped out, shut the bonnet and then drove

down the narrow gravel road. It looked like it was only used by local farmers, environmentalists or Western Power out checking the lines.

Now they were driving down the road, towards the thick bush reserve,
Jaz felt her nerves kick up a gear. She clenched the cold steel of the gun,
checking again that the safety was on.

No one spoke, as if their words would carry and alert their targets.

Soon Cody motioned for Ryan to slow down, then he pointed to a
track leading into the bush. They followed it for a few minutes before they
spotted the two vehicles upfront.

Ryan parked off to the side and killed the motor. 'You two wear these,
okay, especially when burning the crop.' He handed them each a balaclava,
which they put on. Ryan didn't have one. Next he passed them a few large
cable ties. 'If we need to subdue them.'

'There's a container of fuel on the back for burning. We'll come back
for it once the targets are apprehended,' said Cody. 'Let's go.'

Quietly they slipped out of the car and followed Cody's lead. He knew
the way in. They all held their guns out front, ready.

The bush smelled fresh and moist as Jaz tried hard not to step on a
stick. They weaved their way around tree trunks and past prickly shrubs,
with guns at the ready. Cody raised his hand. They stopped. He signalled
for them to split up and head around in an arc.

Jaz knew they must be close. She went to the right while Ryan took the
left. She was even more scared now she was out on her own. Ryan had disappeared from view but she could still make our Cody through the bushes.

Cody signalled for them to pause and listen. Jaz could hear voices,
one left and another right. Cody motioned for her to take the right. She
could see him communicating with Ryan, telling him to get his target on
his signal.

When it came, they all moved forward quickly until they entered a
clearing. Jaz had eyes all over the place, trying to assess the area and situation. A big green drug crop was front and centre, two guys at the edge of it
talking. The biggest man was directly in front of Jaz, her target. She aimed
her gun, and clicked off the safety.

The two men, who looked like your average bogans in jeans, black

T-shirts and red checked shirts, tattoos and a cigarette burning from their fingers, paused at the sound.

They turned, eyes bulging, but before they could utter a word, Cody spoke.

'Don't move.' He walked forward and nodded to Ryan, who had stepped into the clearing. 'You boys are in a bit of trouble, hey? Growing illegal substances.'

The big guy glanced at his scrawny mate with the missing tooth. They did look like deer in the headlights. 'It's not ours,' said the scrawny guy. 'We were just asked to check it.'

'That's not what our intel tells us,' said Cody sternly.

He sounded like a cop, which was probably the effect he was going for.

The big guy's eyes were spinning around in his head, and his hands were twitching like a caged animal. Just as she thought he was going to run, he did just that, straight into the drug crop and out of view. Jaz cursed and took off after him. She heard Cody shout for Ryan to keep the other one under guard. She hoped he was running around to the other side where the big guy would come out. She could see the red flannelette shirt just ahead and as he broke free from the drug crop, Jaz launched onto his back, knocking him over.

Cody was running towards her but she put her hand out to stop him. She had this. As the big guy went to get up he roared and aimed his shoulder towards Jaz's stomach, but she saw it coming and dodged it. With her elbow she came down hard on his back and as he arched in pain she unleased an upper cut to his jaw. The big guy fell back into the dirt, blood pouring from his mouth. As Jaz shook the pain from her fist, she pressed her boot onto his chest and aimed her gun at his head. He wasn't going anywhere.

'Nice. Now be a good man and roll over,' said Cody. When Jaz took her foot off he rolled over and Cody tied his hands together with the cable tie. Then they lifted him to his feet and headed back to where Ryan held the other one.

The scrawny guy was nearby with his hands cable tied, but he was running off into the bush.

'What the —?' mumbled Cody.

Near the bush further up, Ryan was wrestling another man in ripped jeans with a red ponytail. His gun was lying four metres away in the grass. Cody ran off to chase the escapee while Jaz held her guy. Ryan didn't need her help, he'd taken down five guys at once; this one should be chickenfeed.

When Ryan bent over, Jaz realised he'd gone for his knife. Ponytail man saw it too and he reached out, clutching at Ryan's arm that now held his knife. The man was grunting as he tried to keep Ryan's weapon away. But then Ryan dropped the knife. It just fell, as if in slow motion, right into his other hand that was waiting. Ponytail man didn't have hold of this arm and so with a quick move, Ryan had the knife at his attacker's throat.

Jaz felt like applauding. It was a beautiful tactic.

Cody came back with the escapee and they placed them all together. 'Time to burn some grass,' said Cody.

While Ryan kept watch, Jaz and Cody covered the green drug crop with the fuel. 'A mixture of aviation and petrol fuel, just to make sure it burns it all,' he said before flicking a match. The heat was so intense it would have sizzled off her eyebrows. The balaclava was a must. They watched it burn for a while, checking it didn't try to spread.

'Right, our job is done. Just know we're keeping an eye on you, so I'd watch your back from now on. Take this as your first and last warning. Next time we won't be so nice,' said Ryan, his voice deep and menacing.

Turning, they all headed back to the ute, leaving the fire and the three men. Their job was done.

'Fire crew will be here shortly to keep watch on the fire,' he added to them.

'You going to leave them tied up?' Jaz asked.

Ryan smiled. 'It's tempting,' he said as he waved an old hacksaw blade he found on the back of the old ute. 'Maybe I'll leave them some help.' Turning he went back towards the smoky flames and the captive men.

'Well, wasn't that awesome,' said Cody coming to stand in front of Jaz as they pulled off their balaclavas. 'The way you took that big guy down was so hot.' Cody moved closer to Jaz. His eyes were electric. She moved back, only to find the side of the ute.

'Tell me you're not all charged up after that,' said Cody. His voice dropping, soft and sexy. 'You know the best sex comes after an adrenaline high,' he added as he winked at her.

'The Agency frowns upon that,' she said. His close proximity was a little unnerving.

'Na, sex they are cool with. They understand the raw need to let off steam.' Cody reached out and caressed her face. 'So, how about it, Jaz? When we get back, you and me?'

Jaz smiled then reached for his hand and pulled it from her face. She flicked his arm around, twisting him like a pretzel and then kicked his legs out from under him, dropping him hard into the ground. Nothing that would hurt too badly.

'Ohh,' he groaned, his head resting against the earth.

'I told you she could drop you on your arse,' said Ryan on his return.

As he stepped around Cody, Jaz wondered if he'd overheard the proposition.

Bending down she reached out a hand and helped Cody up. As he brushed himself off, he mumbled, 'You could have just said "no".'

She beamed. 'Where's the fun in that?' Ryan masked a chuckle as he got into the ute.

Jaz slapped Cody on the back. 'No hard feelings?'

'Just my hurt pride,' he said, pulling a face before walking to the passenger side.

The ride home was quiet, with Cody staring out the window in the front, and maybe sulking slightly. Jaz was watching the rear-vision mirror or more precisely, she was watching Ryan. His eyes captivated her, so dark and mysterious as if they held all the world's secrets. She studied the contours of his face and felt the heat burning in her lower belly. She craved to touch him. Cody was probably right, sex after all the excitement would be lots of fun. Just the thought of kissing Ryan right now was setting her on fire; she could only imagine how good the sex would be. If only.

Ryan caught her gaze in the mirror and smiled. A few moments later, he was back watching her. Her breathing grew deeper and more intense with each passing second. She lived for moments like these. Moments when time seemed to stand still. Moments when nothing mattered except them. Moments when she could dream of all the possibilities.

CHAPTER 11

'Where were you yesterday?' Simon asked on their way to school. He enjoyed riding in the front of her Jeep; ten times better than having your mum drop you off. Just quietly, Jaz also enjoyed spending that time with her brother. He was a good kid and kinda quirky with his humour.

'I know you weren't sick,' he said raising an eyebrow, which made Jaz smile. It was the exact copy of her step father, Paul's interrogation look.

'I cut school. Pax needed some help in the gym.' Her lie rolled off her tongue.

'Are you going to work there when you leave school?' he asked curiously. 'You spend enough time there.'

'Maybe, and yes I do.' Jaz indicated into the school car park. 'You know, I wouldn't mind running my own gym. Maybe Pax would let me eventually buy it. I could get some more classes and stuff happening.'

'If it doesn't fall down first,' said Simon picking up his bag, which had been stowed near his feet.

'Oi, it adds to the charm.' Jaz studied her brother for a moment. His hair had been brushed flat, his fringe plastered to his forehead. 'School going okay? Anyone bothering you?' she asked, practising her protective-older-sister routine.

'Yeah it's fine. You scared the last problem bully away. Had no trouble since.' His brow knitted together and his lips tightened. His tell-tale sign of deep thinking.

'What is it?'

'Have you ... um ... ever done drugs?'

'Whoa.' Jaz parked and turned off her car before twisting in her seat to talk. 'Si, why are you asking me that? And it's a big fat no from me. You know I don't do any of that.' Jaz suddenly freaked. 'You haven't, have you? Is someone trying to sell it to you or push you onto it?'

'No. I wouldn't touch it. After Nigel's death last year I can't believe anyone in school would.'

Nigel was top of his class, from a nice family and seemed well grounded. He was trying to be cool, took some drugs offered but reacted to them and died. No one expected it.

'But, it's just …' Simon sighed heavily. 'Bryce is letting it be known that he's the "go to guy" for it.'

'Bryce, as in Minka's younger brother?'

Simon nodded. 'Yeah, he's been asking all the people with money if they want the best time out.'

'Shit.' If there was one thing Jaz hated more than bullies, it was drug pushers. 'I never liked that little turd. Just like his sister.' Bryce was in the year above Simon but was a year older after repeating a year in primary school. The wrong sort you wanted staying down with younger kids.

'You won't tell anyone I told you?' said Simon worriedly.

'Course not. Just steer clear of him, won't you.'

Simon nodded and opened the door. 'See ya, sis.'

Jaz sat for a moment, as she watched her brother merge with other students and wondered what to do with this information. She couldn't go to the police or the principal without evidence. But it wasn't Bryce who needed to be caught, it was the line to his dealer and then the main man who was selling it at the top. That's who Jaz needed to find. Luckily, that was what the Agency was all about. Inadvertently, she'd just found another assignment.

Anna and Taylor were waiting for her by their tree. Anna had her hands on her hips while Taylor was eating. Anna already knew all the details from yesterday's events after making Jaz debrief when she got back to the gym.

'Oh Jaz, hi. Tell Tay how you flattened Cody after he asked to have sex,' said Anna frankly.

Tay just about choked on his apple. 'What?'

'I'm surprised you haven't told him about it already,' said Jaz.

Anna flicked her head to the side, causing her high ponytail to flop across her face. 'He's only just got here. Otherwise I would have.'

'Anyway, we've got bigger fish to fry.'

'We do?' said Taylor. 'What could be more important than you getting propositioned?'

Jaz told them what Simon had told her, and her friends' faces grew serious. She asked that they both keep their ears open.

'We will.' The siren went for class. On the way up the stairs, Jaz kept an eye out for Bryce. Would Minka know what he was up too? Would she be in on it? It was hard to know. One thing Jaz knew was that she had a lunchtime date with Bryce.

She found Bryce outside by the basketball area, near the wall in a spot away from view of the teachers. Kids who liked to smoke could get away with a quick one here. Bryce leaned back against the wall, his phone in his hand and two mates on either side. He was the same height as Jaz but solid to the point of almost being stodgy around the middle. He was already shaving, the dark hairs noticeable along with his red pimples. If it wasn't for the blond tips in his hair and the expensive shoes and watch, you wouldn't think he was from money. His green eyes gave off a criminal vibe, the sort that also said he was only in school to please his parents.

'Hey Bryce.'

He glanced up, realised it was Jaz and started some major eye-rapid movement as he looked for an escape. His mates bailed, taking off to play basketball, or at least pretend to.

'I haven't touched your brother,' said Bryce cautiously.

Jaz shrugged. 'I know. I'm here for another reason.' She leaned back against the wall next to him. 'Say a certain person was after a good time. Are you someone who could help with that?'

He didn't move a muscle. 'Maybe.'

'So, if I was after a really good time, enough for a few people, could you get that? Say, a couple of grand worth.' Jaz needed a big amount to make him go to his supplier.

'Yep.' He raised an eyebrow and it looked like a fat caterpillar. 'I didn't pick you for this type of fun.'

'We come in all shapes and sizes. You understand that this does not get out or you know I'll come looking for you. And I won't play nice,' she said, watching as his eyes grew wide. She'd beat him up a year ago when he started giving Simon a hard time breaking his glasses and leaving his chest black and blue from a beating. Since she'd made Bryce apologise, he'd been like the rest and given her and Simon a wide berth.

'How soon could I have it?' she asked.

Bryce tried to calculate the time it would take to get his package together. 'I reckon by tomorrow at school, if you can get me the money today.'

'Sure. Name your time and place.'

He mentioned a nearby park that had lots of trees and hiding places. 'Meet me by the kids' tunnel at four.'

Jaz nodded and pushed off from the wall. The planning was done, now she just had to work on the surveillance side of things. And she couldn't do it alone.

She got the phone Ryan had given her and sent him a message, asking if he could talk and then waited out by the library wall. It was the quietest place she could find without any eavesdropping.

The phone rang moments later.

'Jaz?'

'Hey Ryan. Any chance you could get two grand together for me by end of school?'

'What have you done?' he said worriedly.

'Your faith in me is so reassuring, Fletcher,' she said sarcastically. Jaz went on to tell him about Bryce and the deal she'd made.

'Nice one, great work,' said Ryan. 'I'll wait for you after school, I'll have the money. I'll help with surveillance.'

'You don't have anywhere to be tonight?' she asked.

'No. All good. If you need to get home, I can continue to watch or we can bring Cody in.'

Jaz didn't want that. This was her job. She wanted to stick it out. Anna would cover her for the night, no problems there. Besides, a night of surveillance with Ryan would be rather fun.

After school she found Ryan waiting in his car. 'Hi ya,' she said climbing in. Instantly she was engulfed by Ryan's scent, a spicy deep redwood that sent her into a state of adrenaline like a thrill-seeking jumper standing on the tallest building.

'Hey Jaz. Good day at school?' he enquired.

She laughed. It was weird to have him ask her that while she was busy picturing him without his black T-shirt. But even with it on there was something appealing with how the material stretched across his biceps. She could also see the shape of his pecs under the soft material. On or off, it was still torture. 'Okay, I guess.'

Anna skipped along beside Ryan's car, her tartan skirt flicking up. Taylor strolled beside her with a serious expression. They both waved as they went past. Jaz understood Taylor's pain. 'Are we going to follow that guy soon? I've noticed he's been missing on occasion. Do you think they're dropping their surveillance on Tay?' Jaz turned in her seat, looking for the black car and the man with the sunglasses that was usually watching Taylor.

'Funny you should ask,' said Ryan as he pointed out the guy. 'He's over there. I was going to follow him today—'

'Not without me, I hope,' Jaz cut in.

He smirked. 'Of course not. But this thing with Bryce came up. So, tomorrow we'll follow that chump and see where he takes us. Tay has waited long enough. You also seem ready, you took down that guy yesterday all right.'

'Which one, Cody or the big guy?'

Ryan laughed aloud. 'Fair point.' He turned on his car. 'Nicely handled, by the way.'

'What was?' she said with a frown.

'Cody.'

And that was all he said. Did that mean he'd overheard? What were his thoughts on that? 'Maybe if I wasn't a virgin I'd take him up on it,' she said bluntly.

It was fun to see Ryan's jaw drop. It was hard to get the upper hand on him, so she cherished this moment, even if it mean revealing something personal.

He eventually closed his mouth and turned to her, his brow creased and his head shaking slightly. 'No, you're not, are you?' He looked shocked.

'Yeah, I would know. Why, don't you believe me?' Not everyone walked around with virgin written across their forehead.

'I … well, no. I do find it hard to believe.'

'Why?'

'Well, you're nearly eighteen and—' He glanced out the window, making his voice harder to hear. 'You're every guy's dream.'

Jaz waited until his eyes returned to her before she spoke. 'Really? Cos besides Cody I've had no offers.'

'Marcus?'

'He's different. That's not a real relationship, well, to me anyway. I don't want my first time to be fake, or based on a lie. And it seems no boy wants a girl who they're scared of.'

'Maybe you just haven't met the right man, then?' His eyes darted away as he said the words, his voice deep, husky and tight with innuendo.

Her body vibrated as if each word had plucked at her heart strings, muscles and organs, waking them up. She swallowed the lump in her throat. Ryan had just said everything she'd been thinking lately. She did need a man. Was he willing?

He put his car in gear and drove out of the school car park while they both sat in silence.

All too soon, Ryan had stopped at the park. 'Here's the money. Just be careful,' he said.

Jaz took the envelope, her fingers brushing against his. 'Thanks. You can't miss Bryce: my height, blond tips, pimples and podgy.' She tucked the envelope into her skirt, untucking her shirt to cover it before climbing out. It didn't take her long to find the concrete tunnel near the kids' play area. Jaz walked to it slowly, dragging her feet like a normal bored teenager. The tunnel had sea creatures painted on the outside and graffiti tags inside. She bent over and stepped inside, sat down and waited. The tunnel cut out most of the park, so she couldn't see Bryce approaching, but she knew Ryan would be watching.

A few minutes past the allotted time, the light grew dark as his body covered one end of the tunnel. His face appeared. 'Jaz.'

'Bryce.' She pulled out the envelope and waved it at him. 'It's all there.'

He took a quick look before shoving it down his pants. Gross, she thought.

'I'll have your stuff for you tomorrow. Meet me at my car, the blue Nissan Skyline. Got it?'

'Yep. I'll be waiting.'

He walked off and Jaz got out of the tunnel. Only two kids played nearby on the swings, their mother watching them carefully. Ahead of Bryce she could see his blue Nissan parked on the opposite side of the play area. Quickly she got back to Ryan's car, which was hidden behind the massive pine trees.

'He's on the next street,' said Jaz. 'Blue Nissan Skyline.'

Without a word, Ryan pulled out and together they followed Bryce, always staying a few cars behind.

'Do you think he'll pick it up now or before school?' she asked.

'Not sure. He wouldn't want to risk having it on him at home, so my guess is in the morning. But it also depends on his dealer.'

Bryce pulled into the driveway of a large house. Minka's red BMW was parked out the front. He'd gone straight home. Ryan stopped further down the road.

'I'll just go for a quick walk and see if there's another exit out of the house.'

He left her alone but the whole time Jaz was focused on Bryce's car. If that moved, so would she, regardless of whether Ryan was back or not. Luckily she didn't have to make that decision.

'No other way out, that's it. If he moves we'll see him.'

After half an hour, Jaz's stomach groaned loudly. Ryan reached into the back and pulled a bag forward. He pulled out an array of food and drinks.

'Always be prepared, right?' said Jaz with a chuckle. She thanked him as she took an apple. They watched with only the sounds of their eating or the passing traffic. No words were spoken until Bryce got back into his car. He was out of his school uniform and in dark jeans and a shirt.

'Here we go,' said Ryan.

Bryce stopped at two places; the first was for just ten minutes, the house a standard brick and tile. The next house they sat watching for two hours. It was fancy, bit like Marcus's. Lots of cars – flashy cars – were scattered out the front.

'Could be a mate's place,' said Jaz, thinking aloud.

Before Ryan could reply, his phone rang. 'Hi Steph, what's up?'

Jaz smiled. She liked his sister Steph a lot. She was nice enough to invite her to their special dinner where she announced her engagement to Gazza.

'I see.' He sighed. 'Jaz?' He glanced at her, his mind ticking over. 'Um, well, she's right here if you want to ask her.' He grimaced. No doubt regretting letting Steph know he was with Jaz again. Ryan kept his family at arm's length and away from his private life, so the moment they'd met Jaz as 'his friend' they latched on.

Jaz could hear Steph demanding he hand over the phone. Ryan did as he was told, a defeated expression on his face.

'Hey Steph.'

Ryan kept watch out the window as she listened to his sister talk excitedly.

'Jaz. I'm so glad I caught you. What're you doing next weekend? Feel like a girls' day out shopping for wedding stuff? Mum will be there too.'

How could she say no? A chance to get to know Ryan's family was great and they were such lovely people. 'Of course. Where shall I meet you?'

Steph gave her address and a time early Saturday. 'I look forward to it,' said Jaz trying not to get too excited, when in fact she felt like squealing with joy. With a bit of luck she'd be Ryan's date to the wedding. Him in a tux would be worth it. Maybe she could jag a dance too.

She hung up and handed his phone back.

'Why are you smiling like that?' he asked warily.

'She wants me to go shopping with her next Saturday. Cool, hey?'

Ryan groaned. 'No, it's not.' He pulled his lip through his teeth.

No doubt he was wondering if he'd made the right decision letting his family meet her. It opened up a whole bag of new questions and possible dangers, but he had to realise his family was important and they wanted to share in his life.

'You know they feel closer to you by having me around. You should make more time to see them.' Jaz put her hand up to stop him. She knew what he was going to say. 'I know you don't like all the questions and lying, neither do I, but you have me now, so you can just make up stuff about what we're doing at the gym. You could even let them come to The Ring. Ryan, they just need a few scraps to feel connected. It can't hurt.'

'Maybe.'

Ten minutes later they followed Bryce back to his home. Jaz walked a few blocks to the nearby park where there were public toilets while Ryan watched for Bryce.

Back in the car she rubbed her hands together, the approaching night bringing the cold.

Ryan reached into the back of his car and threw her a jumper. She smiled as she put it on, trying hard to resist sniffing it. 'Thanks.'

He shook his head as if knowing she would try to steal this one too. 'I'm never going to see my other one, am I?'

'No. It's perfect to snuggle in. I'll buy you another one,' she said with a grin. 'Maybe Steph can help me,' she said teasingly. She wouldn't do that, it would make his family think they were dating, and they'd already had to fend off that question.

He groaned loudly and rubbed his face with his hand.

'Hey, seeing as we are stuck together in here for a while, how about we discuss what's bothering you and Pax?'

Ryan's change was instant, like liquid nitrogen had been thrown at him, freezing him rigid.

'Come on, Ryan. Why won't you tell me? I'm pretty sure it involves me.'

His silence spoke volumes.

'I'll take that as a yes. Let's take baby steps, then. Do you think I should know this secret?' she asked.

'I do,' he eventually mumbled.

'But Pax doesn't?'

He nodded.

'Why not? What is Pax worried about?' she pressed.

'He's worried about you, Jaz. It's big.'

It's big? How bloody big could it be? Had she done something wrong? What did it involve?

'And you're not?' Jaz touched the window with her finger where it was starting to fog up and drew a little love heart. Where was her mind at! Quickly she rubbed it out.

'I am, Jaz. That's why I think you need to know. I don't like keeping secrets from you. I like to think this is one relationship I have that isn't built on a lie.'

She turned to him. 'I'd like to think that too. Please tell me, if you think I need to know. If the roles were reversed and you were me, would you want me to tell you?'

'Yes, I would. But Jaz, it's to do with your family. I don't think it would be wise to tell you now before your mission next week. I really need you focused. Could you hang off with all the questions until after we've sorted out Carl?'

A week. Jaz could wait a week, especially since she didn't know what it was she was waiting to find out. She shrugged. 'Sure, if you think that's best.'

'I do.'

Ryan reached over and squeezed her hand. Jaz forgot about the secret and what it had to do with her family. All that mattered now was the warmth spreading through her hand and up her arm like a trail of lit petrol.

CHAPTER 12

As Jaz took hold of the drugs, she felt a wave of sickness. Ten times stronger than the nerves she'd had all morning just knowing she had to do this. 'Thanks,' she barely managed to get out.

Bryce shot her a smile and Jaz felt repulsed. Quickly she shoved the bag of drugs into her schoolbag and headed back to Ryan's car. Bryce got out and headed to school as if nothing had happened. Meanwhile, Jaz could hardly step one foot in front of the other. Her heart raced and she felt like everyone knew.

Once inside Ryan's car she finally drew in a shaky breath and handed Ryan her schoolbag. He found the drugs, took a sample and tucked it away in a small plastic bag.

'You did well, Jaz. I'll get this looked at and we'll keep an eye on Bryce and see if we can follow the links. You get rid of this like we talked about, okay?'

Jas nodded stiffly as he put the package back in her bag. Thank God there were no sniffer dogs at school. She only had to make it inside to the toilet and flush the lot. It was the quickest and safest way to destroy them. The sooner the better. Jaz didn't want them near her a minute longer.

'I'll see you after school.' He gave her a reassuring smile as she slid out of his black SUV.

Jaz began the terrifying walk to school. *Just get to the toilets*, was running through her mind on repeat. She completely ignored her friends who were in their usual spot.

'Hey you, wait up,' said Anna running to catch up.

'Sorry can't stop, gotta do something first.'

'Okay.' Anna tagged along quietly, not saying anything even after they went into the toilets.

Jaz beckoned Anna into the stall, much to her confusion, and then once the door was looked took out the drugs and emptied them into the bowl.

Anna's mouth fell open but she kept her surprise silent.

Once it was all flushed away, they washed their hands and left. It wasn't until they were by their grey lockers that Anna finally find words.

'Was that to do with Bryce?' she whispered.

Jaz nodded. 'Am I glad that's over.'

'What's over?' asked Taylor as he sauntered up to them.

Anna leaned over and whispered what they'd done. His eyes grew as big as blue plates. 'For real?'

Huddled together against their lockers, Jaz quietly told them about her night with Ryan watching Bryce. 'But that's not the important bit.' She told them about the secret Pax was keeping from her.

'What do you think it could be?' asked Anna.

'I don't know. He said it's to do with my family.'

'As in your mum and dad, or Simon? Or your real father? Maybe they're bankrupt?' added Taylor.

'Who knows. Maybe it's something to do with my grandparents. Mum's always said both her parents are dead. Maybe they're not. Maybe they joined a cult and she escaped.' Jaz sighed. 'Believe me, I've been thinking it all.'

'Well, don't worry. By this time next week you should know. It can't possibly be anything bad, can it?' Anna pulled a face.

Jaz just shrugged and pulled her hair up into a ponytail. 'Oh, and Tay, we're following your creepy dude this arvo.' She knew that would put a smile on his face but the glint in his eye was pure revenge.

'About bloody time. I can't wait to get that bastard. What's the plan?' Tay squeezed his hands together as if he were wringing someone's neck.

'You drive home as normal with Anna. Stay inside. Make it look like you're in for the night, order pizza or something. Then when he moves on, Ryan and I will follow him.'

'I want to be there when you get him,' said Taylor.

Jaz grimaced. 'Ryan just wants us to sort this out, Tay.'

Her best friend gripped her arms with an urgency. 'Please, Jaz. I need to be there. Can you at least text me the address?'

The proverbial rock and a hard place. Her best friend or Ryan. Shit. 'I'll see what I can do.'

'Thanks.' He pulled her into a hug. She knew he wanted payback. These men were menacing his father, threatening Taylor's life unless Mr Stewart warned them of police drug raids. They all wanted it to stop. But since Taylor had been the one with a gun held to his head, he wanted it so much more.

After school, they did as planned. Ryan waited for Jaz in his car while Anna and Tay took the Mustang home. A sea of school kids flooded out onto the streets, none of them aware of the danger lurking.

'Is he here?' she asked as she got in. She tried to ignore how hot Ryan looked in his usual black shirt and cargos.

'Yep, over the road on the left. He's getting in.' Ryan pulled out onto the road after the stalker man, who in turn followed Tay's Mustang.

Jaz opened her school bag and pulled out a long-sleeved shirt and her black Adidas track pants. Quickly she changed in the front seat. Jaz pulled her pants on over her leggings but took off her tartan skirt and white shirt. She had no fear about undressing around Ryan. He'd already seen her naked. The memory of him turning off the shower, wrapping her body in a towel and holding her while she lost the plot, seemed like a distant memory or something she'd seen in a movie. It would have been an intimate moment if she wasn't breaking down over the blood and death she'd just witnessed. Not one of her strongest moments, but one she hoped never to let happen again.

The target stopped short of Taylor's house, parking in the street. Ryan pulled over behind a parked car and then they waited.

'I can't believe someone is paying this guy just to watch Taylor. It seems ridiculous,' said Jaz as she tried to get comfortable. Ryan's car was starting to feel like a second home.

'It's not, Jaz. Think about it: when Tay's dad alerts them to a drug raid, he's saving them jail time and loss of drugs, so they're saving millions. What's a small wage to that? Anytime they think his dad is not going to play the game, they get this guy to take a photo of Taylor, at school or with his friends, just to let his dad know they're still close enough to harm him.' Ryan paused and then said in a strained voice. 'Parents will do anything to save their children, Jaz.'

It all made complete sense, except for the last part. The way Ryan said it made her think he had a very good example or firsthand experience. He wouldn't have any kids around, would he? Did she dare ask? Did she even want to know? Maybe his parents had done something to save him or Steph. Yeah, that would be more likely.

Hours later, at around six-thirty, the pizza guy turned up and Mr Stewart arrived home. It was probably ten minutes after this that the target started his car, turning on his lights.

'Didn't think he'd hang around. Not with his dad home now,' said Ryan.

As they tailed him Jaz texted her mum; well, that's what she told Ryan. In fact she'd already let her mum know what she was up to tonight. Staying with Anna and Taylor was the Friday night usual. She was actually texting Taylor, letting him know which direction they were headed. Jaz could picture him dropping the pizza and heading for his car.

Eventually the car stopped at a dark brick house on a quiet street a few suburbs over. Jaz texted the address to Taylor and tucked her phone away as Ryan parked.

'We both should wear these. He might have recognised us from hanging around Taylor.' Ryan passed her a balaclava. 'And these, just in case.'

The gun and knife she'd used for Cody's mission.

'Thanks.'

It was after seven when they exited the car. Dark outside, but not pitch black. The moon and stars bounced light off cars, signs and also the metal on her gun. She'd have to be wary of that.

'We'll do a perimeter check first; look for possible exits and how many targets are inside. If fewer than five, we go in. If too many, we fall back. Okay?' Ryan's voice was deep and commanding. It sent ripples of excitement under her skin.

'Yep.' Jaz checked her gun, and didn't flick off the safety until they had crossed the road into the targets yard.

Crouching, they crept closer to the house. As they edged along the side wall the bricks snagged on Jaz's shirt when she got too close. Ryan paused at the first window, trying to see inside. He shook his head and waved his arm forward. They checked around the whole house, relieved there were no dogs, and became familiar with the exit points. Ryan had told her to crash through a window if she was cornered. Go butt first, he'd said. Jaz hoped that never had to happen.

At the back door, they crouched together. Ryan told her, in hand signals, that there were at least two confirmed targets, likely more. He would go in first to the right, she would follow and cover the left. Jaz nodded while the whole time her heart sat in her mouth like a lump of grisly meat she couldn't swallow.

As quietly as possible Ryan opened the door. Jaz could only see the whites of his eyes while the rest of his face was black from the balaclava. Trying not to trip over the small step, she followed him inside. Their guns were raised and aimed. Jaz wasn't sure what Ryan had in store tonight, but it didn't matter – she'd soon find out.

Inside the TV was blaring, she could hear sport of some sort playing with commentators getting excited like they did when someone was about to score. She could only hope that all the occupants were in that TV room. Jaz looked for clues everywhere, from the boots left by the back door to the keys hanging up on a wall. Nothing personal was in this house; it was not someone's home, more like a bachelor's pad or a party house.

With soft feet, they stepped through the house, clearing a room at a time just like she'd done with paintball. Ryan's arm shot out. Stop. The floor creaked as someone walked towards them. Ryan flattened himself against a wall and Jaz ducked down behind the washing machine.

Once the man had passed, Ryan gave the all clear and they followed him down the narrow passage. The man was humming as he went to the toilet. Jaz would have smiled if her nerves had allowed. Ryan motioned for her to take up position in the bathroom opposite, and he stayed by the wall out in the open. The toilet flushed and he came out. Instantly Ryan had him in a headlock. The dirty brown eyes of the man were huge as he tried to struggle while Ryan squeezed, then he passed out. His skin was a dark Middle Eastern and his hair thick black. Ryan dragged the man, who looked not much older than Ryan, into the bathroom. He pulled out duct tape from his back pocket and stuck a piece over his mouth while Jaz kept her gun trained on him.

Quickly Ryan used the tape to tie his hands and feet together. Then they shut the bathroom door and cleared the bedrooms. Jaz could hear a voice shouting at the TV. Was it one or two? It was hard to tell with the commentators yelling, and the balaclava over her ears didn't help.

Ryan motioned for her to sweep the kitchen; she did: it was clear. Together they went for the TV room, guns at the ready. Ryan went in high, Jaz at a crouch. Only one man occupied this room. The man who followed Taylor was sitting on a brown threadbare couch with a beer in his hands. His dark sunglasses were perched on his head. Finally she saw his whole face. Hazel eyes turned towards them, dull and plain under the single light from the ceiling. They expanded.

'Put your hands up and kneel on the floor,' Ryan commanded.

'Who are you, what do you want?' said the man as he put his beer down. Ryan pushed his gun closer, making the man obey his order.

'Who do you work for?' asked Ryan. When he didn't reply Ryan punched him in the face. The man smiled, blood covered his teeth and dripped from his split lip. 'Who do you work for?' Ryan asked again.

'Myself.'

Ryan punched him again, causing Jaz to flinch. That blow would have surely knocked her out. But the man just shook his head and grinned. Ryan grunted as he reached into the man's pockets. Finding a wallet, he threw it to Jaz. She caught it in one hand; opening it, she held it out for Ryan to read.

'So … Joseph. Who do you work for? Or am I going to have to visit 98 Greenwood Street later?' threatened Ryan.

Jaz saw two tattooed names on Joseph's arm. Arabella and Sophie. Ryan must be counting on the fact he had kids at this address. She remembered his words: *Parents will do anything to save their children.*

The grin slipped from his face. 'Please,' Joseph begged.

Ryan had found his weak point in a matter of seconds. But Joseph still wasn't talking. He moved his gun to Joseph's hand. 'You have three seconds before I put a hole in your hand, then it will be your other hand and then maybe a kneecap. Then I'll still visit your house and deal with your family.'

'He will kill me if he knows,' Joseph stuttered.

'Three, two ...'

'Okay, okay. I work for Jameson Figlomeni.'

'Are you with the Shesha Serpents?' asked Ryan.

'Figlomeni *is* the Shesha Serpents. He started the whole thing when he first came to Australia as an immigrant. His empire is huge.' Joseph almost laughed. 'You take him on and you die. Please, you didn't hear this from me.' Joseph was back to begging.

So, Figlomeni, the Shesha Serpents, Carl and De Luca were all connected. All bad guys seemed to work together. Perth wasn't a huge city, so Jaz wasn't that surprised. Figlomeni and De Luca were probably the two heads of this poisonous snake. Their reach was vast and, between the two, spreading a web of illegal activity all over the state.

Jaz heard a noise over the TV and glanced at Ryan. He'd heard it too. Maybe the guy in the bathroom had come to. Jaz carefully crept back through the house while Ryan kept watch over Joseph.

Opening the bathroom door, she saw their captive still on the floor, his eyes open. His tape bindings were still in place and should hold until they left. Jaz lifted a finger to her balaclava, warning him to be quiet. It didn't look like he could reach anything or do much more than wriggle. Shutting the door, she made her way back to Ryan. As she turned towards the TV room, a rich smell washed over her, like an Indian curry.

Then she heard the cocking of a gun. 'Stop right there,' said a voice with a slight Pakistani accent. He reached forward and tugged Jaz's gun from out of her grasp. 'Where are the others?' he asked.

Jaz felt the barrel of a gun pushed against her head. Would he try to pull off her balaclava? Should she try to fight him before he got a shot off? How big was he? An elbow to the ribs? Drop to the floor and go for the knife? Jaz ran crazy scenarios through her mind, trying to find the right one. Would this bloke be trigger happy? Had he killed before? Could Ryan hear what had happened or was the TV too loud? Just as Jaz had decided on a course of action, she caught a flash of something moving from the reflection on the metal ashtray sitting on the side table.

'Maybe you should put your gun down,' said a familiar voice.

Jaz turned to see Taylor with his dad's gun pointed at a man with a full beard and dark colouring. Her best friend had come to her aid again. She smiled, not that he could see it through the balaclava.

Tay was standing in the kitchen area, his stance strong but his brow knitted together, sweat breaking out and his hand shaking. She knew in that moment that Taylor would struggle to pull the trigger if worst came to worst. He looked like he was reliving a nightmare, one she was all too familiar with.

The bearded man started to move slightly.

'Don't move,' Tay warned using his other hand to hold his gun level. Maybe the bearded man could hear the shaky uncertainty in Tay's voice or he figured he could take him; either way he begun to chuckle.

'You won't fire that, boy.' The bearded man began to raise his gun as he turned toward Taylor. He still had hold of her borrowed Star Fire 9-mm. There was only a second to do something. But what? This could end one of two ways. Jaz hoped she had some luck on their side.

CHAPTER 13

JAZ BRACED HERSELF and hoped she was about to make the right choice.

Out of nowhere, a large frying pan appeared, along with a war cry. 'Yaaaaah!'

Dong! Crack. The bearded man fell to the ground like a bag of flour right in front of Jaz. What the hell?

'Take that, ya mongrel bastard,' said Anna, leaning over the man with a solid frying pan held above her head as if it were an axe.

'Anna!' Jaz couldn't believe it. Taylor had brought Anna! Quickly she reached down and took her gun back. Taylor grabbed the other one out of his hand.

'Remind me not to get on your bad side,' said Tay. He glanced to Jaz. 'What now?' he asked.

Jaz had no clue. She still couldn't get over the fact that Anna had whacked this guy hard enough to knock him out. With a frypan, no less. She smiled at Anna, who was still coiled up like a lion ready to pounce in case the man moved. 'My hero,' said Jaz. 'Brilliant work, I say.'

Anna beamed at her praise.

'What's going on?' yelled Ryan.

No one could think up a reply. Moments later Ryan's head appeared through the door, his gun still trained on Joseph. He took in the scene before him. Jaz, Tay, Anna with her frying pan and a guy on the floor. Jaz could see the WTF expression in his dark eyes.

He eventually shook his head and threw them the duct tape from his back pocket. 'Tape him up and then come and do this one,' he said before ducking back into the room with Joseph.

They secured the curry-smelling man and while her friends stayed to watch over him, Jaz left to tape up Joseph's hands and feet.

'Right. Let's get the hell out of here,' said Ryan, pushing Jaz towards the door.

'Time to go,' he told Anna and Taylor. They all headed for the exit.

'Anna? The frying pan?' Taylor whispered.

'Oh, right.' She used the sleeve of her jumper to wipe the handle down and left it on the floor by the door.

Jaz was biting her lip, so as not to laugh while they jogged towards their cars. Tay had parked behind Ryan's SUV.

'Bloody hell, sometimes I feel like Dumbledore running around with you three,' said Ryan in exasperation as he yanked open his door.

'I hope I'm Harry,' said Jaz with a little chuckle.

'I must be Hermione,' said Anna.

'You're also Ron,' said Tay. 'The whole frying pan proves it.' He laughed.

'I'm glad you lot find this all amusing. Now get in your bloody car and meet back at the gym. Take different routes,' barked Ryan.

Anna and Tay sobered immediately and ran to the Mustang without glancing back.

Jaz jumped into Ryan's SUV, pulled off her balaclava and put the gun back into the glove box, while hoping she wasn't about to get a blasting from Ryan too. As she turned to Ryan, his shoulders began to shake and laughter burst from his mouth.

'Funniest shit I've seen in a while. Anna and that frying pan,' he said between chuckles.

She couldn't help but join him as the image appeared in her mind. 'So, you're not mad?' she asked when she could manage it.

'How can I be when they saved our arses? I didn't hear the other car arrive over the TV.' Ryan shot her a look. 'Don't you dare tell them I laughed! They're lucky it didn't turn out worse.'

It easily could have, with Taylor struggling with his gun and his demons.

'So, how come Anna used the pan when Tay had the gun?' asked Ryan as if reading her mind yet again.

'Yeah, well …' Jaz didn't really know what to say. It didn't feel right to tell Ryan that Tay had choked.

Ryan nodded anyway, as if he understood perfectly. 'Get him to the firing range soon. You should go too.' Then the car grew silent as they drove towards The Ring. Only, Ryan didn't go straight there.

'Where are we going?'

'Just doing a sweep past Jamison's place.'

'Oh. Did Joseph say much else?' she asked as she peered out the window trying to see what Ryan was searching for.

'Bits and pieces. Jamison is running more than just drugs, Jaz. He has a massive operation going on using illegal immigrants. He has free labour and keeps them doing what he wants by threatening to kill them or ship them home. I need to dig a little deeper and see where we go from here. I might need to contact the Commander and also James. See what plan of attack would work best.'

'Is there anything I can do?' Jaz shifted in her seat.

'No. I don't want you near this one just yet. We're going to have to tread carefully. It won't be fixed overnight, that's for sure.'

How long would it take? How long would he have to date Jamison's daughter?

'Once we take Carl out of the picture it will be interesting to see what both Jamison and Salvatore do,' said Ryan, more to himself.

Jaz ended up lost in her own thoughts. Thinking about Ryan and that girl and trying not to picture her hands on his body or her lips on his skin. Instead she tried to remember how he'd touched *her*, held *her* and whispered *her* name. *Jasmine.* The memory of it still made her shiver.

They were at The Ring before Jaz realised. She was a little sad at having to leave Ryan's side and share him with the others.

Tay's Mustang was already parked around the back out of sight. Taylor and Anna leaned against the car in the dark as they waited.

'Let's go inside,' said Ryan gruffly.

Jaz knocked on Pax's back door. He opened it up slowly, peering around the door with his glasses.

'It's just us. Can we come in for a cuppa?' she said sweetly.

Pax opened the door wider so he could see all of them. But they could also see him, standing in his patterned pyjamas and bear-claw fur slippers. Jaz smiled.

'I was watching *Better Homes and Gardens*,' said Pax. 'I didn't think I'd have company tonight.'

'So I see,' Jaz said with a chuckle.

'Come on, kettle's hot.' Pax waited until they'd all trooped in and then shut the door and the many locks. 'So, do I dare ask why you lot are all together slinking around in the night?'

'What makes you think we're slinking?' asked Anna as she got out four cups.

Pax just shook his head. He picked up his half-full cup off the side bench and sat down next to Taylor and Jaz. Ryan leaned against the cupboard in the corner, looking all long and lean.

'Jaz and I went to follow the guy watching Taylor. Then these two decided to join us.' He frowned but Jaz had a hard time believing it was for real.

'Is everyone all right?' asked Pax as his eyes checked over Anna, no doubt looking for broken bones or bullet holes.

'We are, just not the man Anna cracked over the head with a frying pan,' said Ryan. He was fighting the smile, which tugged on his lips. 'I assume Jaz told them where we were,' he added. 'Just as well, because another guy turned up and could have blown the situation out of hand if these two hadn't come in.' Ryan waved towards Taylor and Anna.

Anna handed out the cups, smiling sweetly at Ryan as she gave him his. He just shook his head.

'Is that as close to a "thank you" as we'll get?' she whispered to Jaz as she sat down.

'Probably.'

Jaz glanced up to see Ryan watching her, his brown eyes unreadable and unbelievably sexy. What was he thinking? He sighed as he pushed away from the bench, moving to the table and taking the seat next to her. The table was small, putting him close, his thigh coming to rest against hers. She thought he'd move it, but he didn't. Maybe he was enjoying the warmth just as much as she was.

Ryan put his cup down, licked his lips and told Pax what he'd found out from Joseph. Jaz tried not to stare, but his lips were perfect and she'd tasted them and right now she was visualising them brushing against the skin on her neck.

His words were only half-registering but the others were hooked on every sentence, especially Taylor, who wanted to know everything about Joseph.

'They didn't make you?' asked Pax.

Ryan shook his head. 'No, we were careful. They wouldn't have any clue why we were there. Might have them watching their backs for a while, though.'

'So, how do we get this Jamison guy?' Taylor asked seriously. His hair was cocked up on an angle and that uncertainty she'd seen in his eyes as he held the gun had completely gone. 'How do we break the hold he has over my dad?'

'Right now, I'm not sure,' said Ryan truthfully. 'Anyone have any great ideas?' he said, looking directly to Jaz and then Anna.

Jaz wasn't sure either. How did you get the head of a major business corporation like that? 'We grab him, put a gun to his head and tell him to leave Tay's dad alone? Or do you just make him disappear?' she asked.

'Making him disappear is the easy option but not the solution. There will be a way, we just need to think it through.' He nudged her with his knee, making her turn to him. 'Are you set for Carl?' he asked.

'Actually, I think I am.' Jaz leaned forward and told Ryan her plans. She'd been assessing it over and over, trying to think out each scenario if things went wrong, until she got to a plan that worked best with the least risk.

'Can I help you guys with that?' asked Taylor. 'If you need an extra set of eyes, I'm here.'

Ryan thought about it for a moment. 'Maybe. I'll let you know.'

A few minutes later Ryan got up to leave.

'Leaving already?' said Anna, who was only halfway through her cup.

Ryan glanced at his watch and then ran his hand through his short-cropped hair. 'Yeah, I have … um, a few things to do.'

Jaz raised her brow, already guessing exactly what 'things' he meant. A date?

'Jaz, can you see me out?'

'Sure.'

She got up from the table and followed his firm backside down the passage to the back door. He stopped as he opened the door and Jaz, who was so preoccupied with his butt, face planted into his back. Automatically her hands held onto his back as she collected herself.

'You okay?' he asked with a chuckle.

'Yeah, just tripped. Sorry.' But as she slowly drew her hands away she knew she'd never be sorry. Touching him was a blessing. It made her totally frustrated but still, it was better than nothing.

Outside in the dark she followed him to his car. The lights blinked orange as he unlocked it. But instead of getting inside he turned to Jaz.

'So, what's up?' she asked, knowing he had something he needed to say.

'I wouldn't mind using Taylor but I'd rather know he was doing okay.' He got straight to the point. 'Can you make sure you get him to the firing range and see if he's coping? If he can't get past it like you have then—' Ryan stopped mid-sentence.

'Then you won't recruit him? Is that what you were going to say?' Jaz had half a feeling that Ryan was keen on recruiting Taylor. He'd been looking at recruiting him first before Jaz. 'I thought now you had me you wouldn't need him?'

Ryan shifted his weight to his other foot. 'Jaz, we're always looking for great operatives. I can't help it that he's your best friend. In the end it's up to Taylor. But I won't ask him unless I'm sure he's right for the job. That's why I need to know he can still fire a gun and be in control. If he can't get past Tommy, then it's not even an issue.'

'What makes you think I'm over the shooting?'

Jaz felt the pressure of his hand against her shoulder. He squeezed her gently.

'Jaz, you may not be fully over it but you push through all that and you've had no issues holding a gun and doing what is necessary. One of the reasons I picked you is the strength you have, not only in your body but also in your mind. Sometimes I think you thrive on a fight and the pain you endure just feeds your determination to push on and be stronger, better. I've never met anyone quite like you, Jaz. You're remarkable. All that in such an exquisite and delicate exterior.' His hand moved up to caress the side of her face. 'But don't let all that go to your head, hey?' He let her go and turned to open his car door. 'Take Tay tomorrow morning if you can. The sooner the better.'

Ryan drove away and Jaz walked back to the house.

'Everything all right?' said Anna, who was waiting by the door, her hair slightly glowing from the light behind her.

'I guess so.' Jaz sighed. 'Sometimes I think Ryan knows more about me than I do myself.' Was he always that intuitive with everyone? But he had one bit wrong. Her exterior wasn't exquisite or delicate, it was strong, scary and as many would say 'butch'. 'He thinks I have an exquisite and delicate exterior. Strange, hey?'

Anna shook her head and smiled. 'No honey. That's not strange at all. Ryan just sees what the rest of us do.'

The next morning Jaz did as Ryan asked and got Tay to go to the firing range. Anna tagged along too. To quote Anna: 'A gun would be more effective than a frying pan, right?'

Neither of them had disagreed.

Jaz's phone buzzed as they got out of the car and headed to the brick building. She checked it and sighed heavily.

'What's up?' asked Anna.

'Just Marcus. He's been asking to come to my place and meet my family for a while now. I've been putting him off and was hoping that soon I wouldn't have to, once we've dealt with Carl. But now I'm thinking that Sunday might be our last day together and I'd like to say goodbye, in a way, if that makes sense.'

'I get it,' said Anna. 'He's a nice guy, you've got a bond and I can imagine it will be hard to say goodbye. And really, it's not going to hurt if he visits, is it? It's not like he's on the wrong side of the law and will come back to slaughter you in your bed.'

Jaz pulled a face. 'Thanks, Anna, for that scenario.'

Taylor chuckled and shook his head. 'I'm with Anna on this. Marcus isn't his dad.'

'Thanks, you guys.' Jaz quickly texted Marcus, inviting him over Sunday afternoon. His enthusiastic reply brought a smile to her lips.

'So, why are we really here?' asked Tay as they checked in with Stewie.

Jaz didn't say anything. She didn't have the courage to tell Tay straight out. She didn't want to hurt her best friend.

They walked into the back room where the targets were set up in stalls.

'Well, if you'd ask me I reckon it's because you were shaking so much last night I could hear the bullets rattling in the gun,' said Anna with a grim expression.

Tay looked to the floor. 'Was it that bad?'

Anna was a straight shooter, but she did it with love. 'Tay, I hit the dude with a frypan because I didn't think you were going to do anything. I didn't expect you to shoot him but you could have clobbered him with the gun.' She put her hand on his arm. 'I'm not having a go at you, Tay. I just need to know you can look after yourself if you're going into these tricky situations. I care about you. *We* care,' she added.

'And we're here to help you. Maybe shooting a few rounds will bring your confidence back,' said Jaz softly.

'Is that what you did to get over it?' he asked as he dug his hands deep into his jeans pockets.

Jaz shrugged. 'I didn't really have time to think about it. Ryan just shoved the gun in my hand and we were off on Cody's mission. I guess I just compartmentalised Tommy's death into another part of my brain. It's still there, lurking when I sleep or when I'm tired. But if I'm to do what Ryan does as a job I have to be able to move on. I need to survive.'

Jaz went and got the guns. She held out one to Taylor, daring him to pick it up and confront his fear.

Tay's green eyes brightened. 'All right, let's do this.' He reached for it with determination and took a ammo clip. 'As much as I loved you coming to my aid, Anna, I'd rather be the one saving you.' He shot her a smile full of white teeth.

'I'd like that,' Anna replied as she loaded her gun.

Jaz moved to her booth and shot off her first round, giving Taylor some breathing space. She smiled at her improved aim and then stepped back to watch Taylor fire his last two shots. He had one outside the target's black outline and then each one after that was bang on target. He turned and nodded, a grin twitching on his lips.

'I won't let you down ever again, Jaz,' he said sternly. He meant it with every bone in his body.

Yeah, Taylor was back.

'Are we still paintballing this afternoon?' he asked with a wiggle of his eyebrows.

'You bet ya.' Jaz slapped his back proudly. Then she pulled out her phone and sent Ryan a text.

Tay is on target.

CHAPTER 14

'Okay Mum, don't chuck a party or anything, but Marcus is coming over for lunch,' Jaz said as she sat on a kitchen stool.

Tasha was getting ingredients out to make pizzas for lunch. Her hair was tied in a messy knot on top of her head, her glasses resting on the edge of her nose while her knitted blue jumper fell off one shoulder. 'What!' She nearly dropped the container of tomato puree. 'Now? You wait until *now* to tell me this? Jasmine Thomas, why didn't you tell me sooner?'

Jaz picked at the fraying holes on her jeans. 'You'd have made a big deal about it, and I don't want this to be a big deal. I just want it to be normal.'

'We are normal-ish,' said Tasha with a smile. 'But I'm not dressed properly.' She glanced around the house. 'Oh, I need to tidy up.'

Jaz started laughing as the doorbell rang. 'See Mum, this is why I didn't tell you. You look fine and the house is perfect.' She jumped off her stool and went to answer the door.

'Hi ya,' she said, swinging open the door. Marcus was dressed in good jeans and a nice button-up shirt and his hair was pulled back. He was trying to make an impression. 'You look nice.' She gave him a kiss and while doing that, tugged the elastic from his hair. 'But this looks better.'

'Nice digs,' he said walking in and snatching his hair elastic back.

They didn't quite make the kitchen before Tasha rushed towards them.

'Hi Marcus, lovely to meet you. I'm Jasmine's mum, call me Tasha.' She gave him a quick hug and then offered him a drink.

Jaz rolled her eyes. 'Now you see why I haven't brought you home.'

Tasha frowned. 'Jaz, don't be rude. I'm just a bit excited because my daughter has never brought a boyfriend home before.' Tasha almost clapped her hands but changed her mind as Jaz shot her a murderous look. 'Marcus, come in and make yourself at home, I'm just starting lunch.'

Simon came out of the computer room wearing his glasses and a button-up shirt with some slacks. He stopped when he saw Marcus.

'Who are you?'

'Simon, this is Marcus. Marcus, this is my brother.'

'Hey Si, I've heard a lot about you.'

This only made Simon look more confused and startled. 'Hi.' Without saying anything else, he nodded and turned back into the computer room.

'Did I say something wrong?' Marcus asked.

Jaz laughed. 'No, that's just Si. Come on, I'll show you my room.'

Tasha frowned, her eyes flashing caution as she watched them head upstairs.

Geez, it wasn't like they were going to slip in a quickie while everyone was in the house.

'It's very ... tidy,' he said as he walked around her room. He quickly spotted his drawings hanging up on the wall by her desk.

Jaz liked the smile it brought to his lips. He still didn't realise how just how skilled he was.

'Yeah, well, it isn't usually this clean.' Not until she'd seen Ryan's house. There was something about the order and neatness that made her want to aspire to that. A certain pride.

Half an hour later they were all seated at the table, Jaz's whole family and Marcus. As they talked and laughed, a warm sensation of happiness and normalcy flooded through her. For just a moment things felt real. She was just a kid at school, with a boyfriend and a happy family; no lies or deceit.

But in the real world she was about to bust her fake boyfriend's dad.

What would her parents think if they knew? She doubted Paul could even fathom the work she was doing. That stuff only happened in the movies. And her mum? Well, who knows what she'd think if she knew. Probably try to lock her up or something. Demand the Agency be brought to justice for employing a minor. What a shit fight her mother could cause. Jaz had seen her firsthand berate a kid who'd tried to steal an old lady's bag at the supermarket. The kid would have preferred the police compared to the barrelling Tasha had given him in front of the whole shop while she'd gripped his arm tightly. Jaz had even been embarrassed and had vowed never to steal.

Jaz watched Marcus carefully as he interacted with her family. He had such an easy laugh and smile. She would miss that, and him.

Marcus didn't leave until after a movie in the late afternoon. He had to get back and study for an exam. Jaz walked him to his car, her mind full of things she wanted to tell him.

'Thanks for coming, I had a great time,' she said, giving him a hug. She breathed in his fresh scent, young and vibrant. His arms tightened around her and she knew she'd miss this the most. Having someone to hold her, even if it wasn't the one she loved. Marcus had made her feel special, even if it was for a brief time. 'You are the coolest boyfriend ever, you know that.' He was sweet, kind, sensitive and emotionally available. But Jaz couldn't tell him any of this without arousing suspicion. She stayed in his arms for ages, maybe too long, but she didn't know how else to say goodbye without using the words.

'You're not bad yourself, Jaz. I like your family. We'll have to do this again,' he said as he buried his hand into her hair.

If only.

'I'll give you a call after I've got some study done.' He took her face in his hands and kissed her lips. 'Maybe we could get together without any family,' he whispered against her cheek.

'Maybe.' It was hard to sound optimistic when she knew there was no chance of it happening after her mission. 'See ya.'

Jaz waved him off as he drove away. The next Sinclair she'd see would be his dad on Tuesday. It made her gut twist just thinking about it.

Tuesday came much too quickly. Jaz was thinking of her mission constantly even though she had it planned. The container sale was at three in the afternoon, so she snuck out of school early with Taylor, while Anna stayed behind to cover for them. She would go to The Ring and wait for their return.

'Wish I'd had the need to escape school; this way out is awesome,' said Tay, as they jumped down from the fence into the tree and onto the ground.

'Ready?' said Ryan, who sat in his car, parked on the curb. It added that extra protection from prying eyes.

Quickly they got in and Ryan drove them to The Ring so they could change and prepare.

Dressed in dark pants and a black skivvy, she loaded the untraceable ute that they used for Cody's mission with binoculars and a first-aid kit. Tay was wearing black jeans and a red shirt but had brought a black hoodie for later, while Ryan was in stonewash jeans and a fitted black shirt. It was one of her favourites. Cody and another operative were going to meet them at the address, where Jaz would instruct them. Ryan would pose as a buyer and stand in the crowd with Carl and watch to see if he bid on the sea container. Jaz would watch from a safe distance so Carl didn't see her.

'You okay?' asked Ryan as he checked his gun.

Jaz took the one she'd been using. 'Yep. One day I'd like to have my own,' she said, turning the cold steel over in her hands. How could something so small be so deadly?

'Me too,' said Tay. 'Any chance you can find me one?'

'We'll see.' Ryan got in and they followed suit.

It was a quiet drive to the Fremantle auction yard. A big wire fence, taller than Jaz, topped with barbed wire, ran the perimeter. Ryan parked in a spot where she could see into the yard but was far enough away not to be noticed.

'There's Tilly.' Ryan pointed out the skinny guy on the corner, smoking and reading a newspaper.

'Did you know Tilly was helping today?' she asked. The last time she'd seen Tilly he'd had a bullet hole in his arm, bleeding all over the ute as he drove them through Pakistan after an exchange gone wrong. 'Good to see he's well.' His arm was still attached at least, and he'd managed to get out of Pakistan with everything else intact.

'He was quite keen to meet you again, see how you handle yourself.'

Great, no pressure. Jaz got out and went to meet with Tilly. She pulled her beanie down low on her head, a form of disguise. 'Hey, any chance I can bum a cigarette?' she asked when she approached.

'Sure. Nice to see you again,' he said as he tucked his paper under his arm.

'Likewise.' Jaz smiled at Tilly's chipped-tooth grin. 'So, I need you to watch the north corner,' she said speaking quickly while Tilly took his time getting out a smoke for her, in keeping with their charade. 'Watch and follow Carl.' Ryan had taken her photos of Carl two days ago to show the other operative, who happened to be Tilly. Jaz had included Salvatore in that mix just to cover all bases. 'We expect him to buy and take a sea container back to his warehouse. If all goes to plan we'll then move in.'

Tilly lit the cigarette for her and passed it over. Jaz stuck it in her mouth for a bit before pulling it out. 'Can you pass that on to Cody, and tell him to cover the exit of the saleyard.' Jaz had shown Cody the pictures of Carl and Salvatore personally after their paintball match. Which the boys had won due to Tay's awesomeness.

'Can do, little lady,' said Tilly, who opened up his paper. 'I'll be seeing you.'

Jaz kept walking and did a lap of the block, coming back to the car.

'All set. We have ten minutes until the auction starts. You got the container number?' she asked Ryan.

He held up his phone, the details stored on his screen. 'I'll be off, then.'

'Good luck,' said Jaz. It sounded ridiculous but 'be careful' was a bit too much. 'Now we wait.' Jaz smiled at Tay, who sat quietly in the back, watching, waiting. She turned and tracked Ryan's movements and when her eyes strained she raised the binoculars. They gave her a great up-close view of his backside. Now she felt like his stalker. Ryan raised his middle finger and scratched between his eyes, causing Jaz to laugh. He knew she was watching.

'This waiting business has got knobs on it,' said Tay with a sigh.

'Ha, you think this is bad. Wait until Ryan sets you up watching a target, or worse, waiting for a target. I had to watch a door for hours and I still missed him walk out,' said Jaz, thinking back to some of her training.

'Do you think they'll recruit me?' he asked.

'Depends. Do you want that?'

'Yep. Any chance you can train me to fight? That would have to help, hey?'

'Definitely, and I'd like that. I can set you up with Bags too. We can start tomorrow and every day after. Within no time we'll have you able to defend yourself.' Jaz hoped he'd be well and truly able to take down a human before he was put into the field.

'What's happening? Has it started?' asked Tay. If his face were any closer to the window he'd leave an imprint.

'I can see Carl. Ryan is about five people behind him and to the left.'

It was half an hour before Ryan gave the signal that the special sea container was next. Men shuffled through the yard, standing before each container, bidding. Jaz checked out the container, which looked like every other one there. 'Ryan just upped the bid, crazy bugger. Carl raised his hand straight up again. Yep, Carl won the bid.' Everything was going to plan. Jaz allowed herself a quick sigh of relief.

Sweeping the binoculars around she found Tilly, pausing by the building over the road near a homeless man. He fitted right in and could probably stay there the whole time undetected. Cody was also moving about but keeping his eyes on the exit road. She saw him light up a cigarette a few times and other times with his phone out. He also changed his appearance by taking off his jumper, tying his hair up or putting on his beanie. Ways to go unnoticed.

It wasn't very exciting but as each minute crept by she knew it would intensify. Ryan came back to the car and they waited until Carl's crew arrived to load the sea container. She saw Rich, his face still scarred with healing scabs, and cringed. How did she do that? A simple moment of hurt or be hurt.

He was there with a new guy, Jaz guessed Ethan. Carl was the first buyer to take away his purchase, which wasn't surprising considering the amount of drugs it was harbouring.

By now, the sky was growing dark as clouds moved above them like a blanket over the earth, covering the setting sun. It would make it a little easier to move in undetected.

'Tilly and Cody are behind the truck, we'll leave in front and set up,' said Jaz. When they arrived, after parking behind some trees and out of sight, they readied their weapons. 'Tay, you're the sharp shooter, can you take out the dog, please.'

'Sure can,' he said as he took the dart gun with the tranquiliser.

She was relieved when Ryan said it would be no problem to get hold of one. Killing animals wasn't something she planned on doing, even if Cujo had taken a liking to her foot.

Carl pulled up, unlocked the gate, let the truck in and then locked up before opening the warehouse. When the truck and everyone had disappeared inside, Jaz knew it was nearly time. She waited five minutes for a bit more darkness before giving the hand signal and whispered. 'Let's go.'

Outside they crept through the semi-dark. Tilly and Cody had been waiting by the line of trees and now joined them. At the fence, Tilly pulled out wire cutters and made quick work on the mesh. Once inside the yard, Jaz motioned for them to split up, Cody and Tilly to the left while Jaz's team went right. She pointed to Taylor and gave the signal.

He took out Cujo with one shot. His hand never quivered. They watched the dog flinch and then after a few seconds lie down groggily.

With soft steps, they moved in closer. A man was by the side door, keeping watch. Jaz indicated to Ryan that there was one target. She drew her gun, so did Ryan and Tay, who slipped the tranquiliser gun into the back of his pants. They passed Cujo, who was deep in sleep, and hid behind Carl's car, parked just by the door and between them and the guard.

Jaz picked up a rock and threw it into the dark in the opposite direction. The man guarding the door heard it and moved towards the sound, showing them his back. Without being told, Ryan ran towards him silently. His strong arm went around the guy's throat while a hand covered his mouth. Jaz was right behind him, pulling the roll of duct tape off her arm. One piece went over his mouth just before he collapsed from the choke-hold. Tay slipped a cable tie over his hands and one on his feet. Then they left him there, out of play.

Jaz peered inside. Carl was talking to the two men as they stood within the open sea container. Just as she'd hoped, they had already unloaded it off the truck and gone to work extracting the drugs.

Holding her arm up, she instructed them to wait. Cody and Tilly came around from the other side; this was the only door in and out.

'Is that the last one?' said Carl as Rich walked out of the container with another small white plastic bag. Jaz didn't hear Rich's reply but the nod of his head was all she needed. She gave her team the go-ahead to move in. With guns drawn, Jaz went straight for Carl while Ryan shouted, 'Don't move!'

Jaz pushed her gun to the back of Carl's head so he wouldn't turn around. Tay and Ryan grabbed the two workers while Cody swept the area for more. Once he'd cleared the office and toilet, he came back and helped Tilly move all the drugs into a metal drum they found, he took photos for evidence. Tilly found some fuel in a jerry can for a nearby generator and poured some over the drugs before lighting a match.

'No!' cried Carl. 'You can't. They'll come after me.'

The Carl Jaz had originally met seemed like a different person to this drug dealer, who suddenly seemed slimy in his gold chains and fancy dress pants. His voice gave away his fear. She had to try hard to force away the images of Marcus's face.

Ryan turned to him. 'You shouldn't make your deal with the devil.'

'They made me an offer I couldn't refuse,' said Carl. 'Please, who are you? The police? Can we work out something?'

'Nup,' said Tilly, ditching the match into the drum. With a *woof* the bags ignited, filling the shed with an orange glow. The flames danced across his face and the metal walls of the shed.

Carl swore and his hands went to his head in frustration, pulling at his hair. Jaz watched carefully in case he made a move for her gun.

'So ... are you going to kill us?' Carl asked. 'I have a family,' he begged.

'You'll never know. We'll always be watching.' Ryan shrugged.

Tilly laughed. 'We all have families, mate. And you're the bastard helping to kill them all, selling this shit.'

The smell of the burning drugs was something Jaz didn't know if she'd ever forget, different again from the green hemp.

Suddenly Ethan, whom Taylor had his gun trained on, darted for the door. He must have thought his captor was too young or distracted by the flames. His mistake. Taylor turned and shot him in the leg, the suppressor on the gun muffling the sound. Ethan fell as he cried out. Taylor went and stood over him. 'My next one won't miss.'

Jaz knew Taylor could have run him down but maybe he was trying to prove to Ryan that he was capable of firing his gun when needed. He was no longer weak. Taylor did look rather badass standing over Ethan, who clutched at his leg while blood ran over his hands and seeped through his baggy jeans.

'Please, I'll do whatever you want,' Carl said, his voice quivering.

Ryan glanced to her. This was her gig, they left when she said it was time.

'Turn around, Carl,' said Jaz, making a split-second decision.

As Carl slowly turned, his eyes grew as he realised what he was seeing. His son's girlfriend with a gun. 'Jaz? Is that you?'

'You're in way over your head, Carl. I suggest you move overseas before Salvatore finds you. That *is* who you work for, correct?'

Carl nodded his head but his mouth was trying to form words. 'But … you …'

Jaz ignored his surprise and went on to interrogate him. 'Where do the drugs go from here?' Carl glanced at the others before coming back to her. She knew he was still trying to piece it all together. She pushed the gun closer to his chest, near his heart. 'Yes, I met your son on purpose and yes, I am working with these guys. Now answer my questions or you'll end up like Ethan.'

His eyes flashed with panic. The fact that she knew Ethan's name was working to her advantage too. Quickly she repeated her question about the drugs.

'To Tony.'

'Tony who, Carl? Don't make me have to visit Marcus tonight.'

Carl paled and blinked rapidly under the bright shed lights. She could see he was confused, still trying to understand how she could have been in his house with his son one minute and then pointing a gun at his head the next.

'Tony McNally. He works for Salvatore.'

'Salvatore De Luca? Where do you meet?'

He nodded. 'It's a different place each time. Rich is supposed to hand over the shipment at eleven tonight. Tony texts me the address each time. It's our only contact.'

Jaz thought for a moment, wondering what other intel she could gather from Carl. 'What country does the container come from? Do you know where the drugs are made?'

'I don't know. Honestly, I don't. I'm just the extraction point. I'm told when it's here and the number of the sea container.'

'Who tells you?' said Jaz, keeping her questions coming while Carl was happy to talk.

'Daniel. I don't know his last name, I just know he works in customs.'

'Where are you supposed to deliver the shipment tonight?'

Carl gave her the address. 'It's an abandoned warehouse we've used before. Tony switches it up over a dozen sites.' Jaz asked him to list some of the other sites and tried to lock as many as she could to memory. No doubt Ryan was doing the same.

'You can tell Tony his shipment was destroyed, that you're out of the business because you fear for your life,' said Ryan. 'But she doesn't get a mention unless you want us to visit your family.' Ryan nodded towards Jaz.

'Please don't hurt my son, he's all we have left.'

Jaz glanced to Ryan, who gave her a short sharp nod of approval. They'd got enough from Carl.

'Carl, why don't you find a country that has a great arts program and let Marcus be your focus from now on.' She gave the gun a little jiggle so he'd remember she was holding it. 'I'd hate it if anything ever happened to him,' she said it like a threat and meant it.

Jaz raised her free hand and gave the signal to leave.

They all retreated, guns aimed at Carl and the other men until they were clear of the warehouse. They escaped back through the cut fence and to the safety of their cars. There was no thank you to Tilly and Cody, it wasn't needed. Jaz gave them a thumbs up before they went their separate ways. Tilly stopped, raised his hands and gave her a silent clap. With a nod he disappeared. She didn't know where Cody and Tilly went but she had other plans. Ryan sat behind the wheel and started the ute, Jaz watching him until he turned to her.

'Are you thinking what I'm thinking?' she asked.

'An eleven o'clock appointment? Definitely.'

CHAPTER 15

HER BLOOD RACED through her body, as if being pumped by a massive oil rig at double speed, while Jaz checked over her gun. Ryan drove them through the lit streets in silence. Jaz googled the address and gave Ryan directions to the warehouse.

After ten minutes Ryan finally spoke. 'That was good, Jaz. How you handled that. You too, Tay.'

Tay sat in the back quietly; in the rear-view mirror she could see his smile from the streetlights that flashed past. Jaz would tell him later how awesome he was. She'd feel safe with him covering her back any day.

'So, are we going to catch Tony?' Tay asked.

'No.' Ryan's voice was deep and serious. 'We'll watch, see what transpires and then we'll decide.'

When they were close to the address, he pulled over.

'Right, we have half an hour till Tony arrives. Tay, you stay here, don't leave the car but keep watch. Jaz, you're with me. Let's go check it out.'

'Here, take this,' said Tay, handing her his black hoodie. As she reached for it, he gripped her hand. 'Be careful.'

Ryan reached for his jumper and they both pulled them on, before slipping from the ute and merging with the dark. It was cold, making her nose prickle. With her gun tucked in her pants, she crouched over and followed Ryan. He led them down the long street, with only one working streetlight, to the warehouse in the dark. It was a metal building with two large roller doors at the front. Jaz could see enough from the glow of the moon through the thin layer of clouds that covered the sky to make out padlocks on each door.

Ryan walked the width of the warehouse. It was up against a wire fence but the building alongside had a driveway down to the back of the block. He indicated that he was going to see if he could do a lap around the warehouse. She was to stay, hide and watch.

Jaz nodded, watched Ryan disappear and then turned back to try the other end of the warehouse. There was an old wooden door, covered in graffiti, but it was also locked. The fence on this side had a hole where the wire had been pushed aside. A chunk of tin had been put in front to try to hide the hole, but it was loose and sitting on an angle. Jaz moved it carefully and cringed as the tin scraped loudly against the fence. Gripping the cold hard wire, she climbed through the fence into the yard of the warehouse and stood silently, listening until her ears hurt. A breeze picked up and rattled some loose tin nearby, making her jump. Once she'd got her wits back, she checked out this side of the warehouse, looking for another entry point, whether it was a broken window or a loose panel, anything. On closer inspection in the mottled moonlight she saw that the side was covered in graffiti; it looked like kids snuck in regularly, and maybe the odd homeless person.

A noise made her pause and drop down automatically. Rats? Cats? Vagrants?

A hand came over her mouth. Jaz crunched her teeth together to control her instant panic. A warm arm snaked its way around her waist and a familiar scent put her at ease.

'Shh, it's just me. Thought I told you to stay put,' whispered Ryan. His lips brushed against her ear as he spoke, sending tingles along her skin. 'One roller door at the back but it's locked too. Rest looks abandoned.' He took both his hands away but stayed close to her ear. 'We'll hide out in here and hope we can hear what goes down.'

And be quick enough to get out and follow Tony, Jaz hoped.

She nodded and pointed to a pile of building materials leaning up against the warehouse wall. Together they squatted behind it. Jaz put her hand on the ground to steady herself and found wire mesh. It felt rusty. No one had used this yard in ages.

A car rumbled its way down the street. Jaz breathed heavily, trying to calm herself but noticed her breath, like a mouthful of smoke, wafted in the cold air. Quickly she covered her lips with the sleeve of Tay's jumper to stay undetected. If only she could stop breathing altogether, it sounded as loud as the approaching car.

Ryan put a hand on her arm as if to say 'get ready'. The car pulled up out the front. Jaz moved so she could see through a gap and caught the back end of a sedan. It looked green in the sliver of light that was available from the closest working streetlight. A door opened, keys jangled, feet shuffled, a groan, click of a lock and then screeching as the roller door was lifted up.

Jaz felt Ryan tense beside her, his grip on her arm becoming like a vice. He'd pulled his gun out, and the moonlight made his eyes look like deep black pits of hell. He had murder on his mind.

In that very instant Jaz remembered his mate Chris, who was shot dead by Tony. The same Tony who was hardly ten metres away. Shit.

Maybe following him tonight was a bad move. Would Ryan be able to stay in control or was this revenge? Was he planning to leave here with blood on his hands? Jaz had no way of asking him either. She knew how badly Ryan wanted revenge for Chris's death. It was the reason Ryan had come to The Ring in the first place, the reason he'd met Jaz; she'd been the first person he could talk to about it. He hated Salvatore with a passion for giving the order, and Tony even more for following it with a point-blank shot to Chris's head.

With a steady hand, she calmly touched Ryan's leg and then gave it a squeeze, just to let him know she was there. Was it enough to stop him doing anything foolish or dangerous? Well, maybe just foolish.

Instantly his grip on her arm eased and she breathed a bit easier.

Tony's feet shuffled back to his car and it roared into the warehouse and shut off. No lights came on. It remained quiet.

A squeak of a door opening echoed out before it was closed with a thud. A click of a lighter followed by the hiss of car shockies. Jaz could see Tony in her mind, getting out, lighting a cigarette and leaning on his car. Soon the waft of smoke leaked out through the nail holes in the wall.

Maybe one of them would be big enough to see through? She didn't dare move yet, she was waiting for Rich to arrive. That would be her chance.

They waited for a few more minutes. The chilly night made her shiver but she didn't feel cold, it was more from the anticipation and danger. Tony cleared his throat and spat.

AC/DC's 'Thunderstruck' suddenly rang out into the night, making them both jump.

'Yeah … I'm here … All right I will … No, not yet … I can hear a car now … Righto, bye.' Tony ended the call as another vehicle approached.

Jaz quickly moved to the warehouse wall, using the car's noise to full advantage, and felt across the tin, searching for a hole as the car turned in. As lights lit up the inside of the warehouse, it caused pin pricks of brightness to escape through the holes in the wall, like sunbeams through clouds. She quickly found a big one and stuck her eye up close. Presto. She could see Tony's green car in the light. It was an SS commodore. She couldn't make much of Tony except that he was taller than his car and had a small bald patch at the top of his head.

'Right on time,' said Tony, after Rich turned off his car and got out.

Only, it wasn't Rich. Maybe Carl didn't trust him not to mention Jaz?

'Carl, why are you here?' asked Tony cautiously.

'We don't have the shipment. Tell Sal we were overrun by a group and they burnt the drugs right in front of us while we were held at gunpoint.' Carl's voice was hard to hear, especially as it wavered.

'What!' yelled Tony clearly.

'Ethan got shot. I think they let us live as a warning. I swear, Tony, I don't even know who they were. Police, a gang, some secret mob. I don't know. Please tell Sal there was nothing we could do.'

Tony stalked through the car beams like the Terminator on Judgement Day, pulling his gun from his back pocket. Jaz stood up automatically to warn Ryan. She couldn't let Marcus's dad die, no matter what trouble he'd got mixed up in. But Ryan wasn't there. She took a few seconds to focus into the dark, only to see a shadow of movement out the front near the roller door. Oh shit.

Did she help or did she stay?

With her gun held firmly in her hands, she stepped in the direction of Ryan's last whereabouts.

She could hear Carl and Tony's voices clearly as she came to the open door. If she stayed in the shadows, they might not see her. Pulling up her hoodie, she leaned against the wall and glanced in as far as she dared, her heart rattling like the loose tin in the wind. Crouching down, she waited for her moment.

A crunch rang out, fist on bone. Jaz darted inside and behind a metal pillar. Luckily the lights from Carl's car were pointing in the opposite direction. Jaz took a moment to see what was happening. Carl was bent over holding his nose while Tony shook his fist. Jaz went rigid as Tony reached into his pocket, but he only pulled out his phone.

'Sal, bad news, the shipment has been destroyed.' Tony grimaced. 'I'm with Carl. He said some guys came in and burnt it … No, no idea who they were or where from … Yes, I'll clean it up right now.' He disconnected and smiled. It was the smile of a psychotic killer, one she'd seen in many movies.

Jaz felt like she was going to be sick.

'No, please,' begged Carl. Blood was pouring down his chin, either from his nose or a split lip. Maybe both.

Jaz had heard that same plea earlier, only this time he seemed more certain of his impending death. Maybe he knew how Tony operated.

'Sorry, mate. Just business,' said Tony, as he lifted his gun.

Carl's hands went up as he stepped back while Jaz rose and took aim. Tony saw movement and glanced her way just as Ryan appeared in the light behind him. 'Drop the gun on the ground and kick it away,' he instructed, pushing his own gun into the back of Tony's head.

Tony grunted but did as he was told.

'Hands behind your head.'

The dark jacket Tony wore crinkled as he moved his arms up, exposing his belted jeans and a leather pouch at his waist.

'Get out of here, Carl. I suggest you get away from Perth as soon as possible,' said Ryan.

'Thank you.' Carl didn't wait a moment longer. Jumping into his car, he reversed out. While his lights bounced up into their eyes, Tony went for the leather pouch and dropped to the ground. Jaz tried to aim a shot but as Carl departed, so did all the light, dropping them into instant darkness.

Grunts and shuffles were all she could hear while she waited for her eyes to adjust. It was so infuriating. With shapes starting to take place, Jaz moved towards them with her gun aimed, hoping she wasn't about to find Ryan hurt.

The scrape of a metal gun sliding across the concrete floor scared her; it could only be Ryan's. Pulling out her phone, she turned on the light and held it up next to her gun as she kept her aim. Ryan was on the ground with Tony beside him, locked together wrestling.

Hell.

'Don't move!' she yelled to Tony. But her words didn't register as he elbowed Ryan in the face. Ryan returned the gesture, and added a hard knee to Tony's groin, causing him to contract in pain.

'No, I've got it,' growled Ryan.

Was he worried about a shot fired into the night? Or did Ryan want Tony all to himself? Jaz pondered the outcome as they wrestled on the floor like two pythons, twisting and wriggling. Ryan was younger, stronger and he had a dangerous look in his eyes. He wanted Tony dead. The way things were looking, he might just get his wish. Then what would happen?

A glint in the light made her catch her breath. A knife. Tony gripped it firmly as he moved to bury it into Ryan's ribs. Before Jaz could shout, Ryan latched onto Tony's arm, stopping the knife millimetres from his chest. A test of strength raged between them, the point of the knife coming to rest against Ryan's skin. Jaz had to do something, she couldn't watch Ryan die. She stepped closer just as Ryan jerked his knee into Tony's groin again. Already tender, Tony doubled over. Ryan used this to his advantage, turning the knife towards his attacker.

Jaz didn't see anything but heard a hiss of air, whether it was from Tony's mouth or his possibly pierced lungs, she couldn't be sure.

'Start the car, Jaz, turn on the lights,' came Ryan's command as he stood up.

She did as he asked. As the light lit up the inside of the warehouse, Ryan found his gun and quickly picked it up, while Jaz kept hers trained on Tony. He was holding his chest, blood ran through his fingers and over his hand, turning his white shirt red. Ryan put the knife on the car before hauling Tony to his feet and shoving him into the back seat. Tony didn't fight, he was too busy holding his chest. He looked at his blood in disbelief.

'Get in and drive, Jaz,' he ordered as he grabbed the knife and sat in the back with Tony.

'Lock up the building too. If we don't, it will implicate Carl. We need it to look like they came and went,' said Ryan.

Jaz did as instructed. The screech of the roller door as she pulled it down made her pulse jump as if she were hanging onto an electric fence. Surely half the city heard that? Clicking the lock closed, she got back in the car and reversed out onto the road. She glanced back to see Ryan with his gun pushed against the deep cut in Tony's chest, causing him to groan. Ryan looked as if he wanted Tony to try something, anything to give him a reason to kill him. As if sensing Jaz, he pulled his gun back.

'Drive to the ute, tell Tay to follow us and head to the cemetery, Becky's one.' Ryan's eyes didn't leave Tony.

Jaz pulled up alongside the ute. Tay got out, relief on his face when he saw her.

'I was getting worried,' he asked as he glanced in the back. 'What's happening?'

'Just follow us, okay.' She shot him an I-really-can't-go-into-detail look and drove off. Jaz was trying hard to remember how to get back on the right roads to the cemetery. Just her luck she'd get them lost or worse, pulled over by the cops for forgetting to indicate. She could see it now: *Sorry officer, I was too busy worrying about the guy bleeding out in the back. You know, the one we're holding at gunpoint.*

Biting her lip, she blinked and focused on the road ahead. Soon they were back where the streetlights all worked and the roads were familiar.

'I've waited for this day,' said Ryan.

For a moment, Jaz thought he was speaking to her.

Tony grunted, causing Jaz to glance in the rear-vision mirror. As they passed a light she caught a glimpse of Ryan with the knife in his hand; fresh blood ran down the blade.

'Tell me about Salvatore. Has he got another shipment coming in?'

A wheezing sound came from Tony's lips, his attempt at an evil laugh.

'Do you want this slow and painful, or quick?' offered Ryan. 'Give me something and I promise I will end it fast. Just like you did for my best mate, Chris.'

Jaz couldn't tell if Tony recognised that name, she had to keep her eyes on the road. They were fifteen minutes from the cemetery. Would Tony even make it that long? And what was at the cemetery? An agent who knew first aid? A secret lair they used to hold prisoners? She really didn't want to dig any further than those few questions; the other possibilities scared her.

Ryan was still talking to Tony, but his voice had dropped. There was an awful gurgling sound coming from Tony that was starting to turn her stomach and the next time she glanced back, there were blood bubbles along his lips. Gross.

Five minutes from the cemetery and everything was very quiet in the car. The metallic blood scent was so thick she faced the air vents towards her and started to breathe through her mouth. It felt like the longest bloody drive in history.

'Where to now?' she asked as she pulled into the parking area.

'Turn left here,' said Ryan as he directed her into the cemetery.

She had to stop at a gate but Ryan gave her the PIN, which was a little unnerving. Did all operatives know it? Should she?

Ryan now had her driving through the cemetery.

'Pull up here.'

Jaz stopped, killed the lights and got out. There were nothing but crypts, headstones and decaying bodies underground. Tay came running up after leaving the ute back in the car pack. 'What's going on?' he whispered.

Fucked if I know, was her first thought. She went with a shrug instead.

Ryan had opened his door and held out his gun. 'Tay, take it.' Then he pulled out Tony.

Jaz scrunched her hands into fists. 'Is he ...'

'Dead? Yep. Grab his feet.'

She pulled a face but did as she was told. Jaz focused on Tony's leather shoes and not his dead facial expression. She had no clue where they were taking him, they were in the middle of the cemetery at night. It was as freaky as all hell.

Ryan led her past old graves with broken headstones and sloping slabs, where flowers were a thing long forgotten. The only fresh material were the deposits the local birdlife had left on top of the headstones. The clouds had thinned, breaking open in sections allowing the moon to shine down, which bounced off the polished stone graves casting eerie shadows around them. Goosebumps covered her body and Jaz thought of the age-old saying that 'someone had walked over her grave'.

'Here,' said Ryan, dropping Tony's dead body to the ground, leaving Jaz still holding his feet.

She let them go and wiped her hands on her pants because she felt the need to.

Ryan stepped towards a large old crypt with an engraving she couldn't quite read in the darkness. With a sigh, he pulled on the door. He grunted with the force and eventually it creaked open. 'There've been no recent funerals, so this will have to do.'

Jaz glanced at Tay. She didn't even want to ask what the heck that all meant.

With the door open, Tay helped Ryan drop Tony's body inside. Jaz wouldn't walk in there, just in case the room was full of dead bodies. Well, there were bound to be some, but she certainly didn't want to see ones like Tony – fresh ones. How often did the Agency do this?

Ryan turned on his own phone for light, double-checked Tony's body for his phone and ID, pocketing them.

'Help me push it shut.'

Jaz did, only to rid the vision of Tony's bloody lips and wide-eyed expression. Nightmares. More nightmares, she was sure of it.

'Right, let's go.' Ryan took his gun back from Tay. 'Jaz, you go with Tay. Follow me. I'll torch the car, text Sal and tell him Carl was dealt with and then we can go home.'

Ryan took the plates off Tony's car and doused it in petrol from the jerry can in the back of the ute. It was done in some abandoned blocks off the highway down south. They didn't hang around to watch the flames lick over the body and blister the paint, but they heard the explosion from the fuel tank not long after they'd left.

'Well, that was a little intense,' said Jaz in the car as Ryan drove. Tay sat in the back silent. The metallic blood had been replaced by a strong stench of fuel and smoke. Ryan had a small blood smear across his chin. He looked tired, as if Tony's death had taken a toll on him; there was no sense of relief. A shiny patch on his jumper caught her eye. 'Is that your blood?'

Ryan glanced down after stopping at the lights. He frowned at the offending mark and with quick hands ripped off the hoodie.

Jaz leaned over and lifted up his shirt. 'It's your blood,' she said. 'Tony must have cut you.' While one hand held up his shirt, she pressed the other one against his stomach to get a better look at how bad it was. She had to try very hard to see the cut and not feel his abs.

'Will it need stitches?' Ryan asked dragging her from her inner turmoil.

'Maybe one, if you're lucky,' she teased and dropped his shirt, pressing it against his wound to help clot the blood. He didn't even flinch. After what he'd endured over the years, this was probably like a paper cut.

'Did you get anything out of him?' Jaz asked. She didn't want the ride home to be in silence. Her thoughts were too frightening.

Ryan cleared his throat and nodded. 'Yeah. He told me about a new shipment coming in.'

Jaz frowned, finding it hard to believe that Tony would give up such big intel.

'Just like that?' asked Tay, as he leaned forward. He'd been quiet this whole time too. She knew he'd have a million questions about what had happened. Jaz was still trying to piece it all together herself.

'No. I threatened to kill every last member of his family if he didn't. Guess he believed me,' said Ryan, deadpan.

Jaz watched him as he drove. In this moment, he seemed so much older and harder, like a war vet who'd survived too much. Would she become like this? She wanted to reach over and hold his hand, to remember the fun-loving guy she'd first met at the gym. She knew he was in there. Even though he'd killed Tony, she wasn't appalled or sickened by Ryan. If anything, she admired him more, his ability to do what was needed by any means and to remain totally in control. He was amazing. The things he did and the life he gave up for his country and its people made him her hero. Ryan glanced across, his eyes swimming with so much she didn't know what to make of it all. He turned away before she could get a fix on any one emotion. He may be a hardened soldier but Jaz could always see the turmoil that lay beneath. Maybe because she loved him.

At The Ring, Tay jumped out and ran to catch up with Anna. Jaz dawdled, standing before Ryan in the dark.

'I know that must have been hard, with Carl … and Tony. But I'm proud of you,' he said with a thick voice.

Jaz stepped into his arms because it felt right and because she really did need a hug. It had been hard to face Carl but she hoped he made the right choice for Marcus's sake. And to see another dead body – well, she really needed his arms to help her sleep. Jaz felt emotion welling up in her chest. She took a shaky breath and squished herself closer to Ryan, needing his strength.

He kissed the top of her head. 'It's okay, Jasmine. It'll be okay.'

His murmured words warmed her body and she knew that if Ryan said it would be okay, then it would.

'Can you tell me the big secret now?' she asked.

Ryan untangled her and held her at arm's length. 'I'll pick you up after school tomorrow and we'll talk then. You've earned the truth. And we need to talk …'

Jaz reached up and caressed his face, covering the blood mark. 'I know.' They stood staring at one another for a long moment. Jaz felt the night's events fade away as her concern and love for him took over. Her whole body ached to be with him; to have Ryan touch her would erase all the bad ugly thoughts.

Could this secret be any worse than what she'd just been through?

Ryan reached for her hand and gently pulled it from his face. Then his hand slipped away as he let her go. He drove off into the night, leaving Jaz wondering just how life-changing this secret could possibly be.

CHAPTER 16

JAZ WAS WALKING down the school corridor when Bryce winked at her.

'Oh gross,' said Anna after he'd ambled past. She pulled a face like she'd just bitten into a rotten apple. 'Seriously, did he just do that?'

'Yep, I think we're supposed to be best buds now.' Jaz paused by her locker and collected the books she'd need for study and chucked them in her bag. Taylor found them just as she locked it.

'Hey guys. So? Is everything all set?' he asked.

'Sure is,' said Jaz. 'Tick is going to meet you there and he'll take you through a few things.'

'Awesome.' Tay grinned. 'I can't wait to start.'

'You do realise he won't take it easy. Tick will make you work harder than I probably would.' One of the reasons Jaz asked Tick to train Taylor was because she knew he would be tough and she wanted Taylor to be prepared for the worst. 'But between all of us, we'll make sure you end up a fighter.'

Anna clapped her hands quickly. 'Can I come and watch?'

Tay frowned. 'No.'

'Oh. Ruin a lady's fun.'

'Maybe when I know what I'm doing and Tick's not laying me out on my arse,' he added with a chuckle.

'I can be waiting with the ice?' Anna offered.

'Actually, that's not as silly as it sounds.' He grimaced as they headed out of school along the corridor. 'I have a feeling I'm going to be battered and bruised.'

They stepped outside into the blindingly bright sunshine. It took Jaz a moment to adjust. As soon as she could see, she searched for Ryan.

'It's a sin that he should look so damn good,' said Anna. 'Oh, and that bike is hot.'

Taylor scoffed and grabbed Anna's hand, pulling her with him down the steps.

Anna had a point. Ryan was sitting on a big black Harley. Sunnies on, thumbs hooked into the loops on his stonewash jeans, grey short-sleeved V-neck shirt and a pair of black boots. He looked relaxed and not so military.

Taylor paused at the bottom of the steps, waiting for Jaz to catch up. She was a little distracted; just the thought of being on a Harley with Ryan was making it hard to breathe.

Taylor reached for her arm and gave it a squeeze. 'Let us know how it goes. If you need us, you'll know where we'll be.'

'Thanks Tay. I'm sure it's nothing major.' That's what she kept telling herself. What could Ryan possibly tell her that would be ground-breaking?

Anna's face portrayed everything she wanted to say, she was so easy to read. 'Tell me the moment you get back, okay? Oh, and be careful on that bike, all right!' Anna smiled. 'I'm channelling your mum; did I do a good job?'

Jaz laughed and hugged Anna while wondering if her hair was still fine after a day in school. 'I will. Can you take my bag to The Ring? I don't think I'll be needing it.'

Tay took her bag and slung it over his shoulder, along with his own, as they walked to Ryan.

'Hi Ryan! Bye Ryan,' said Anna on her way past.

Tay gave him a wave. 'Nice wheels.'

'Hi guys, catch ya later,' said Ryan.

Jaz stopped just beside him, not saying anything but admiring the view. Was she the luckiest girl here or what!

'Up for a ride?' he asked. 'Nice day for it.'

'That it is,' she said with a smile. 'Is it safe?' She wasn't worried about the bike, more about how she was going to hold onto him without drool-ing on his back.

'I got you through Pakistan safely, didn't I?' He lifted his sunnies, amusement sparkled in his deep brown eyes.

'Now that is debatable.' Ryan reached for the black helmet strapped to the bike. 'Thanks.' She glanced to his strong chest, already imagining the hard muscles she'd have to hang onto. 'Is your cut okay?'

'Yeah, it's fine. Get on.'

He could have lost two fingers and said the same thing.

Jaz put on the open-faced helmet before swinging her stocking-covered leg over the bike. The padded leather seat was soft and she couldn't help slide closer to Ryan, her pleated tartan skirt riding up a fraction.

'Hang on tight,' he warned as he put on his own helmet.

Jaz put her hands gently on his waist as he kick-started the bike. This was not like the Yamaha. The throb under her legs and the deep throaty sound of the motor pulsed through her, bringing a nervous giggle to her lips. Ryan gunned the throttle and they roared from the car park like thunder.

She almost squealed as her hands latched tightly around his chest and she hung on for dear life. The wind caught her hair not held by the helmet, flicking it out like a pirate flag without the skulls.

When they were down the street, he brought it back to cruising speed and Jaz laughed. She stuck her hands up towards the sky and felt as free as a bird.

'Wow, that was amazing,' she said when he finally stopped. He'd taken her to Kings Park near the CBD. It was a little slice of heaven in the hustle and bustle of city life. Her folks had brought her here a few times when she was younger.

'I know, right? I should get it out more often.'

'Come pick me up when you do.'

He chuckled and tucked her hand into his elbow. 'Come on you, let's go for a walk. I know a great spot.'

As they strolled along the pathway past the breathtaking view of the city and towards the natural bush, Jaz felt like they were a real couple. They talked about Tay's training and the beautiful day. She wished it could be like this for longer, when she could at least pretend.

'Over here.' Ryan led her to a bench seat that sat alone in a small clearing. It was off the path ten metres, so it was private enough from anyone passing.

Jaz sat down. 'I like this spot.' The natural bush helped dull the street noise and in front, it thinned out enough that they could see the Swan River, busy with boats.

Ryan sat down and rested his arm behind her along the top of the seat. He smelled so good she had to try hard not to turn and bury her nose into his neck.

Clearing her throat, she asked, 'So, where do we start?'

'How did you sleep last night?'

Great, he wanted to start there. Why not go straight to the good stuff? She wanted to know the secret. 'Yeah, better than I thought. I mean, it wasn't great but better than last time.'

He nodded understandingly. 'Yeah. Well, I'm here if you ever need to chat about anything that happened.'

Jaz shrugged and shook her head. 'Not really. I kinda get it. Well actually, not the cemetery part. Is that normal?' she quizzed him.

'Sadly, yes. Best place to leave them. We prefer to use a fresh grave but if there are none, the crypts work well.'

'Great,' she said sarcastically. 'I had a dream last night where I opened one and there were, like, rotting bodies piled up to the top.' Jaz shuddered and Ryan moved his hand from the bench seat to rest against her shoulder.

To his credit he didn't laugh. 'You wouldn't be the first, Jaz.' He took a deep breath. 'I didn't think last night would go down like that, I hadn't planned it but getting Tony was … I guess … something I've been dreaming about for a while now.' His voice dropped to nearly a whisper. 'Even though he's dead it still doesn't ease the sadness and anger. Revenge or paybacks never really make you feel any better. If anything, it just means one less dirtbag is out in the world.'

Jaz felt his turmoil and understood how mixed he was feeling, but was also honoured that he was comfortable enough to share it with her.

'And we identified another shipment to go after, if Tony was telling the truth. One for you and me to tackle in a few weeks, up north by the beach. How's that sound?'

'Really? A beach?'

'Yep. It will be a big drive up to Geraldton and we'd have to look like camping backpackers or something but it should be an easy one. You keen?'

Jaz grinned. She didn't care what they did. All she heard was 'long trip', which meant them in a car together, and camping near a beach, which meant sharing a tent. Well, hopefully.

Yes please. She was completely excited by the prospect. 'I'm in.'

They fell silent. Kids nearby were squealing as they ran around playing, causing birds to fly from tree to tree.

Ryan was staring at the river but he wasn't seeing it. A muscle in his jaw was pulsing. Jaz waited patiently.

'I suppose I'd better let the cat out of the bag, hey.' He turned to her, smiled weakly before turning back to the view. 'I'm not sure how to really tell you this. Pax doesn't want anyone to know. I found out by accident and pressured him for the truth. I've known a while, Jaz, and I'm sorry I couldn't tell you sooner. Please don't kill the messenger.'

'Ha, after last night I doubt I even could.' Her teasing didn't help ease his discomfort. If anything, she felt like she was making it worse. He was really struggling with this, and she had no idea why. 'Just start at the beginning, Ryan.' She lifted her legs up beneath her and turned to face him on the seat. 'I'm listening.'

'It was not long after we'd met when I worked it out. I know James quite well and often spend time catching up. He oversees our unit in Perth and, like you, I did all my paperwork through him when I joined.

'One time I saw a photo of his sister, a small one on his desk, and he told me how she died young, that she too was an agent, following in his family's footsteps after they started up the Agency.'

'Yep.' Jaz was wondering where he was going with James. Not the direction she thought he'd take. What did it have to do with her?

'Anyway, I was chatting with you at the gym and you showed me that photo of you and your mum, you remember?'

'Yeah, the one Pax has in his office of me when I was just walking. And?'

'And she looked familiar.'

'Who, my mum?'

Ryan nodded, his dark eyes latching onto her. 'She had different hair but the face was exactly the same as James's sister.'

Jaz frowned. 'What do you mean?' She was struggling to understand where he was going with this.

'It was too close a match, Jaz, and then with her connection to Pax, I just had a hunch the two were the same woman. So, I asked Pax straight out—'

Her hand flew up into his face like a large red stop sign. 'Wait, *what*?' She tilted her head to the side and scrunched her face up. 'You think my mum is James's sister?'

'No, Jaz. Your mum *is* James's sister. When I confronted Pax, he came clean. Your mum, Tasha, is really Natasha Montenegro.'

'You're shitting me?' Jaz stood up and then paced around with her hands on her hips. Every now and then she'd stop, look at Ryan, who'd nod, which would send her off pacing again. 'No. No fricken way.' Jaz tried to picture it, her mum as a Montenegro. How was that even possible? Her mum was, well, her mum! 'Are you sure?' Jaz trusted Ryan, but this? This was loony-bin stuff.

Ryan reached out and grabbed her hand, pulling her back to the bench seat. 'Listen. This is what Pax told me. Nineteen years ago, your mum was working as an operative when she fell pregnant. She didn't want to bring you up in her world and risk someone taking you away or her dying. So, she went to Pax and asked him to help hide her. She disappeared off the earth. Pax gave her a new identity and he brought her home to Western Australia so there was less chance of anyone recognising her.'

Jaz put her hand over her mouth.

'James believes she's dead. He thinks she was caught during one of her undercover ops, was murdered and they hid the body,' said Ryan.

All she could think of was Ryan's friend Chris; if Ryan hadn't been watching, then Chris too would have just vanished without them knowing what happened. Wow. Jaz got up and walked over to the shrubs, staring blankly at the tiny boats cruising along the river. Situation normal for them. But Jaz felt anything but normal. How was any of what Ryan said even possible? As the seconds ticked by, her mind raced, searching for the signs she'd missed. It was true her mum had an unknown past, no siblings, dead parents, no photos or connections from her childhood. It was possible she was hiding something. Then the way her mum was when she was young, teaching her to fight, being at The Ring all the time with Pax and being so paranoid about Jaz being out of her sight. Not to mention her avoidance whenever Jaz asked about her father. Jaz always thought her mum was just highly strung, but could it be that she was scared of being found out? Had she lived this life in fear that her past would come back to haunt her?

The thing Jaz was finding the hardest to swallow was her mum being an agent, like Ryan. The same woman who sang off-key in the shower, whose cooking wasn't great and who worked in an office in heels. Nothing said agent, except the commando boots Jaz had found in her closet.

Her mum always seemed a bit skittish when they were out at new places: was it possible she was scouting the place, keeping note of the exits and looking for possible tags? 'Oh my.' Jaz held her head. Brain overload.

'You okay?'

Ryan had come up behind her. She turned to see his uncertain face. He looked like he wanted to comfort her but wasn't sure if he'd be attacked.

'I think.' She leaned against him, resting her head on his shoulder. 'I don't blame you, Ryan.' The moment the words left her mouth, his arms wrapped around her. They stood like that for a while before he finally spoke.

'Thank God. I wasn't sure if you'd believe me or not.'

'Of course I do. When I think about it, it fits. How else would Mum have known Pax? They are so different. And she taught me how to protect myself from a young age. Even though it fits, it's still bloody weird and hard to imagine.'

He rubbed her back and she closed her eyes.

'You can't tell her, Jaz. Pax said she'd have a pink fit if she found out you knew, and even more so if she learned that you now work for the Agency. She uprooted her whole life to escape it and yet here we are.'

'My destiny, maybe? I was born to do this job,' Jaz scoffed, not really believing her own words. 'What about James?' Could she talk to him? Tell him the truth?

'I don't know, Jaz. Do you think he could leave Tasha alone after finding out the truth?'

'Maybe he'd be happy just knowing she was alive and well. He under-stands what it's like in this business, he would know how to keep a secret.' Jaz scrunched up her face. 'Wow, James is my uncle. It's so surreal.' And yet when she'd first met him there was something about him that put her at ease, something familiar. It had been his eyes, just like her mum's. So many things were making this unbelievable secret a reality.

They stood together for ages in their quiet patch of native bush, not really enjoying the panoramic view on offer. Nonetheless, the smell of the eucalyptus, rotting leaves and nature itself had a calming effect on her, not to mention Ryan's warm body.

'Come on, I'll take you back to the gym. Don't tell Pax I told you. He won't let me near you again otherwise,' he said with a grin.

Jaz felt the cold as he stepped away but his words continued to warm her insides. *He won't let me near you again otherwise.* He liked being with her?

'So, when's this big eighteenth birthday party happening?' he asked as he began to walk back to his bike. 'Am I invited?'

The way his lips curled up into a cheeky grin left her almost lost for words.

'Um … I don't know. Tay and Anna are organising something, so God only knows what it will be. Probably something fancy and over the top, maybe a river cruise.' Especially if Anna had anything to do with it. Balloons, fine dining, champagne. 'I hope you're invited. I'll need some back-up.'

She knew he was trying to brighten the mood after the bombshell he'd just dropped but it didn't work for long.

As Jaz got behind him on the bike, her mind kept returning to a question she had about her mum. It was an awful thought, and one she couldn't ask Ryan about for fear of what he'd think. Maybe she could talk to Anna about it? But without asking her mum, she'd probably never know the truth.

With the pulsing thud of the bike beneath her and the man she loved, but shouldn't love, in her arms, they headed back towards The Ring as the afternoon sun warmed her skin.

CHAPTER 17

ANNA RUSHED THROUGH the front door of the gym as Ryan pulled up outside, and before Jaz could get her helmet off Anna was reaching for it.

'Can you take me for a spin, please?' Anna yelled.

'Sure, jump on.'

Jaz almost laughed at the pure delight on her friend's face as she did the helmet up and climbed on. Wrapping her arms tightly around Ryan's waist, Anna yelled, 'I'm ready!' Anna squeezed her eyes shut as if she wasn't sure about the whole experience.

Jaz was about to ask why she was doing it if she was scared, but then she realised it was Ryan on a Harley. How could you not.

As he roared off, Anna's squeal could just be heard over the rumble of the bike. Jaz stepped into the gym with a chuckle. Inside Tick and Taylor were over on the large mat, facing each other without their shirts on. Up the back, Bags was giving a woman covered in tattoos a boxing lesson. Her hair was held back by tiny braids and her moves were strong, she could throw a punch. What was her story, Jaz wondered: bullied, anger issues, gym junkie or future fighter?

'How's it going?' said Jaz as she stood by Taylor.

'Early days, Jaz.' Tick threw a punch her way, which she quickly deflected. 'Good to see you haven't lost your touch. It's been a while. You up to a fight, give Tay a rest?'

'I vote for that,' said Tay, raising his hand. He had a shiner on his cheek already and a sheen of sweat over his naked torso.

Jaz grinned. 'Tick, I thought you'd never ask. I'll just change.' She headed to the change room and got into her yoga pants and sports top. She always made sure she had a clean set ready and waiting.

Grabbing a nearby skipping rope, she quickly warmed up. Her leg twinged a bit, but it wasn't anything she couldn't handle.

'Right, I'm ready,' she said. 'Just don't hit here, please. It's still not quite healed.' She touched her thigh and Tick nodded. He didn't know it was from a bullet but if he saw the wound he'd know; he had his own similar scars on his arm and shoulder. Both were hard to see due to his tattoos.

'I'll take notes,' said Tay, who sat against the wall.

Jaz and Tick circled each other for a while before she threw the first punch. Tick raised his eyebrows and smiled, as if she'd just given him a tell. But they weren't playing poker, so she spun and kicked out. He hadn't expected it but nonetheless he was fast enough to react and turn it into a glancing blow.

Tick jabbed, then tried an elbow. She blocked them but missed his uppercut. Even though she moved, she couldn't avoid it altogether and took a weak hit to her kidneys.

'Ooh,' said Tay.

Jaz didn't let it slow her down and went for a couple of jabs to Tick's face. She was limited, finding it hard to duck quickly because her leg was still stiff and sore. To compensate she found other ways to dodge Tick's punches and only kicked her healthy leg. Before long, she was covered in sweat and both of them had got in a few punches. They stopped for a breather.

'Awesome,' said Tay, getting up and passing Jaz his water bottle.

She squirted some water into her mouth. 'Thanks.'

'I've gotta get home to my sis, I'll catch you tomorrow?' said Tick as he reached for his shirt and phone. He gave Jaz a wink.

'Sure, man. Thanks Tick.' Tay fist pumped him before he left.

'So, wanna show me what Tick taught you?' she asked.

Even though he'd probably been beaten up the last hour or so, he didn't pause to decide. 'Yep. Let's go,' he said with determination.

Tick had taken him through the basic jabs and kicks, exercises to strengthen his muscles, as well as some dirty tricks to get out of sticky situations. Instead of teaching him anything new, Jaz just got him to go over what he'd learnt.

'Look at you go,' said Anna as she came back into the gym. Her face was flushed and her smile huge.

Ryan stood beside Anna, his eyes doing a slow long crawl over Jaz's sweaty body. 'How'd the leg hold up?' he asked.

Jaz was too flustered to respond.

'She did good. Even with a sore leg she was even pegged with Tick,' answered Tay.

'Na,' said Jaz, finding her voice. 'He was taking it easy on me.' She should know, she'd fought with Tick enough times.

'Really?' Tay frowned. 'Damn.'

'You good?' asked Ryan.

She knew what he was implying. 'The spar with Tick was good. Gave me a break from everything,' she said with a weak smile.

'Good. Look, I gotta go, so I'll see you guys later. Stay out of trouble,' he said with a smile.

'Thanks for the ride,' said Anna as he left. They both watched him leave and sit on his bike, which was parked out the front.

Tay clapped his hands to draw their attention. 'Hello. So, what was the big secret? Can you share it?'

There went her blissful moment. 'Yeah.' She glanced towards the office. 'Is Pax here?'

Anna nodded. 'He's actually reading the latest Matthew Reilly book, why?'

Jaz took a slow breath. 'Maybe we could go for a drive in the 'Stang?'

Tay and Anna both raised their brows curiously but didn't ask why. 'Sure. Let's go get a coffee.' Tay reached for his Birds of Tokyo T-shirt and pulled it on.

Jaz went and got her grey hoodie and told Bags they were leaving.

'Righto, have fun kids,' he said, before instructing his student. His big-muscled arms could give Vin Diesel a run for his money.

They drove to Molly's, picked a spot in the back corner, and huddled together after their coffees arrived.

'So, is it as bad as you thought?' asked Anna after sipping her drink.

Some of the froth stuck to the top of her lip. Tay grinned and wiped it off with his napkin.

'Yeah, and what's it have to do with Pax?' he added.

Jaz dropped her voice and told them everything Ryan had said. Coming from her own mouth didn't make it any more believable.

'No fricken way,' said Anna.

'That's what I said, but it makes sense,' she said and went on to explain the unknown things about her mum.

'Yeah, I guess,' said Tay. 'Wow, that's heavy stuff. Still doesn't get you closer to knowing who your dad is, though.'

Jaz leaned back and stared out the window while twirling a small sugar packet between her fingers. Tay had hit the nail on the head. 'I was thinking … Mum was an agent when she fell pregnant with me. What if my father is some drug-selling, coke-snorting, abusive idiot? What if she was raped?' She finally turned to see their reactions. This was the one thing she couldn't ask Ryan today. What if she came from everything wrong he was trying to fix in the world?

'No way, Jaz. As if your mum would let that happen. For all you know she had a secret boyfriend.' Anna's eyes lit up. 'Oh my God, maybe she fell for an agent and knew it was against the rules and ran.'

Jaz knew they were thinking of her and Ryan. 'I never thought of that.'

'As long as you're not related to Ryan, it's all good,' she added.

'Well, no chance of that, I've met his folks and they know nothing about the Agency.' She didn't mention that his uncle was an agent. But Tasha had come from Victoria, so she didn't think that was likely. 'Who knows. He could have been a married man for all I know.'

They fell silent until they finished their drinks.

'It's funny, all those little things your mum did we put down as quirks, which made her fit with your dad. But now?' Anna shrugged.

'I know. Maybe Mum liked Paul for his quiet nature and slight gawkiness. Maybe that's what she'd been craving after a life of killing, lies and pain. Something real and normal.' That's where Jaz and her mum differed. Jaz was attracted to the dangerous, risk-taking bad boy with a dark past. Not that she'd dated any, but that was her preference on TV. Damon on *Vampire Diaries*, Oliver on *Arrow*, or Jax Teller on *Sons of Anarchy*.

'So, um … about my birthday,' she asked, changing the subject. 'Is Ryan getting an invite?'

'Maybe.'

'Gee Anna, don't spill the beans, will you.'

Her friend grinned. 'I'm not telling you anything, it's all a big fat secret that I can keep from you.'

'Is this payback?' Jaz asked.

'Maybe.' Anna laughed. 'Don't worry about it, it'll be fun. Just wear something hot for Saturday night.'

'Finally I'll have someone as old as me,' said Tay, rolling his eyes.

Outside a black BMW pulled up at the curb and Jaz sat up, her heart racing. Her friends noticed and followed her gaze.

'Is that …' Anna began.

An old man climbed out of the car and they all seemed to deflate like a bouncy castle at the end of a fair.

'Thank God,' Jaz mumbled. 'I really thought that might have been Marcus.'

'Have you heard from him?' asked Tay.

'No, nothing. I haven't been game to text him. I just hope they're somewhere safe.' Jaz tapped her fingertips on the table. How would she ever know if Marcus was okay? Had Carl come clean with them, telling them why they had to leave? Maybe he'd told Marcus that Jaz was bad and not to contact her? It had only been a few days since she'd last seen him but already she felt the loss. Something told her she'd never see him again, which was a shame but it was probably for the best. Maybe he'd be some famous artist in years to come.

'He'll be all right. Carl wouldn't let anything happen to his son.' Anna gripped her hand and gave her a reassuring smile. 'So, you still going shopping Saturday with Steph?'

'Yep.'

'Get her to help you find a sexy outfit for your birthday bash next week.'

'Can't I just wear my jeans?'

Anna looked appalled. 'No, it's a fancy affair,' she said with a grin.

Tay shot Anna a wink and Jaz wondered what that was all about. Was she missing something? What were they planning? 'Just remember, yours is only a month away.'

'And I can't wait,' said Anna.

It was after six when they left Molly's and collected their stuff from The Ring.

'Hey Pax,' said Anna as she grabbed Jaz's schoolbag from the office.

Pax was sitting there doing a crossword puzzle. Since his stay in hospital, Pax had lost some weight. His face seemed leaner and his button-up coloured shirt didn't pull across his middle.

'Hi Jaz,' said Pax.

She smiled and greeted him. But for some reason she couldn't make herself go up and hug him like normal. It was still too raw. Not that long ago she'd had a moment with Pax where she felt closer to him than ever. They could share the MTG Agency secret and confide in each other. Only now he was hiding something again, this time it was huge and it was about her life. Pax had been there when she was born, he'd known her longer than her own stepdad, Paul, and yet he'd kept this secret about her mum and her life. Sure, she knew it was to protect her but it didn't make it hurt any less.

Pax's eyes narrowed, he sensed something.

With a huge smile, she slung her bag on her shoulder. 'Well, we gotta go. Mum's making her famous shepherd's pie.'

He leaned back in his chair, while rolling a pen through his fingers. Did she have him fooled?

'Righto, catch you all tomorrow. You did good today, Tay,' he said, causing Taylor to grin like a kid at a race wearing a blue ribbon.

'Cheers. Later, Pax.'

After Tay dropped them home, she ran upstairs to her room and flicked on her computer. Simon was home playing Final Fantasy, Mum wouldn't be far away either. So, time was short. Jaz typed in Natasha Montenegro and pressed search.

She didn't know what she would find, but it was worth a shot. She wanted to know more. Did her family put out 'missing' posters when she didn't come home? Did it ever make the news, or because of her being an agent did they not do anything?

Nothing came up except the name belonging to people on Facebook and LinkedIn. Jaz knew none of them would be her mum, she'd disappeared long before all that was in. Maybe she'd find out more if she knew what school she'd gone to and where in Victoria they'd lived. The only person she could ask about that was James. Maybe she'd find out when he was next in WA and see if she could set up a meeting with him and then slyly ask about his sister.

'What're you doing, darling?'

Tasha's voice made her jolt. 'Jesus, Mum. You scared me half to death.' That and the fact she had Natasha Montenegro on her search bar. Quickly she shut the laptop and got up. 'What are you doing sneaking around the house?'

Tasha laughed. 'I wasn't sneaking, you were just deep in thought. I actually called out before but you didn't hear me. Everything all right?'

No, I just found out you were an agent who's probably killed more people than a bus full of tourists crashed over a mountainside.

Tasha stood against the doorframe. She'd changed out of her work clothes and into her worn jeans and a cream cashmere sweater. Her hair was out of its normal harsh bun and fell loose around her face. Her eyes grew dark and for a moment Jaz saw a hidden strength and the ability to see signs of lies. No wonder she'd never been able to get anything past her mum over the years. Tasha wasn't as clueless as she made out.

'Just a few boy troubles,' she said with a shrug, hoping the topic would throw her off.

'Marcus?'

'Yeah. I think we're through.' Jaz didn't have to pretend to feel sadness or confusion. Not hearing from him made her feel like she was missing something, like a clock without a tick.

'Oh, Jaz. He seemed so nice.' Tasha came in and gave her a hug.

Jaz was surprised at how much she needed one, with everything that had happened over the past few days. 'I know. It might be all right, we'll see.'

Tasha leaned back and brushed a strand of her hair back. Then she held Jaz's face in her hands as she studied her face. 'My beautiful girl.' She kissed her forehead before letting her go.

Jaz felt the motherly love and understood, to a degree, why her mum must have done what she did. Imagine leaving everything you knew to start fresh. She'd done that for Jaz. 'I love you, Mum.'

'Aw.' Tasha's eyes got glassy and she blinked them clear. 'I'm just about to start dinner. Feel like helping me? I could use a veggie chopper.'

'Sure, why not.' It had been a while since they'd spent some quality time together. 'I'll be down in two seconds.'

Her mum left and Jaz opened up her laptop and deleted her browser history. If her mum had been an agent then she'd have to be more careful with what she left in her room. Snooping was something that probably came naturally to Tasha. Before she went downstairs, she checked her phone again. Still nothing from Marcus, not even a goodbye. That made her sad. She touched the drawing of them he'd done and then tugged it from her wall. That was in the past, time to move forward.

CHAPTER 18

THE REST OF the week went on as normal. Get up, go to school, then head to the gym so Taylor could practise. The fact that Taylor was fit and strong, combined with his fencing practice, meant he was at least halfway there. They just had to teach him how to kick, punch, evade and harm. It would all take time; Jaz had nearly sixteen years of learning karate, and then boxing and street fighting when Bags and Tick came to The Ring. Only now was she finally doing something with it.

Jaz was at The Ring early Saturday morning to train with Taylor.

'Show me something cool,' he asked as they stopped for a rest. Tay was wearing a white singlet and shorts, his hair spiked with sweat.

In a fluid motion, Jaz spun around, pushing her good leg out and up. Her foot stopped just short of Taylor's nose. She held this position, her abs contracted as she stood firm.

'Nice one. Will I be able to do that one day?' he asked.

Jaz retracted her foot and smiled. She wore black shorts and a fitted racerback tank top, her hair up in a high ponytail. 'Sure. You can start doing yoga with me.'

Tay pulled a face. 'Sounds a bit girly.'

'*I* do it,' said Ryan as he walked in the door. 'You calling me girly?' He stopped before them and flexed his muscles, causing his white T-shirt to strain tightly against his biceps. He wore comfortable jeans and his favourite commando boots. His hair had recently been trimmed short again, causing Jaz's lips to curl into an appreciative grin.

Taylor coughed and took a step back. 'Of course not.' He smiled.

'I liked that move,' he said to Jaz. 'I take it the leg's fine?'

'Good enough to take you out,' she said cheekily.

'Oh, right. You want some of this?' said Ryan, pointing to himself. 'Let's go, then.' He pulled off his T-shirt and boots before joining her on the mat in his jeans.

'Ha, this will be fun,' said Tay, clapping them on. 'Should you have gloves?'

'No bad dude's gonna wait for you to put gloves on,' said Jaz with a chuckle.

'Exactly,' said Ryan. 'You need to learn what it's like to punch knuckles to skin.'

Jaz and Ryan circled each other. He glanced at her leg, her wound visible but nothing more than a raw scar.

'Don't go easy on me cos you think I'm still hurt,' she said.

'I won't.' Ryan shuffled forward and threw out his right fist but she deflected it with her arm. He attempted a few more jabs, which she ducked or covered.

'Come on, Fletcher,' she teased. 'You're just playing with your food. Afraid to get a little dirty?' Jaz launched an attack: jab-jab-cross and finished with an elbow.

He deflected the first two but was a little slow and her elbow caught his lip, splitting it. He touched it with his finger, looking at the blood, then at Jaz.

She smiled while jumping on the spot.

'You little bugger, Thomas.' His eyes danced with playfulness.

'Bring it.' She waved him forward and she noticed the switch as he focused on the fight.

Jaz didn't have time to tease after that, it was game on. Deflected punches, kicks that were caught and jabs that were ducked. Jaz copped a hit on her chin, making her blink a few times. An even up, maybe? She tried to get him in a headlock but the waft of rich perfume caused her to recoil.

'What?' he asked, seeing her face as she stepped back.

'You reek of women's perfume.' It was like a dog marking its territory, he was covered in the stuff. She wiped the end of her nose, hoping to rid herself from it. Jaz didn't even want to know if that was from rolling around in the sheets last night.

'I had to meet Annaliese this morning for breakfast,' he said quickly.

Jaz was relieved, but still fire raged inside her gut. Bending over so her hand brushed the floor, she kicked her foot out and got Ryan in the chest. Her connection was good. He doubled over, winded.

'All right, you two. I think that's enough before you kill each other,' said Tay, who had Ryan's white T-shirt and was waving it in front of them. 'We still have a game of paintball to get through.'

'I'm going to have a quick shower,' she told them and left before her hurt gave her away. Hopefully a shower would wash that perfume from her memory. As she walked to the change rooms, Jaz questioned the raging jealousy that had spiked. It made her angry and territorial. If she saw Annaliese now she was likely to rip her head clean off her pretty neck. It didn't matter that their relationship wasn't real, Annaliese got to be close to Ryan. Intimate. That really jerked Jaz's chain.

The guys were still in the gym after her shower. She walked out wearing a stonewash denim skirt, a soft white top with lace detail and tan strappy sandals with a small heel. 'You still here?' she asked.

'Just waiting for Anna. Cody will meet us there,' said Ryan, who glanced away when she looked at him. 'I was just about to tell Tay that James will be in next week, so I've set up a meeting.'

'Brilliant,' said Tay, punching his fist into his palm.

'I can take him,' she said quickly, shooting up her hand as if she was in school. Why was she such an idiot, couldn't she just be naturally cool like Taylor? She dropped her hand quickly, resisting the urge to slap her forehead.

Ryan licked his lips, his eyes narrowed. After mulling it over he said, 'Sure, why not. I am busy next week.' He knew why she wanted to go. 'I trust you.'

'You can.' Jaz smiled reassuringly. She wasn't about to tell James everything, she just wanted a chance to see him now she knew he was her uncle, to get another look at him and see if there was a family resemblance. 'You lot take it easy on Anna,' she said as she walked to the office to grab her tan bag.

'Sure you don't want to join us?' said Tay.

'I'd love too,' she groaned. 'But I can't pull out on Steph now, her maid of honour is at home sick with the flu and her other bridesmaid can't make it until later.'

'Where are you meeting her?' asked Ryan.

'She's picking me up here,' she replied.

'What!'

'It can't hurt to let her see a part of you, Ryan. If seeing this gym makes her connect you to something, then she'll feel closer to you. Trust me, it won't hurt.'

Ryan rubbed his forehead as if he had a headache. He probably did – it was called Jaz.

'She's here.' Jaz pointed to the car outside on the curb. Steph climbed out, looking gorgeous in a soft blue baby-doll dress and matching sandals.

'She's hot,' said Tay.

'She's taken,' added Ryan.

Steph glanced up at the sign on the building before entering through the open door. Her nose wiggled as she entered and Jaz smiled at her reaction. She never got sick of seeing that on people on their first visit to the gym.

'Hi Steph,' said Jaz, waving her over to the mat.

'Hi Jaz. Oh Ryan, you're here,' she said almost running to him and giving him a hug. 'Oh my God, what happened to your lip?'

'Jaz did it.'

'Only cos you're too slow,' Jaz retorted.

Steph leaned over to look at Jaz's face and the red swelling on her chin. 'And I guess he did that?'

Ryan laughed. 'Yeah, cos she was too slow.'

Steph rolled her eyes. She turned and looked around. 'So, this is the place you talk about. It's got a rustic charm,' she said as she glanced up at the photo of Mohammad Ali on the exposed old red brick wall.

Ryan's eyes were on Jaz as he replied. 'Yeah, it's pretty cool.'

'Steph, this is my best mate Taylor,' said Jaz, doing the introductions. 'Tay, meet Ryan's sister Steph.'

'Aren't you cute,' she said shaking Tay's hand, causing him to blush.

'I'm here, I'm here, sorry I'm late. Mum was having a pink fit cos she couldn't find the car keys, but I'm here now,' said Anna, charging into the gym with her usual gusto. 'Oh, hello,' she said finally spotting Steph.

'And this is my other best friend, Anna.' Jaz put her arm around Anna and whispered, 'This is Ryan's sister, Steph.'

'Oh, hi.' Anna leapt into her arms and gave her a warm hug. 'I've heard lots about you. Gosh, I can tell you two are related,' she said, glancing at them both.

'What are you wearing?' said Tay, glancing at Anna.

She looked down at her army pants, black boots and grey singlet. 'What? I thought I'd dress for the occasion. You don't like?' She had her hair in a braid. 'I was going for a Lara Croft look.'

Tay's face lit up. 'I totally love it. But I don't think it's going to help your aim.'

'Maybe distraction was her aim,' said Jaz with a smirk. Tay was not going to concentrate with Anna's tight top showing off her chest. Different from the more conservative clothes she wore.

'I love your friends, Jaz. We'll have to catch up again,' said Steph who'd been watching their banter with interest. 'I can see why you like it here,' she said to Ryan.

'Eh, they're all right,' he said crossing his arms.

'We've grown on him,' said Anna.

'Like mould on cheese,' he teased.

'Let's go, Steph,' said Jaz. 'No love here.' She headed to the front door, with Steph a few steps behind after saying goodbye to everyone.

'Don't have too much fun without me,' Jaz called out when she reached the doorway.

'Don't let Steph lead you astray,' Ryan yelled back.

Jaz turned, taking in his form. He stood there, jeans, bare feet, his hands on his hips and the dark mysterious eyes that she fell for first. The sight of him drove her heart up into her mouth. Would that feeling ever disappear?

Steph, who had paused beside her, was watching the interaction with an amused expression – one Jaz hoped didn't get her into hot water. 'So, where to first?' she asked, hoping to shift her thoughts back to the wedding.

'Everywhere, Jaz. I have a whole list.'

And she did. Steph had found her wedding dress with her mum a few days before and now was trying to find bridesmaids' dresses and her wedding shoes. The worst thing was without her bridesmaids, Jaz became the token mannequin. But it wasn't as bad as it sounded and was more fun when Steph's friend Suzie finally made it. Even if she did have baby spit on her shoulder and the token messy mummy ponytail. Steph and Suzie even helped Jaz find an outfit to wear to her birthday party, along with matching shoes.

'This will knock his socks off,' said Steph, admiring their choice.

'You don't think it's a bit much for an eighteenth?' said Jaz. The soft white strapless dress hugged her bust, her waist and then fell in soft folds to mid thigh, just enough to cover her scar. Jaz frowned when she thought back on Steph's words.

'What do you mean "his"?' She changed out of the dress, and decided she had to buy it.

'Ryan. He'll love it.'

Jaz was trying to put her top back on but put it on backwards. She felt a little flustered and was glad Steph couldn't see the red face she could feel burning her skin. 'Um, we're just friends.' Finally she got her shirt on the right way but she was too scared to go out and face Steph.

'What I saw begs to differ.'

Jaz grabbed her bag and the dress, walked out of the change rooms and straight to the counter to pay for it. Steph came and stood beside her.

'Tell me I'm wrong?'

She fumbled handing over her credit card and then looked for Suzie – anything to avoid facing Steph.

Suzie was walking to the change rooms with an armful of dresses.

'Well, am I? Jaz?'

After taking her bag and thanking the assistant, Jaz turned to Steph and shrugged. 'I like your brother, what's not to like?' Jaz knew she couldn't get away with lying to Steph, so she tried the truth, of sorts.

'Ah huh. I thought so. Are you more than friends?' she asked. They hung about near Suzie's change room, waiting to see if she'd found anything good.

'No, and I don't think we ever will be. I'm happy with being friends.' Bullshit. Jaz almost smiled at her own lie. Well, it was sort of a lie. Yes, she wanted more, but she knew that wouldn't happen, so staying friends was better than nothing.

'Really? I'm sure he cares about you.' Steph touched her arm gently. Her concern just made her so much more likable.

'Oh, he does, in his own way, I'm sure. But that's it.'

'Well, I think we can change his mind. This dress will be a start. Then when I tell him he has to bring you to the wedding we can work on him some more.'

Steph's wedding was still a few months away.

'What do you think of this one, Steph?' said Suzie as she came out with a bright pink strapless dress.

'I said no pink, Suze. Take it off,' she said with repulsion.

Suzie laughed and went back to change. 'I have a blue one here that I think is the one.'

Lucky for Jaz that was the last of the talk about Ryan. It was sweet that Steph cared, but it only made Jaz get her hopes up dreaming of what could be instead of what it really was. No dress was good enough to change that.

CHAPTER 19

RYAN HAD BEEN busy for most of the week, leaving Taylor's training to Jaz with the help of Bags and Tick.

'Ryan came in earlier,' said Pax after they finished working on choke holds.

Jaz missed the cinnamon-with-a-hint-of-coffee smell that used to follow Pax; it had been replaced by something resembling mothballs and breath mints.

'He did?' Jaz picked up her towel and wiped away some sweat. 'What did he say?'

Pax nodded towards Tay. 'He said you have an appointment with James tomorrow at four-thirty.'

'Yes,' Taylor said with a fist pump. 'I thought it'd never happen.'

When it came to patience, Tay had as much as Jaz.

'Hey, Jazinator.'

She turned, confused by the voice coming from the front door. Cody was walking towards them with a cocky smile, looking every bit the surfie in board shorts, a singlet and thongs.

'What're you doing here?'

'Come to see you, is that okay?' He gave her a wink.

She couldn't help but smile. Even after she'd put him on his butt after propositioning her, he still didn't give up. 'What did I do to deserve that?' she said.

'I've got a gig for ya.'

Jaz frowned but Pax was nodding.

'Ryan mentioned this. You're to help Cody out this arvo if you can?' said Pax.

A loud curse rang out from through the office followed by quick footsteps. 'Pax, I think I've stuffed it. I need your help,' yelled Anna as she ran out of the office. She stopped her panic mode when she saw the extra person. 'Oh, hi Cody.'

'Anna banana, hey sweet thing. How's my partner in crime?'

Anna didn't take offence, nor was she swayed by his flirtatious ways. But she did laugh. They were all getting used to Cody.

'Not going on *your* team again, that's for sure. I bags Ryan next,' she said.

They were slaughtered by Ryan and Taylor in their last paintball game. Tay had taken great delight in reliving the whole event many times during their afternoon gym sessions.

'So, you need help?' Pax asked, getting back on track.

'Oh yeah, it's stuck and I think it's melting the plastic.' She pulled a face and together Pax and Anna headed back to his special room.

'Let's go into the office, Bags is due in soon for a session.' Cody and Tay followed her in and shut the door. 'So, what you need me for?'

'We're keeping an eye on a guy. We take over the shift in twenty minutes.'

'Right. You do know I'm busy,' she said.

Tay nudged her shoulder. 'It's okay, I can spend time on the punching bag and do push-ups and stuff. I'll cope.'

'All right, good plan.' Jaz asked Cody, 'How long will we be? Do I need a cover?'

He shook his head, making his hair move like a scraggly mop across the floor. 'Our shift ends at seven, so you can get home in time. Okay?'

'Yep. I'll just get changed.'

When she came back in her jeans and sweatshirt, she pocketed her phone and wallet. Tay had gone back to working out, hitting the bag with gusto, while Cody waited outside, sitting on the hood of his old Jeep.

'Let's go.'

She jumped in the front, flicking food wrappers off the seat and kicking the iced-coffee cartons at her feet. 'Gross, Cody.'

'Yeah, sorry. Didn't have time to clean up, the waves were good.'

He took off while her eyes were still rolling. 'So, fill me in. What's the go?'

'We got a hit about this bloke selling drugs. We've been following his every move waiting to see who his seller is, which will hopefully lead us further up the chain. We're just watching from a distance, not to interact or be seen.'

'Righto.' On the drive to their target's location they ran through their signs again to refresh their memories.

Cody drove down a busy street, cars were parked in every available spot along the road. This part of Fremantle was popular with locals and tourists alike. 'Good luck finding a spot,' said Jaz.

The old Jeep slowed and Cody put his flicker on to park, but there were none. Just as she was about to explain this, a blue Mazda, parked in front, indicated to leave, giving Cody the perfect park. 'How?'

'They're the ones we're taking over from.' Cody grinned like a school boy as he parked. 'You thought I was awesome, didn't you?'

'No. Just lucky,' she said with a chuckle. 'So, where's our target?'

Cody described the guy, who apparently worked in a record shop that sold old vinyls. 'See that green building ahead?'

It had one big window next to a door and was sandwiched between a coffee shop selling coffee and cake for six dollars, and a souvenir place for tourists. Painted boomerangs and stuffed koalas spilled out onto the path.

'So, we wait and see if he leaves? Can I go in there and get a good look at him?'

'Sure, good plan. I already know what he looks like, I've been doing this gig all week with the others.'

Jaz strolled down the path slowly and paused when she got to the record shop to peruse the small box out the front with CDs on special. Grabbing an old Rolling Stones CD, she headed inside and walked along the back wall, checking out what else was on offer. A girl with black leggings, black Doc Martins and a check shirt was sorting through a row of CDs in the back corner while a man fitting the target's description sat behind the counter reading a magazine. Was this his shop? Good way to switch money through, maybe.

Putting the Stones CD on the counter she pulled out her wallet. 'Just this, thanks.'

'Yep,' said the guy, putting down his magazine. He groaned as he got up. If he moved any slower, Jaz would likely age three years. On the plus side, she had plenty of time to study him. Mid twenties, scrawny, jeans held up by a black belt, tattoo sleeve up one arm, nothing specific about any of them besides the usual cross, lion, gun and roses with thorns. His face was gaunt, eyes brown but red-rimmed. She wouldn't want to be stuck working with him, that's for sure. He handed her the change and sat back down, leaving Jaz to collect her CD and leave. She stopped at the coffee shop and brought two coffees. She sat on one of the outside tables and after a few minutes Cody joined her.

'Sorry, but I don't fancy sitting in your messy car any longer than I have to.'

'Fair enough.'

After their coffee they walked the streets, but one of them had eyes on the shop the whole time. After five minutes they returned to the car in preparation for close of business. Sure enough, the target locked up and headed down the street a minute later. 'I'll follow on foot.'

Jaz jumped out and kept the man in her sights. He didn't stop but went straight to a car park. Cody was driving past after doing his second loop and Jaz waved him down. Together they followed the man. He went to the bank, stopped at the bottle shop and headed to the TAB.

'I'll go in and see if he meets with anyone.' Cody was gone for half an hour before he returned after the target had left.

'He's just got back into his car,' she said as he started his Jeep.

'Nothing unusual inside.'

The man drove back to a house and pulled into the driveway. Jaz craned her neck as they went past. 'I know that house.'

'You do?' said Cody.

'Yeah, Ryan and I followed a kid at my school here. We think this dude was his supplier.'

'Ah, well that makes sense, then. This came from Ryan.'

He did a lap of the block and came back to park a few houses down in a position where they could see the car and front door.

'He's leaving again, that was quick. He has a package,' said Jaz.

'Do you want to check out the house while I follow him, and I'll text you when it looks like we're headed back? He has no housemates.'

'Hasn't someone done that already?'

'Yep, but you never know when they'll leave something incriminating behind. And address, an number. Think you're up to it?' Cody asked.

They ducked down as the target's car drove past. Jaz opened her door. 'I'll be waiting for your text.'

'If I'm not back by seven, there's a bus stop a block away.'

She nodded, shut the door and watched him drive off. It was still light, so she had to walk up the street as if she belonged there. Jaz headed up the driveway and into the carport area.

The side window was locked and there were no dogs in the backyard that she could see or hear. Jaz climbed over the metal fence as quietly as possible and checked out the back of the house for an entry point. The back door was locked but there was a dog flap, which might just be big enough.

Shimmying like a wriggly worm, she eventually got through but had to twist her body on an angle. The house reeked of stale smoke, dirty dishes and mouldy carpet. Jaz crept through every room, checking for cameras or any kind of traps only because she'd seen that in movies. You really could learn a lot from film. In the dining room, she went to the table covered with bills and other bits of paper. The name on the bills was Mr Paul Turner. She carefully searched through them in case something had been scribbled on the corners. Meeting points, phone numbers or names. It wasn't like he had post-it notes.

Her phone beeped. It was Cody.

MOVE!!

Followed by another.

He only went to corner store for smokes. I hope ur out Jaz!!!

She didn't need telling twice. Jaz ran to the back door but wasn't even halfway through the dog flap when she heard the car pull in. Shit. Could she get out of the flap in time? She'd have to just open the door and run. Pulling herself back, she stood up to open the door when the front door began to open. You could see the back door from the front. She couldn't compromise this by being seen, it would stuff up future surveillance and cause him to be more cautious.

Jaz stepped into the nearby laundry and swiftly hid behind the door. Her heart pounded with the shot of adrenaline. She pressed her lips together, forcing herself to breathe quietly and evenly through her nose.

Hell, how long would she be stuck here? She prayed that this guy was as good at doing his laundry as he was doing his dishes.

She pulled out her phone, switched it to silent and sent Cody a text.

Stuck in house. Have to wait for right time to escape.

Feet shuffled towards her. Jaz quickly tucked her phone away in case she needed both hands to defend herself. The target, Paul Turner, farted and lit a smoke. A risky move on his behalf in this small house, she thought. The fridge door opened and a can cracked open. Then he shuffled away, maybe to the lounge room? With a bit of breathing space she slipped out her phone. Cody had sent her three messages.

Fuck

Are you safe? Shit

Maybe I can create a diversion? Yes?

She quickly told him she was fine and wondered if she should wait for him to go to the toilet, then escape.

The feet returned, she could hear the bottom of his jeans dragging against the floor. Jaz held her breath. Something went into the microwave and he turned it on. Minutes later, she heard him slurping.

'Shit!'

He swore loudly, jolting her alert. Had he seen her?

Suddenly he appeared in the laundry. Jaz held her breath, keeping herself hidden behind the door. He stepped towards the back corner to the old washing machine. Jaz leaned her head to the side as Paul pulled off his shirt and shoved it in the open machine. He was all skin and bones, the ink on his arm making his skin look even whiter. A circle on his back, right between his shoulder blades, caught her eye. She squinted, wondering if what she saw was right.

Paul began to move, so she snapped her head back behind the door just as someone knocked at the front door. Paul went to answer it while Jaz remained still but her thoughts raced on.

Who was at the door? A drug pick-up? Did he have a stash hidden in the house? Crap, was it in the laundry?

'Yo dude, I'm looking for Jimmy?' Cody's overly loud voice travelled through the house.

'No Jimmy here, man,' replied Paul.

'Yeah, Jimmy said he lived on this street, dude. Red brick house, dude.'

'You sure it's not the one down further. What number?'

'I don't know, dude. Red brick.' Cody was doing a great impression of a wasted guy; hopefully it worked to draw Paul outside.

She heard the flywire door bang shut and their voices grow quieter. Jaz quickly glanced around the corner, out the front door and saw Paul, shirtless, pointing further down the street. Jaz didn't waste another moment, she went for the back door, unlocked it and slipped out, closing it as quietly as possible. Around the side she lifted herself over the fence. It rattled as she jumped down. Quickly she hid behind Paul's car and waited. Had he heard that?

She listened until she heard the front door shut and then worked her way along the side of the car, ducking down in case he glanced out the side window. When she was clear, she sprinted down the driveway and turned right into the neighbour's shrub on the fence line. Hidden behind the bush she waited a minute, just to be sure, before walking up the street to Cody's empty car. After two minutes Cody came running around the corner; he'd done a lap of the block.

They got into the car before either of them spoke.

'You okay?' he asked when he caught his breath.

'Yep, thanks. It worked a treat,' she said giving him a free smile. 'His name is Paul Turner, but I'm guessing you guys already found that out.'

Cody nodded but kept his eyes on Paul's house.

'Did you know he was a member of the Shesha Serpents?'

He snapped his head in her direction. 'What? How do you know? We haven't been able to find a link.'

Jaz smiled. Lucky for her she already knew what the Shesha Serpents tattoo looked like and extra lucky that Paul slopped his meal down his shirt. If he hadn't been such a slob they might never have found out he was connected.

She told Cody how she got inside and saw his tattoo. His first reaction was to laugh.

'What?' Jaz frowned but it only made Cody splutter even more.

He brushed his blond hair back as he tried to speak between chuckles. 'It's just … I'm just trying to picture you wiggling your way through that doggy door.' He shook his head. 'I would have paid money to see that.'

Jaz punched him in the arm. It only made him laugh louder. It was infectious and she found herself smirking too.

CHAPTER 20

'PLEASE TELL ME what you have planned for my birthday. I promise I won't let on,' Jaz said as Taylor drove into the city for his appointment with James.

'No way. You know Anna would take one look at your faked surprise and then I'd be in the shit for telling you. Sorry Jaz, you may punch harder but I fear Anna more,' he said with a grin.

'Gotta give a girl points for trying,' she replied with a shrug. If the roles were reversed she'd do the same. Anna could be hell scary but in the sweetest way. Besides, Jaz wouldn't be able to handle seeing the disappointment on Anna's face knowing her surprise was ruined. Especially because Anna put her whole heart into everything she did. 'So, how's things going at home? Is your dad any better?' she asked after a few minutes.

His reply took time. 'A little. Ryan said the man who'd been following me was also the one receiving Dad's information calls. Ryan destroyed his phone but it will only be a matter of time before they make contact again. Even if Ryan had killed him and the other guys, they'd just replace them. In saying that, I haven't noticed anyone following,' he said glancing in the rear-vision mirror. 'If I do I think I just might stop and shoot their arse.'

It was habit now for Jaz to watch the mirrors, looking for tags. Since that night with the frying pan, she hadn't seen any. It was good but also a little unnerving. Like Tay said, it was probably only a matter of time before they came back like flies to a roast dinner.

'Shall we do that?' she said turning her eyes back to the road. 'I saw it on a TV show once. These guys were being followed so they jammed on the brakes, jumped out with guns aimed and ran at the car. I think it would be awesome! Totally catch them out.'

'How funny would it be if we'd got it wrong and they weren't following us,' he said with smile. 'Give someone something to talk about to their mates.'

'They'd probably want to send you their dry-cleaning bill,' she joked.

Tay pulled into the car park Jaz had told him about and found a vacant spot. 'Hey Jaz?'

'Yeah?'

'Thanks. For everything. Helping me out and coming with me today. I'm just glad to have this chance to be included, you know. To be apart of what you, Ryan and Cody all do. Especially with Anna involved. I feel as if we have this great big family now. It's not just us three against the rest of the world anymore.'

Tay dragged his lip between his teeth, a sign he was a little nervous.

'I get it, Tay. And I agree, it's great having you all at The Ring. And not having to lie anymore to you guys, we share the same secret.' Jaz watched a woman a few cars down as she tried to strap her resisting child into his pram. Outside life went on as normal, yet her mind was drawn into her mum's lies and secrets.

'I'm sorry about Pax and your mum, Jaz. Must suck to find out like that.'

Neither of them made a move to leave the cosy interior of the Mustang. The old leather seats were similar to the leather in the gym, making her naturally at ease in Taylor's car.

'It does but I'm glad I know.' She hadn't really talked about this much with Tay. He was more the listener and Anna asked all the questions. 'It just hurts knowing that Pax and Mum are still keeping it from me. I'm sure you guys felt exactly the same when you found out about me and the Agency.'

'Jaz, they are *so* not in the same league.' Tay waited until she glanced at him. 'I know you must be confused about whether you're a Montenegro or a Thomas, but your friends know exactly who you are. Just look to us if you ever forget that, won't you?'

A massive lump had worked its way up her throat with Tay's speech.

He didn't say much, but when he did it left a lasting impression. She would throw herself in front of a bus to save him. 'Thanks, Tay.' Her words came out at a whisper, her love for him choking her.

'Shall we do this, then? Go see your uncle?'

Clearing her throat and sucking in a breath, she nodded her head. 'Yep, let's.'

On the way to the building, Jaz had to remind herself to slow down when all she wanted to do was sprint. Tay reached for her hand and pulled her back, grounding her.

'It's okay,' is all he said as he shook their joined hands.

They headed inside the building and Tay shot her a look of disbelief. He'd been past this place many times, as she had. It made you wonder how many more secrets were hidden in the city behind the big corporations and businesses.

'Hi Janice. This is Taylor,' she said when they reached the reception desk.

Janice smiled, creases fanned from the corner of her eyes. 'Hi Jasmine. I can't get over how young you kids seem these days, but yet I wasn't much older either,' she said with a bemused smile. 'James is waiting for you both, head through.'

'Thanks Janice.'

One day Jaz would love to ask Janice what her life with the Agency had been like in the beginning. Now she knew her family legacy was the Agency, it interested her tenfold.

'This way,' she said, directing Tay through the big door, which Janice unlocked with the push of a button.

She stopped down the corridor at the second door on the right. Last time she was here, she was just as nervous, only this time her nerves were for a completely different reason. Raising her fist, she knocked on the door.

'Come in.'

Jaz turned the knob and stepped inside James Montenegro's office, Tay right behind her.

James got up and came around his desk to shake both their hands. Right from her first meeting with him she felt comfortable around him, he didn't big note himself by hiding behind his big desk, instead he made you feel on the same level as him. The touch of his hand was warm, she stared at it in wonder and almost forgot to let it go. It could have been worse, she had contemplated giving him a hug.

'Hello,' said Tay and introduced himself, which was great, because Jaz's throat had gone as dry as the dead plants that Pax neglected to water.

'It's good to see you again, Jaz. I've been informed of all your current work and your successful Sinclair operation,' said James.

Opening her mouth, she hoped the words she formulated worked. 'Thank you.'

'It's quite unusual to have someone of your age doing what you do. You seem to have an apparent knack for these things.'

'Trouble has always found Jaz, sir,' said Taylor with a smirk.

James didn't seem deterred. 'Nonetheless, it produces results, and results are what we are all about.' He indicated for them to take a seat while he sat on the end of his desk. His navy suit jacket hung from his chair, the sleeves of his white work shirt rolled up his lean arms and his blue tie loosened.

Jaz studied his features. His eyes were definitely like her mum's and her own. His face structure was similar, high cheekbones, as were their smiles. It took every ounce of strength not blurt out the truth. She'd never had an uncle, no close family except on Paul's side but that wasn't the same, not blood relations. James noticed her expression, maybe felt her assessing eyes on him.

'Would you like me to wait outside?' she added, trying to throw him off her scent.

He stood up. 'No, you're fine. Seems like you two work well as a team anyway, be a shame to split you up. And I believe your other friend Anna is learning the ropes from Pax? A deadly trio you guys will make,' he said, pleased.

'Yes, she'll be great. Very smart,' said Tay.

As James made his way back behind his desk to find the paperwork for Taylor he added, 'Ryan did well to stumble upon you all. He thinks you'll make a formidable team, and my gut feeling is the same.'

James did his little spiel on the Agency, filling Taylor in on what was expected, and the dangers, but none of it deterred Tay. The firm expression on his face and in his eyes said nothing would change his mind.

Tay began his formal paperwork while Jaz discussed the latest findings with James.

'So, did you really crawl through the dog flap?' asked James.

Jaz pressed her lips together, surprised and a little embarrassed.

Taylor snickered but went back to filling out his forms when she glared at him.

'Don't look so worried, Jaz,' said James. 'Cody told me.'

Jaz resisted the urge to roll her eyes. God only knows how Cody would have explained that situation.

'And he was impressed. Don't let it worry you. The fact that you could fit through there is another reason women are so important as agents. You have ways of accessing information some of us just can't gather. And spotting the tattoo – that's something we may never have found. So, be proud of how you gather intel, by whatever means necessary.' He glanced at his desk as if in deep thought, but continued to speak. 'My sister was slight, like you, and she'd always be the one to go through a small bathroom window or under a low fence. But she loved it because it meant she got to be the one to do the hard yards and put herself at risk for the mission. Sometimes I think she felt she had to prove herself because she was a woman.'

'Were you an agent, sir? I mean before the desk,' asked Taylor.

James frowned. 'Call me James, and yes, I worked in the field. My father believed you couldn't sit behind a desk putting agents in danger without first experiencing what it was like. I would have stayed out in the field longer except he passed away and I ended up here.' He waved to his desk.

Jaz saw a familiar glint in his eyes, the excitement of a mission. James missed the action. It was a hard thing to give up, the adrenaline rush, the feeling of accomplishment and saving people.

'And your sister? She loved it too?' she asked, hoping he would tell her more about her mum, this new side of her, which seemed strange and still a little unbelievable.

'Oh yeah, Natasha – we called her Nat – well, she loved going out in the field. She had an uncanny way of attracting people to her. Not because of her looks, more because she made people feel good when they were around her, she lifted their spirits.' James smiled and reached over his desk. 'I take this with me everywhere, just so I don't feel like an only child.'

It was a small photo frame and Jaz just about launched off her chair to reach it. Ever since Ryan had told her about seeing a photo she'd been curious to see it herself. It's not that she didn't believe Ryan, more that she couldn't believe this is how he found out her secret.

'Oh, can I see?' she asked, reaching out a shaky hand. Quickly she latched on with both, hiding her excitement and nerves. Her eyes remained closed for a long second as she tried to control herself. Any display would make James curious, and she couldn't have that. No tears, no recognition, she had to be neutral.

When she did open them she found herself looking at the first photo she'd ever seen of her mum at a young age. Dark hair fell to her shoulders in gentle waves and her blue eyes were bright. It was amazing to have something from her past, if only Jaz could keep a copy. She would love to take a photo with her phone but unless James stepped out, that wouldn't happen. Her heart raced while she forced a calm smile. 'She's young and pretty. Was she an agent then?' Jaz showed it to Tay, just so she could hold onto it a bit longer. His eyes widened at the familiar person.

'Yes, she was. This was taken at her twenty-first.'

Her mind spun. Jaz was born when her mum was twenty-two. Could she have been pregnant with her here in this photo? With a new identity would have came a new birth date. 'Oh, what date was that?'

Tay's pen paused for a half a second. Was she pushing it a little too far? Jaz took a last look at her mum and handed it back to James, aiming for nonchalance.

'Um, in February.' He put the photo back and then crossed his arms.

February. Tasha celebrated her birthday in April now. How weird would that be?

'So, the Shesha Serpents are quite big,' Jaz said. She didn't want to change the subject but she didn't want to draw too much attention to herself or the photo of her mum.

'Yes. Ryan told me about your dad, Taylor. It just shows how much leverage they think they have over this city. I know your dad's not a supporter but there are many in high-powered positions who are. Politicians, judges, lawyers – the list goes on. People can be bought for the right price or if they're threatened in the right way. It even reaches governments, and sometimes it's the rules and regulations that keep us from catching some of the high-powered ones. That's why the Agency came to be: we needed another avenue so they couldn't get away with it. And yes, Jaz, the Serpents have grown, but that could end up being their downfall. We'll use it to our advantage to get inside the group and take it apart from the inside out.'

'Do you think Salvatore controls them?' she asked. It was so interesting listening to him, she was learning so much.

James rubbed his chin. 'There's no intel that suggests it at the moment. Salvatore has mainly dealt in drugs and weapons whereas the Shesha Serpents have their finger in every pie. People-smuggling, underage prostitution, terrorist cells and countless others.'

Tay lifted his clipboard of completed paperwork and set it back on his desk while he listened.

'The worst ones get into this country as illegal immigrants like Jameson. They say they're poor but they've paid handsomely to get here. And within a few years they have set up cell groups or are rolling in money. How is that possible? Look at what Jameson has: his business, the money. You can't tell me he didn't come here without this being his plan. He had connections already in place just waiting for his signal.'

'Wow, I didn't realise. I thought he must have lived here his whole life to be where he is money and structure wise.'

James shook his head. 'Hard to believe, isn't it. But what can we do? We just keep recruiting and work hard at fighting them. It's an ongoing war, one we may never win, but we won't give up fighting.'

'Sounds like a good motto,' said Taylor.

James chuckled. 'You should ask Ryan about our mottos. We have a few. Now, Taylor how is your combat training going?'

'It's going great,' answered Jaz. 'Between me, Ryan and the guys at the gym we'll have him dangerous and deadly in no time.'

'Well, from what I hear we don't need to worry about your shooting skills.'

Tay smiled. 'About that? Can I get my own gun?'

'Me too,' said Jaz.

The delight on James's face was as plain as day. 'Eagerness, I love it. I'll discuss it with Ryan and we'll see. I don't normally give eighteen year olds guns just after they've signed up. This is new territory for me.'

Jaz felt like saying 'You're the best!' but pressed her lips together. Some degree of professionalism was required, and it was hard enough already when she wanted to know everything about James, his life and his sister. One day soon, she hoped that she could confide the truth to him and have a real uncle. She'd get to go to Victoria and learn about the Montenegro side of the family. Surely the universe had this in its plan all along?

CHAPTER 21

HER FINGERS TWITCHED. Jaz felt nervous. Actually, a little scared was more the truth. Sure, she wasn't overly worried about crawling into a drug dealer's house, but attending her own birthday surprise? That terrified her. A room full of people, some she probably didn't even like, all staring at her. That kind of limelight petrified her more than being in the dark with Cujo trying to bite off her foot.

With a sigh, she reached for her white dress. Facing her fears was something she was getting good at and she'd do it a hundred times over if it meant not disappointing Anna.

The soft material was cool against her skin as she slipped on the dress, and she was pleased to note that it covered her newly acquired bruise on her ribs from yesterday's sparring session with Taylor. Copping that blow from Taylor had made her so proud; he'd finally managed a solid hit after a long week of getting belted by all of them. Jaz had shown Anna the mark, like a proud mum showing off her talented kid's first drawing.

He still had a long way to go, but this just proved how determined and focused he was to succeed. Jaz couldn't wait to show Ryan. It had been a few days since she'd last seen him, and each day seemed dull without him.

She hoped he was coming to her birthday party tonight. If he did, it meant he wasn't with the other woman. Jaz didn't even want to think her name, that would only make her more real.

'Oh, look at you,' said Tasha as she walked into the bathroom and did up the back zip on Jaz's dress. 'It's a very beautiful, grown-up dress,' she said.

'Thanks Mum. Feels like it's taken forever to get here,' said Jaz, meaning her eighteenth.

'Well, for me it's all come far too quickly. Just the other day I was helping you tie your shoelaces and showing you how to do a high kick.' Tasha frowned as she watched Jaz slip on her white high heels.

'You're not going to cry tonight, are you, Mum?'

'I might,' Tasha said with a smile. 'Mums are allowed to do that. It's our given right to cry over our children.'

Jaz rolled her eyes. 'I'll pack some tissues.'

'Ha ha. Come on, are you ready? It's time to go.'

'Go where?' Jaz asked, trying again for birthday details. She reached for her father's medallion and slipped it on over her head.

'Somewhere fancy,' said Tasha, who was looking gorgeous in a long flowing sapphire dress. 'Do you really have to wear that? I've got some pearls that would go nicely?'

Jaz looked at the mirror, seeing the metal circle resting just above her breasts. It went with her dress, simple and understated. Plus, how did she tell her mum it made her feel like she had a piece of her real father with her on her birthday? 'I like it. It's me.'

Tasha lifted the medallion; she didn't turn it over to see the engraving but her fingers moved across it as if feeling the words. Something Jaz did quite often. Tasha let it drop and smiled sadly. 'I can't believe this day is here.'

'Now that I'm eighteen, will you tell me more about my real dad?'

Tasha swallowed quickly and her face almost screwed up as if she'd bit into a sour lemon, but you could see she was trying to control her expression. Was she a little out of practice after nearly nineteen years out of the Agency?

'Let's not talk about this now, we're running late.' With that, she turned and headed out of her room.

Her real dad was in her mum's old life; did she worry that in discussing him, she would risk revealing the secret of her old identity? No wonder she'd never given Jaz anything on him. She always assumed he must have been bad or done something wrong but it all made so much sense now. To divulge him was to divulge her past.

Minutes later Jaz sat in the back of the car with Simon while her dad drove through the night.

'You excited, sis?' Simon asked as he pulled his dress jacket together.

'About being eighteen, yes, the party, not so much,' she whispered.

'It'll be okay, you'll see.' Simon kept her busy with talk about school and a few questions about girls. He must have his eye on someone, she thought as she glanced out the window.

It had been a nice birthday. Pancakes for breakfast before she'd gone to the gym to train with Tay. Then on her way home, she'd detoured past Marcus's house, just because. Seeing the 'For Sale' sign out the front made her feel a little sad and she'd even sat at the beach where they'd shared their first coffee. No matter who you are, you can't just forget people and the effect they've had on you. She didn't want to forget Marcus. He was a good guy. She just hoped wherever he was, he was happy and safe.

Jaz focused on the passing buildings, realising they were familiar. 'Hey, why are we here?' she asked as they pulled up at the gym.

'Getting Pax. You didn't think we'd leave him out of your birthday celebrations, did you? We even brought him a suit to wear,' said Paul, turning in the front seat.

'Oh my God, really? That I gotta see,' she said, relieved that someone else would be out of their comfort zone.

'Well, then you can go and get him,' said Tasha. 'Be quick – we don't want to be late.'

'Okay, okay.' Jaz got out and went to the front door of the gym, wondering if she'd need her keys. But the door was open. She stepped inside the dark room and reached out for the light switch. The lights flickered on and Jaz turned to head to the office when an almighty roar scared her.

'Happy birthday!'

A crowd of well-dressed people were in the gym with drinks in hand. Anna, the first person she recognised, was walking towards her with a huge grin. She wore a blue dress with silver accessories and her hair gathered elegantly at the top of her head.

'Happy birthday, my gorgeous friend.'

It took Jaz a moment, or two, to comprehend what she was seeing. The gym had been decorated in balloons and streamers, tables were set up with food and drinks. She'd never seen it look so colourful. Nor had she ever seen this many people in it.

Faces became clearer as she focused on them: Pax, Bags, Tick, Niles, Ryan, Steph, Cody, Mr Stewart, Anna's parents and her own parents as they snuck in the door beside her.

It wasn't the fancy affair she thought, instead it was perfect.

'And you doubted me,' said Anna beside her.

Jaz hugged her friend and before she knew it, everyone had come forward to hug her and wish her a happy birthday.

'Here, have a glass of champagne,' said Taylor, handing her a glass flute. 'You can legally drink now.' He bent his head close to her ear and whispered, 'No more need for fake IDs.'

Jaz downed the champagne, hoping it would take the edge of her nerves. 'Thanks, I needed that.' Tay rolled his eyes and took the empty glass away.

Steph and Ryan were mingling closer her way; even so, she knew where he was the whole time, keeping him in her peripheral vision. He looked relaxed in dark jeans and long-sleeved fitted white shirt with three buttons near his neck, which were undone. He laughed with his sister and her eyes danced with delight at having her brother beside her. Did Jaz look as mesmerised when near Ryan? Probably.

The pull to go to him was great, she wanted to know what they were laughing about, wanted to be close enough to feel his heat, and she wanted her birthday hug.

'Who's that, Jaz?' said Tasha, who appeared beside Jaz.

She'd been so caught up on Ryan she'd missed her mum's approach. For an old retired agent, she still had some stealth moves.

'Who?'

'The cute guy you're watching,' she said softly.

Jaz turned to face her mum. She was sure Tasha remembered meeting Ryan at the hospital when Pax had his heart attack. She was just fishing for more information. 'You met him at the hospital when Pax was taken in, remember?' she said, playing along.

'Oh, yes. He's very handsome. And older.' Tasha's eyes narrowed slightly. 'Is this what *happened* with Marcus?' she asked.

'I don't really want to get into that here, Mum,' Jaz whispered harshly. 'And he's just a good friend.'

'Uh huh.' She didn't sound convinced. 'Just be careful. Something about him worries me.'

It was too late to be careful. Jaz had to turn away from her mum to hide her smile. She'd thought the same thing about Ryan when she first met him. It was the darkness in his eyes, mysterious and dangerous, or maybe it was just his sexy muscled body. Either way she'd been drawn in and seen past all that to the man inside. Watching him with his sister, he seemed almost normal, but nothing could erase the scars he carried, permanently on his skin, and mentally.

As if sensing her, Ryan glanced across and met her gaze. They shared a smile. The pull was too great as she sauntered towards them. Each step felt slow and the party around her seemed to fade away into a soundless blur. All she could hear was her heartbeat pounding in her ears.

'Happy birthday, Jaz.' Steph launched herself in her arms, hugging her madly.

'Thanks, Steph, great to see you here.' Even though she was talking, all she could think about was Ryan as he moved towards her. He wrapped her up in his arms and wished her a happy birthday. Every part of her body tingled as she hugged him back. He smelled so good she forgot herself and the gym full of people. The embrace was much too long. Quickly she pulled back.

'Thanks, Fletcher,' she said with gusto. His brown eyes were shining under the lights and she forced herself to focus on Steph.

'I'll go get us a drink,' said Ryan, wandering towards the drink table.

Thank God, she had time to breathe again.

'That was a little intense,' said Steph. 'I'd say the dress was a winner.'

Jaz had no words. What could she say to Steph to deflect her feelings for Ryan? Absolutely nothing. At this moment she couldn't be bothered with a lie.

'I'm so glad you're here. You look lovely,' said Jaz as she admired Steph's pale pink dress.

Steph's eyebrow raised as she noted the change of subject. 'Thanks. Anna said you wouldn't mind. And I'm loving being here with Ryan. Since meeting you, I've seen more of my brother in the past few months than I have the past five years. I can't thank you enough.'

'Thank you for what?' said Ryan as he brought them champagne; he'd settled for a beer.

Steph ignored him. 'Jaz, come and open your presents. This one's from me,' she said, tugging her towards a table piled high with pretty wrapping-papered shapes.

When she glanced back to Ryan, he was chatting to Tick. Maybe they were discussing Taylor's training.

It took her half an hour to open all her presents. Vouchers, money, clothes and more. Her friends got together and got her a sky-diving jump, which could come in handy if the Agency ever decided to hurl her from a plane. She did notice that there was nothing from Ryan, not even a card. Had he not known what to get her?

Jaz knew what he could give her, she'd been thinking about it for a while. The only thing she needed was the courage to ask. Maybe after a few more champagnes? Just watching him across the room was enough to get her hot under the collar; she could only imagine what the sex would be like.

'Time for cake!' yelled Anna as she brought it out, candles blazing. As if she were still five, they all sang 'Happy Birthday' and Jaz blew out the candles in the middle of cake a boxing ring with rope sides. She loved it.

'Here's my girl,' said Pax, who wasn't wearing a suit like she was told, but slacks and a plain button-up shirt. It was quite tame for him, except for the brightness of his orange shirt. 'You know how hard it is to find something for the girl who has everything?' said Pax. 'Bloody hard, but I hope this will come in handy.' He gave her a wink and pulled out a box from his pocket.

'Aw Pax.' Jaz lifted the lid off to find a beautiful Swiss army knife with more attachments than she could count. Included was a leather pouch to hold it onto a belt or her pants. 'Oh my God, I love it, Pax.' She hugged him tightly and couldn't wipe the smile from her face. Sometimes she felt he knew her better than most. 'I could have used this a few days ago,' she said softly before kissing his cheek.

David Guetta's 'Lovers on the Sun' grew louder. Jaz saw the iPod dock set up in the corner, Taylor with the remote. He shot her a smile and raised both his arms in the air in a dance move. As the night wore on, more and more people started dancing.

Her mum was sort of dancing with Paul, doing some funky moves from their youth no doubt. They looked happy and in love. Something her mum probably wouldn't have had if she'd stayed with the Agency. Is that what Jaz might be giving up?

'Jaz?' Ryan's voice was for her ears only as he came up behind her. 'Can you come with me?'

'Okay.' She would follow him into a burning building if he so desired.

He led her into Pax's office, Anna was standing by the door with Taylor. They both grinned as if they both knew what was coming. Instead of following, they shut the office door, leaving them alone. Ryan took her into Pax's house and to the room she shared with Anna.

He shut the door.

Right about now, Jaz's mind was going into overload. Had he guessed her birthday wish? Her knees trembled at the thought while her face started to burn. 'It's warm in here,' she said. It was probably only ten degrees; this part of Pax's house was always freezing.

'Sorry to take you away from your party but I wanted to give you your birthday gift and it's … um … best done in private.'

It was so damn hot in here. 'You didn't have to get me anything,' said Jaz. 'Although I do have a birthday request. Something I really want, that you can help me with,' she said. Her chest pounded as she said the words, there was no taking them back now.

Except Ryan hadn't really heard her. He was busy picking something up off the bed. A box.

'Here. Happy birthday, Jasmine.'

It was wrapped with brown paper and tied up with red ribbon. Sex didn't come in a box. She was momentarily confused before accepting the gift. She undid the bow, wondering what it could it be.

Opening the lid of the box underneath she found a hand gun. A Star Fire to be exact.

'Do you like it? It's all yours.'

Jaz sat on her bed, and Ryan joined her. She pulled out the gun in awe. It was so new and shiny. And it was hers. 'I love it.'

Something on the gun caught her eye. It was engraved with what looked like a bird of some sort with long tail feathers. 'What's this?'

'That, I had put on there. It's a phoenix. A symbol of fire, resurrection and immortality, also grace and kindness in Chinese mythology. It's something that I hope brings you a long life, Jaz, and it's also something that reminds me of you.'

With a finger, she traced the engraving. She couldn't look at Ryan, not now. This gesture was too amazing and she was overwhelmed by this thoughtfulness. It took her a moment to be able to speak.

'It's perfect.' It was now her most prized possession. Putting it back in its box she leaned over and hugged Ryan. 'Thank you.' Jaz didn't want to move from this position, locked in his embrace and riding on an emotional high. She moved back just enough to shift her hands to his face. 'How do you do that?' she asked, searching the depths of his eyes.

'Do what?'

She was going to say 'understand me' but her eyes had dropped to his lips and without thinking, she'd kissed them.

'Jaz,' he mumbled.

It only spurred her on, moving her tongue against his lips. She felt him stiffen, his hands went to her waist but he didn't push her away this time.

She stopped. 'Sorry, I wanted my birthday to be memorable,' she said, feeling far too confident.

He cleared his throat and picked up her gun. 'What was this thing you wanted that I can help you with?' he asked.

Here he was trying to avoid what had just happened, thinking he was changing the subject. A wicked little grin tugged at her lips.

'Well, we've talked about my lack of experience in the bedroom, but I want to change all that now. I can't go into the Agency without experience, and quite frankly I don't want it to happen with some undesirable.' Jaz thought she might have more of a chance if she made this more about work than her heart.

'Jaz, I don't think we should be having this conversation now.' Ryan glanced around the small room as if the walls were closing in on them.

But she would not be derailed. 'Was your first time with someone you had to get close with for the Agency?' she asked, hoping to God that it wasn't. Grabbing his chin she make him look at her. 'Was it?' she asked again.

'No. No, it wasn't. It was with a girl I fancied at school before I was recruited.'

'See. My point exactly. That's why I want it to be with you. Someone I know and trust.'

His pupils dilated. 'Jaz, no.'

'Why not? Would you rather I be with some low-life drug dealer?'

'No. I don't want that for you. But I can't,' he said softly.

'Well, I doubt I'm going to have time for a real boyfriend while working for the Agency. So, I wanna do this now before I'm in a position where I might have to, or I'm raped.' Jaz thought back to that moment she was attacked by five guys and shivered. If it hadn't been for Ryan … well, she didn't even want to think about it. Shaking it off, she continued. 'Besides, there's no rule that says it's not allowed between us, just for one night?'

Ryan looked up at the ceiling. She would love to know what he was thinking. A few long seconds passed, he remained silent and it drove her insane.

'Can you not see where I'm coming from?'

'I can, Jaz.' His eyes found her but flicked away just as quickly. 'But it's not that easy.'

'So, you won't help me?' She sighed. 'Then the only other option I have is Cody.'

That snapped his focus back to her. His brow creased. 'Cody. No. He's …'

'He's what? At least I know he's keen. And he knows me and my secrets. There is no one else. Can you see my predicament?'

Ryan dropped his head into his hands, squeezing it as if that would help him think. She couldn't do much more, and begging just seemed a little pathetic. She had more dignity than that. Reaching down, she picked up her gun. 'Thanks for this, I absolutely love it and can't wait to use it.' She stood up and put the gun away under her bed. It would stay here at Pax's where it was safe from prying eyes.

Then Jaz walked out of the room, leaving Ryan to his thoughts. As she joined the party, which was in full swing with everyone dancing, she wondered why this was such a hard thing for him. Was he that afraid of breaking the Agency rules?

Cody came by and put an arm around her shoulders. 'There you are, my lovely.' His hair was brushed back and was only just long enough to tie back into a knot. He was wearing stonewash jeans and a black button-up shirt. It was open at the neck, revealing his suntanned skin. He shot her a cheeky grin, making dimples appear.

'Hi Cody, thanks for coming.'

Why was Cody happy enough to break the rules for her but not Ryan? Was Cody just younger and less disciplined?

'I've got your birthday present,' he said with a grin. 'But first you have to dance with me.'

Jaz laughed and let the frustration from being so close with Ryan ease from her limbs as Cody tugged her into the middle of the dancing crowd. He held her hand as he spun her around before pulling her back into his chest. She laughed at the expressions on his face, as if he were a dancing professional.

'So, what's my present?' she asked as she caught Ryan joining the crowd. He was standing next to Anna and they were chatting. She watched their lips. Anna asked if Jaz liked her present. Ryan was all smiles but she missed his reply as Cody brought her closer to him.

'You sure you want it?' he teased.

Jaz nodded. 'Sure.'

'Big finish,' he added as he swept her through his arms and bent her back in his arms. Her back arched and she felt her hair touch the floor. Then Cody was kissing her.

The position he had her in meant she couldn't push him away or she'd end up on the floor in a very unladylike fashion. He lifted her back up and spun her around. The room was clapping, along with the odd wolf whistle.

When she stopped spinning, she faced Cody. She had two moves, punch him or laugh. He smiled sheepishly at her, hoping to avoid what he guessed could be coming.

'You wanted it,' he added.

Seeing as she'd already belted him before, she began to laugh and laugh. After all, the kiss wasn't that bad. And the way things were going, she might just have to settle for second best.

When Cody realised he wasn't going to end up with a fist in his face he reached for her and brought her back to his arms for some more dancing. He didn't try to kiss her again but they did have a ball dancing up a storm.

Anna was moving beside them with Taylor, who was clearly delighted. She saw Steph chatting in the corner with Pax, but after a good search around the rest of the room, Ryan was nowhere to be seen.

CHAPTER 22

Jaz got out of bed on the wrong side on Monday. From the get-go everything had been shit. She'd burnt her toast at breakfast, found a hole in her black stockings, had a flat battery in her car and had to catch a lift to school with her mum, had a spot test in math (which she only just passed), and then to make it all worse Minka was going out of her way to get in her face today, no matter how hard she tried to ignore her. Being eighteen sucked.

With her big biology and history books on her hip, she headed down the corridor for her next two periods before school finished. Jaz was so focused on her bad mood that she didn't see the glint in Minka's eye as she walked towards her with her best friends in tow.

'Whoops,' said Minka as she caught the corner of Jaz's books, sending them to the ground with a thump.

Her pencil case, which had been resting on top, burst on impact, causing pens to roll across the floor like pick-up sticks. Jaz saw red.

Ignoring everything on the floor she spun around, grabbed Minka by the shoulders and slammed her up against the lockers hard enough for fear to flash through her made-up eyes.

'Do you want me to fight you? Because I will. Just keep pressing my buttons, I dare you.' Jaz shook her hair back but kept her eyes pinned on Minka. She realised her fingers were digging into her skin, enough to leave bruises.

'Yeah, a black eye would go great with your uniform,' came Anna's voice behind her. 'Jaz, why don't you let the scared animal go before it dies of shock?'

Jaz knew one of Minka's friends had run off to find a teacher, and she didn't need a suspension. Stepping back she released Minka. 'Don't piss me off unless you're prepared to deal with the consequences,' said Jaz, as she watched Minka head off down the corridor through the crowd that had begun to gather.

Bending down, Jaz started to collect her pens while everyone went back to their classes.

'Feeling a bit testy today?' asked Anna as she helped.

'A little.'

'I'm glad you didn't deck her.' Anna smiled. 'Kind of.'

'Well, I'm trying to be more in control of my feelings. If I can resist hitting her, then I'm stronger than I think.'

Anna laughed. 'I'm glad.' She stood up with the books and handed them to Jaz as they walked to their shared biology class. 'Wanna tell me what's really bothering you?'

Jaz stopped grinding her teeth. 'I don't know. Maybe it's Ryan, maybe Marcus, maybe it's my mum. Hell, maybe it's the whole bloody lot of them. I thought I was coping.'

'You're dealing with a lot, Jaz. Give yourself time and don't feel like you have to cope. What you're dealing with is not normal teenage stuff.' Anna stepped in front of her and gripped her shoulder. 'Talk to us, lighten the load. You don't have to be so tough all the time.'

Jaz sighed and felt her body relax. 'Thanks.'

When they got to class, they took their seats near the door.

'Hey, who is Tay talking to?' Anna whispered.

A pretty brunette was sitting next to him and they were talking as they waited for Mr Green arrived.

'I don't know, never seen her before. Have you?'

Anna shook her head slowly. 'No. Must be new. I don't like her.'

Jaz laughed but cut it short when Mr Green strode in the room.

At the end of school, they all headed towards Tay's Mustang.

'Jaz!'

Jaz turned at the sound of her name. It was her mum, who'd come to pick up Simon. She was still wearing a long grey fitted skirt and matching jacket with a white blouse. She'd be heading back to work after settling Simon at home. 'Hey Mum, I'm going to the gym with the guys, I thought I told you that this morning.'

'Yeah, I remember. I just thought you might like this. It came in the mail today.'

'Who's that from?' said Simon, as he arrived and tried to look over her shoulder.

The envelope was plain, with a stamp from Qatar. Strange. The handwriting was familiar. Turning it over she saw two letters on the back: MS. 'Marcus,' she said more to herself.

'Oh, is that all.' Simon went and got in the car.

She could feel her mum's eyes on her, watching, waiting.

'You okay, honey?'

'Yeah. His family have moved overseas, so it's definitely over.' She had to give her mum something.

'I'm sorry.'

'Jaz, come on,' yelled Tay from his car. He reached in and honked the horn.

'Thanks for this, Mum, I'd better go. I'll see you at home.' She sprinted to the Mustang, the letter gripped firmly in her hands.

'Sorry. Let's go,' she said as she jumped in.

'Tay, who was that chick in Bio?' asked Anna, who'd claimed the front seat.

Jaz sat in the back watching out the back window for any tags, while the letter burnt a hole in her hand.

'Nina. She's just moved here. Her dad's a bigwig at some mine. She seems really nice and down to earth. I reckon you'd like her.'

Anna remained silent.

'I'll introduce you tomorrow.'

'Yeah, sure,' said Anna quietly. She turned in her seat, obviously to see what Jaz thought of this new girl. Except Jaz was too busy with the envelope in her hand. 'What's that?'

'Mum, just gave it to me. It's from Marcus.'

The car fell silent. Her friends knew what this meant to her.

'Aren't you going to open it?' asked Anna. She turned back to the front, giving Jaz some privacy.

She slipped her finger under the paper and edged it open. She pulled out a napkin with Qatar Airways written in maroon in the corner. Marcus had written on it.

Dear Jaz,

You must be going crazy wondering where I am. Dad didn't want me to talk to you but I couldn't leave without saying goodbye.

I'm on a plane to another country because my dad did something stupid, that's why we had to leave. He told us about it. I can't really tell you much about it but please believe me. I'm so angry with him, not just for what he's done, but the lies and the fact it means I have to leave you.

Jaz flipped over the napkin. His writing grew smaller and cramped as he tried to fit his words.

On the up side he's letting me go to an art school. I think he's trying to win me back. It's a start. But all this means we won't be coming back to Australia.

I wish we could stay in touch, but it's safer if we don't. I wish I could have said a proper goodbye, held you in my arms one last time. I won't forget you. This is the hardest thing I've ever had to write. But I'll have you forever in my dreams.

Marcus. xxx

He'd even drawn a little picture in pen at the bottom. It was them hugging goodbye.

Jaz blinked away her tears and handed the napkin forward for Anna to read while she watched the world flash by her window.

Marcus was okay and he'd given her closure. Even though she was upset, she felt weight lift off her shoulders.

'Aw, that's so sweet.'

Anna handed it back and Jaz read it again before tucking it into her schoolbag. She hoped for Marcus's sake that they were safe from Salvatore's reach. She also wondered what Salvatore thought of Tony's disappearance. What had he thought happened? What had Ryan texted him from Tony's phone? Would he ever look for Carl? Her brain ached with the unanswered questions.

When they arrived at the gym they went inside and changed. It was funny to see it all back to normal after the party. It brought back memories, good and bad.

'I'll just be a minute, Tay. Just wanna check something,' she said ducking into Pax's house.

She pulled out the box from under her bed and held her new gun as she sat on the floor.

'And here I thought I was the only gun-mad person,' said Tay as he poked his head inside the door.

'It's just so cool. Have you seen it?'

He nodded. 'Ryan wanted to double check you'd like it. Personally, I thought the phoenix was a rather special idea.' He knelt down beside her and reached for it, checking out the engraving. 'It's like giving you a nickname. Out on ops you can be called The Phoenix.'

Jaz laughed. 'I like it. I might have to get the matching tattoo.'

'Nice.'

'What about you? We'll have to find one for you too. I'm thinking something relating to your Mustang,' she said with a chuckle. Jaz reached for the gun and popped out the empty clip. She'd love to take it to the firing range but that wouldn't happen, seeing as she didn't have a gun licence.

Pax paused by the door. 'Oh look at you two, sitting there like kids with a new toy,' he said.

Jaz shot up as an idea hit. 'Pax. Can you make me a gun licence so I can take this to the firing range?'

Pax puffed out his chest and held the front of his shirt. 'Why yes, yes I can. I'll do it up now for you. Another thing I can teach Anna too.'

'Awesome. Thanks Pax.' She threw her arms around him then turned back to Tay. 'How about we take this puppy out for a test drive tomorrow?'

'Jaz, you just made my day.'

Putting the gun back, they went out to the gym and spent a few minutes getting warmed up. Then they started the lesson.

'One thing Ryan taught me, Tay, was "no rules". When it comes to unarmed combat, use anything imaginable as a weapon.' They walked around the gym and pointed out things that they could use and how. 'We can use our belts, shoes, dirt, whatever.' Jaz nearly said bricks but stopped herself. The sound of her hitting Rich in the face with a brick churned her stomach as she momentarily relieved it. 'And he also said to maim, not hurt and anger. Making them angry just gives them strength, so we have to fight hard and dirty. In the situations we'll face, it will be either them or us. So, go for eyes, hit the nose upwards and go for the groin.' She got him to hold her tightly and then went limp to show him how hard it was to control her. 'While I'm down here I now have access to your family jewels,' she said with a grin.

'I don't need that demonstrated,' he said with a frown.

'I think we should also practise some knife fights. It's not something you can really prepare for,' added Jaz. She hadn't been prepared for her knife attack and would surely be dead if Ryan hadn't come to her rescue.

'What if we hurt ourselves?' he said looking at her strangely.

Jaz shrugged. 'How else are we going to learn? You know Cody said that most of the injuries the SAS get are from their training, not the actual missions. Maybe we need to go hard too. And if we get cut, then we just sew it back up, just like Ryan does.'

'Oh yeah, I can see myself doing that.' Tay screwed up his face. His singlet had a circle of sweat at the neck. 'Actually, he did say we should do a paramedics course.'

'Really? Huh, good idea. Do you want me to see if I can enrol us in one?'

'Yeah, I think that would be good.'

Anna walked in as they were talking and she was shaking her head. 'It's a big course, they can go for months. You'll have to see if you can fit it in with school, otherwise you'll have to do it next year at uni. In the meantime, you can do a heap of ambulance courses that are shorter. Could probably do one during school holidays. We'll all go.' She held out a piece of paper.

Jaz reached for it. It was her gun licence, looking all official on the right paper.

'You have a gun because you are a part of a pistol club and a member at the rifle range yada yada,' said Anna with a smile. 'I can whizz them up like that.' She clicked her fingers.

'It seems so wrong,' said Jaz with a smirk. They had access to stuff above the law. It was a strange feeling.

'Not for me,' said Tay. 'Shall we get back to fighting?'

'Yes, let's.' They went back to the mat and begun to spar. Anna stayed to watch for ten minutes. In that time Jaz had connected kicks five times, as well as punches, but Tay deflected many more and got one punch in.

Tay bent over, breathing heavily.

'Good. Again!' she ordered. She didn't wait for him to get ready, instead she went straight into attack mode. Through being with Ryan on a few missions, she'd come to realise the difference between the sparring and play fighting she did to the survival fighting that happened out there. You couldn't go easy, or take your time. Everything was urgent and instant. She really wanted Tay to understand this too before he was put in a compromising position. And that meant going hard on him. So, he ended up with a few bad bruises, but at least he wasn't dead.

His arm flew up quickly, deflecting her jab. After another ten minutes she called it quits and got him to spend time punching the bag. 'Harder, Tay, throw everything into it.'

Sweat was now running down his face, drenching his singlet. He paused to rip it off and throw it in a wet heap on the floor. Jaz motioned for him to get a drink too.

'Okay, let's do a run of push-ups, then squats, kicks then back down to push-ups.' Jaz did each one with him and when he began to tire and slow she pushed him harder. 'Last one.'

He collapsed on the floor with a groan. Jaz sat beside him, also covered in a sheen of sweat. 'Awesome, Tay.' She held out her fist for him to pump.

'Now you can go for a run with a heavy pack on and weights on your hands,' said Ryan as he entered the gym. He had on a zip-through hoodie with his black cargo pants.

Tay flopped back and groaned again while Jaz laughed even though she knew Ryan was serious.

'What you up to?' she asked as he sat down with them. It was the first time she'd seen Ryan since he'd slipped out from her party on Saturday. Now wasn't the time to ask why he'd left. The cool, level-headed Ryan was back.

'Sorting out our trip up north. Anyone here?' he said, glancing around the gym.

Jaz checked the clock on the wall. 'Tick will be here in ten and Bags' lesson called in sick.'

He nodded. 'Okay, well, we need to be on the road Friday so we can get there and set up camp. The ship is passing through that night and the drums are supposed to be thrown overboard where the tidal waters meet and should wash up in the morning. We need to keep watch on who comes to collect them. Can you get Friday sorted?'

'Yep, you can stay with me,' said Tay, giving her a wink. He would be her alibi.

'Good. Be ready here at nine, pack like a tourist and we'll head off. It'll take us nearly five hours to get there and set up.'

'I'll be ready. Will I need my gun?'

'Bring it. It's yours to take where you feel fit, which means most ops.'

Jaz couldn't help her smile. Was it normal to get excited over that? She really was a little different, but so were her friends and that's why she loved them and why they all connected.

Jaz reached for her towel and dried off some of the sweat on her chest and arms.

Ryan stood up and slipped his hands into his pockets. 'I'll leave you to it. I'm busy until Friday, so if you need anything send a text and I'll try to stop by the gym.'

All three of them had instructions to text Ryan saying the boxing lesson time at the gym had been changed. He'd know that meant they needed to talk to him. Other than that he didn't want them to use his number.

'Okay, see you Friday,' said Jaz. He waved as he headed back to the front door. Jaz watched him the whole time. Friday they had over four hours in a car together. He couldn't run or avoid her, so it would be the perfect time to really talk with him.

'You're so gone, aren't you?' said Tay, who was staring at her.

'Maybe,' she said. 'Just a little.'

'Gonna be an awesome trip,' he said wiggling his eyebrows.

Jaz threw her towel at him. 'You need to get back to work. Besides, I think you have your own love life to worry about.'

Tay stood and helped pull Jaz up. 'What'd you mean?'

'Is this new girl of interest or are you just teasing Anna?' For the first time in what felt like ages since she'd worked out that Tay liked Anna, she said something about it.

He chewed his lip. She could see his mind trying to process it.

'Do you think it's working?' he asked.

There was no trying to deny his feelings and that in itself made her think he was getting close to doing something about it.

'Do you think it's wrong? I mean, will it ruin our friendship?' Tay whispered.

'You need to weigh up whether you think it's worth it.'

Jaz should know, she'd wondered if Ryan had been wondering the same thing. Maybe that's why he kept backing away. He didn't want to take the risk? Maybe she wasn't worth it? Was he? Yes, she thought so.

CHAPTER 23

JAZ WAS AT the gym early. She'd left home under the disguise that they had a science project to finish, which they'd been working on at Tay's. Lucky for them it was half true: they did have a project due for science but it had been last week and they'd already completed it at school. Jaz showed her mum photos of it, saying it was nearly done, a few bits to finish before taking it to school. 'Good job,' her mum had said. 'Are you still staying at Tay's tonight with Anna?'

'Sure am. I'll see ya Sunday maybe.'

It was a lot easier lying to her mum when her friends were in on it.

Jaz had hugged her mum goodbye, carried her overnight bag to the car and headed to the gym where her friends were waiting.

Once there she changed out of her uniform and into black leggings, white Chuck Taylors and a long blue knitted jumper.

'I know I'm only away for a bit but I've done up a list of things for Tay to do,' she said, handing it to Anna. 'Make sure he gets through all these after school.'

Anna grinned. 'So, I'm the boss. I like this,' she said shaking the page at Tay. 'Twenty push-ups then burpies. Man, I am going to make you sweat.'

'Don't let the power go to your head,' said Tay teasingly.

He wasn't fazed one bit and Jaz had to wonder if he was looking forward to it being just the two of them.

'We should be back Saturday arvo sometime. It will all depend on if what Tony said was true and drums do turn up. If he's right, then we'll end up back here somewhere,' Jaz added. She was assuming it would be a building belonging to Salvatore.

'Let us know where you are and what's happening, okay?' said Anna.

'Will do. I'll text, don't worry.' Although most of it would be in code in case they were ever found and someone decided to go through her phone.

Tay started laughing and they all turned to the road. 'No way, Jaz. Look, you're travelling in style.' Out front was a white Wicked van, the funky type seen driven by backpackers all around Australia.

They all rushed outside as Ryan got out. He was wearing thongs, denim shorts and a white shirt. She'd never seen him in shorts before, or thongs.

'Wow, what a ride, Ryan,' said Anna. Putting her hands up to one of the windows, she glanced inside. 'Not much room,' she added while glancing back at Jaz.

The worst thing with Anna was that Jaz knew exactly what she was thinking. To hide her burning face, Jaz admired the spray job on the outside. It was covered with graffiti characters – who exactly she wasn't quite sure, but they were certainly bright and colourful. Funny to think being this outlandish meant they'd blend right in.

Ryan slid the side door open, revealing a little table and seating area. It no doubt folded down into a bed also. How was a person not supposed to think about the bed arrangements when it was clear there was only one bed!

'Chuck your bag in and we'll get going,' said Ryan.

'Good luck,' said Tay.

Her friends hugged her after she'd thrown in her bag. Not because they were worried she wouldn't make it back, but because they were best friends.

As she climbed in beside Ryan in the front of the little van, Anna put her arm around Tay and they both waved. They were in their school uniforms, ready for a day of school without her.

With all the missing days of school, Jaz would have to be careful. Maybe Anna could write a letter to say that Jaz was suffering from an illness, or anything that might stop the school from calling her parents.

'All right, let's get this bus on the road,' said Ryan, pulling out and heading down the road.

It was a quiet ride north out of the city, both focused on their own thoughts. When they hit the open road Jaz glanced around the mini-van.

People had written on the inside, leaving their names and dates, writing sayings and funny comments. In the back she saw Ryan's bag, some sleeping bags (she wondered if they were joinable) and bags with food. 'Wow, you've thought of everything,' she said.

He laughed. 'It pays to be organised and cover every base. I've got some binoculars and dark clothing for when we're crawling through the sand dunes.'

'Now that sounds like fun. I hope there's no creepy crawlies in the dunes.'

Ryan laughed again.

'What?'

'You're afraid of creepy crawlies? That I find hard to believe.'

'Hey, everyone's afraid of something. I just happen to dislike ticks and leeches. The fact that both suck your blood ...' Jaz pulled a face just thinking about it. 'And get all fat and gross. Simon had a tick once under his armpit after we went camping. It was freaky.'

The morning sun was warm through the car windows. Jaz took off her jumper while Ryan wound down his window and rested his arm out.

'But I guess you're not afraid of anything, are you?' she said teasingly.

He wore his sunnies, so Jaz found it harder to read him.

'I am afraid of some things, not bugs though.' He shot her a smile.

Reaching over he turned up the radio, putting an end to their conversation. Was he worried she was going to ask what scared him? Actually, she was curious but she guessed now she'd never know. A man like Ryan, who faced danger head on, would probably not fear much at all. Except maybe losing his commando boots or his favourite gun, she thought with a smirk.

After two and a half hours, maybe more, they made it to Eneabba and stopped at the roadhouse for lunch. The owners there were a friendly couple who made them both fresh burgers with the lot. So good that Ryan opened up the side of the van and they sat there eating, dropping bits of lettuce and smearing sauce over their faces. It was worth the mess.

Ryan reached behind and held out a tissue box. Jaz grabbed one and cleaned her face. 'Best burger ever,' she said.

'I can't believe you ate all that. Where do you put it?' he asked.

'In my muscles,' she said and flexed her arms. She knew hers were no match for Ryan's but the amused look on his face was worth it. 'Want me to drive for a bit?'

'Sure, I could use some sleep. I'll be up most of the night doing checks.'

Jaz had maybe an hour's sleep earlier. She couldn't help it, with the warmth on her skin and the drone of the old van motor she'd fallen asleep, using her jumper as a pillow against the window.

'Here, you can use my jumper. Works a treat.' Jaz threw it at him before jumping in the driver's seat. Ryan settled in quickly, tucking her jumper up into a ball. From the corner of her eye, she saw him turn his head into the material for a moment. Was he smelling it? Jaz pressed her lips together to fight off her hopeful smile.

It was over an hour before they reached Geraldton. Ryan stirred the moment she began to slow down.

'Good,' he said clearing his throat and trying to stretch. 'We'll get some fuel and a few drinks before we make camp.'

Jaz wasn't sure what he meant by drinks; she guessed it wasn't water, because he had a five-litre container in the back. Unless that was in case the mini-van overheated.

But after getting fuel he drove them through a bottle shop and got a six pack of beers. She raised her brow at him. 'Drinking on the job?'

'Maybe. One or two won't hurt. Maybe none for you,' he said with a cheeky grin. 'Na, just props to look the part. There wouldn't be many back-packers' camps without some drinks lying around. If I'd notice that detail, then it's possible they would.'

'Yeah, true.'

'We aren't dealing with your average guys off the street, Jaz. These ones are careful and untrusting, they have to be. They're on the wrong side of the law, which makes them extra vigilant.'

'That's what makes you a good agent,' said Jaz in awe. She was a bit biased, but he could do no wrong in her eyes. 'You don't leave anything to chance, all details are covered.'

'Not all the time. I've had to learn from my mistakes. This one time I got caught in a bomb blast overseas. I thought the area was clear around this bridge we were blowing up, but I missed a kid playing by the river.

Bomb went off a few seconds after I'd grabbed him. Ended up with debris in my back.'

'Kid okay?'

'Yeah, silly bugger thought it was awesome. Except I had a hell of a time making our rendezvous point with my back bleeding. People notice stuff like that.'

Jaz never got sick of hearing his stories. It just amazed her, the things he'd seen and done. She knew he'd only just scratched the surface. She could imagine what it would be like to hear the Commander's stories.

Ryan turned off the main road before they reached Northampton and headed towards the water. They went along the gravel road, past farmers' paddocks, before reaching bush that turned into dunes. A few tracks led off to the left and right, as well as one heading straight to the beach. He took the right one.

'We won't get this old girl bogged, will we?' said Jaz a little nervously.

'Don't feel like pushing?' he teased.

Luckily it didn't get to that. Ryan found a sheltered spot to park. 'They shouldn't be able to see us from here, and we have the height of that rise to give us a good vantage point all up the coast.' He turned off the Wicked van and shot her a big smile. 'Right, let's get this campsite set up. Then we can do a little patrol of the beach.'

'You ruined that whole sentence with "patrol".' It almost sounded like a real holiday.

They got out, Jaz stretching her legs while Ryan opened the sliding door. The area out the side of the van was flat, so he set up the two chairs he'd packed and a fold-out table. 'I'm impressed,' she said as she put a lantern on the table. Ryan went to the back and lifted up the door, which revealed a tiny kitchen. There were also a few rolls of toilet paper stashed down the side gap.

'Afternoon snack,' he said, reaching for a bag of chips. He had a small esky, which she'd not noticed before, inside held sausages, butter and milk.

'I'll go camping with you anytime, Fletcher,' she said, opening the chips.

'We can't light a fire – it's not permitted – so it won't feel like real camping,' he said. 'At least we won't attract attention.'

With most of their stuff out of the van, Ryan made up the bed. She stood there, a little awkwardly.

'Don't get any ideas,' he said reaching for the pillows.

Jaz turned away from him, feeling caught out, as if he could read her innermost thoughts. She felt bad and wanted him to be wrong for once. 'I'm just feeling a little lazy. You've done everything, brought everything. I just turned up.'

'When you're in charge, then it can all fall on your shoulders,' he said with a grin.

Ryan grabbed a beer from the esky and put a pair of binoculars around his neck. 'Shall we check out the beach?'

With a nod, she followed Ryan up through the bushes growing on the sand dunes. The bushes got thinner and smaller the closer to the surf, and within a few minutes they stood watching the waves crash against the shore. The sun was beginning its descent towards the water. The beach was empty, no four-wheel drives, no one fishing, just the seagulls ambling along the wet sand.

The wind was quite strong. Jaz had to stand into the wind to stop her hair from wrapping around her face, choking her. 'It's so beautiful,' she said closing her eyes and inhaling a deep salty breath.

Ryan was using the binoculars, checking along the beach and the deep water.

'Anything yet?' she asked.

'No,' he said dropping them down. 'I didn't think there would be. It's still a few hours before we have to start watching.' He sat on the dune and took a sip of his beer. 'This is the life though, right?'

'Yep.' Jaz took off her shoes, pulled up her leggings, then threw her arms out and ran. She charged down the steep sand dunes, flicking up sand behind her. It was a steep drop but the sandy path was clear of twigs and she reached the bottom without falling. She kept running towards the water, scaring the birds and dodging the seaweed patches. The cold water pulled her up short, but she persisted and kept her feet immersed up to her ankles.

Ryan was watching her from his perch, she waved and he waved back. After ten minutes of watching the sun drop, the water began to feel warm but not enough to entice her to swim. She didn't bring bathers, but that didn't really matter. Skinny-dipping would have been fun, especially if Ryan joined her. Maybe on their next camping trip.

Feeling rejuvenated she ran up and down the beach, stopped to look at shells, collected cuttlefish, carved patterns in the wet sand with her toes and then did some flips and handstands. Time to oneself on a deserted beach should be a must. It was freeing, as if the water had washed away her fears and the wind had driven away her nightmares.

As the sun started to dip into the ocean and fill the sky with golden colours, she joined Ryan back on the top of the dune.

'You looked like you were having fun.' His eyes flicked over her face, as if drowning in her rapture.

'I was. You should have joined me. We could have built a big sand-castle,' she said, bumping his shoulder. 'When's the last time you were at the beach?'

He scratched his chin. 'For fun or work related?'

Jaz rolled her eyes. 'Both.'

'Fun was probably with Chris the last time we went surfing together, well over a year ago. And work – well, last week.'

Ah. Probably with little Miss Red Dress.

'You?'

'With Marcus, and then Tay and Anna but I guess you could call that work related too because I was looking for Marcus. But before that probably a few years ago with the family. Simon got roasted.' She remembered calling him lobster for a while. 'I heard from him, you know.' Ryan frowned. 'Marcus. He sent me a letter.'

'Right. He's okay, then?'

'Yeah. It was good to hear from him. I kind of needed it. I think it might take a while to get into this whole business,' she said. 'Or do you always make a connection with the people you're undercover with?' Was she asking specifically of his time with Annaliese? Probably.

'Sometimes. You wouldn't be human if you didn't.' He shrugged. 'I had to befriend these guys to try to get into their gang once. There was this bloke Gordo, covered in tattoos and a shaved head, seemed like a tough bastard but underneath all that he really had a gentle heart. Loved his dog and had such a sense of humour. I enjoyed my time with him and after the op was over, I actually missed him, you know? It's hard to have friends in this line of work, so you kind of take what you can get.'

'Yeah, I get that. I got so used to Marcus calling me that when it stopped I felt like I'd lost something.'

Ryan's shoulder came to rest against hers. An explosion of warmth spread throughout her body and it wasn't from the golden rays along the water.

'You really cared about him?' he asked softly.

Jaz couldn't look at him, so she focused on the blinding sun, letting it scar her eyes with bright dots. She couldn't find her voice, so she just nodded.

They sat in silence for another five minutes before Ryan stood up. 'Well, I might go get started on dinner.' He handed her the binoculars and walked back to camp. Jaz stayed, happy to enjoy the serenity. After a moment, the sun disappeared as if swallowed by the sea and only the last of the rays lit the sky. She stood and used the binoculars, checking the water for any bobbing drums. Hopefully the moon was bright tonight otherwise it might be hard trying to see things.

Jaz looked up the right of the beach, then down left. Seeing as the road split into three she knew there was a possibility that the men could be waiting. Ryan said the middle track went right to the beach and he believed the men would wait for their shipment there. They might even set up on the beach like fishermen. But as Jaz searched she didn't see any vehicles. She dropped the binoculars, thinking she should probably go and help Ryan. He might even have dinner cooked by now.

Just as Jaz turned something caught her eye, movement on the beach. A man was tucked back against the dunes and had begun to move. She didn't need the binoculars to see him, but that meant that he could see her too. He wore jeans and boots, tattoos on his arm and something bulky under his shirt. A gun? Crap. They were here ready and waiting. She had to move before he saw her. Turning she grabbed her shoes and walked off slowly. If he did see her, she wanted him to think she was just a tourist.

When she was out of sight, she broke off a branch from a nearby shrub and dived down into the sand, shimmying her way slowly to the edge, using the bush as coverage, to see if he was still there. He wasn't in his last known position because he was heading directly to where she'd been standing. Oh shit. Ryan was going to kill her.

Would this guy keep looking for her? Would he come to kill them?

She had only a few minutes to decide what to do. She couldn't kill him or capture him, because the others would know he was missing. Would their presence as backpackers be enough to convince they were harmless or would he kill them anyway? She needed something that would make him leave. But what? Jaz was sprinting back to the mini-van, everything felt grey around her with the sun now gone. Shadows were everywhere and she couldn't really see what she was stepping on as the night inched closer every second. Her mind was running at warp speed, hoping that the man behind her didn't find his way to the van.

CHAPTER 24

'RYAN!' SHE SAID as loudly as she dared. It was enough – that and the fact that she was running towards him. He'd just set down a plate of cooked snags on the table, next to the cans, sauce and buttered bread. He also had a light rigged up off the side of the van ready for the dark. Jaz threw her shoes towards the van and pulled off her top, so she was running to Ryan in just her black bra and gold medallion necklace. The look on his face would have been priceless if this wasn't an emergency. 'Take your shirt off,' she demanded as she reached him.

Ryan was clever enough to put her distressed face and the fact that she was getting undressed together.

'We being watched?' he whispered as he pulled his shirt off.

'Yes, I think I was followed. He has a gun,' she murmured against his ear as she wrapped her arms around his neck.

She didn't have to explain her plan of making the guy think they were too involved in their own desires to bother him. Ryan had probably played this game many times before.

Jaz was trembling, from the run, from the direness of this moment, and from the contact of Ryan's skin against hers. She kissed his neck and ran her hands down his back to his shorts. Ryan's hands pulled her closer, a finger slipped under her bra strap pulling it from her shoulder. Then his lips kissed along her shoulder to her collarbone. Jaz leaned back and groaned. In seconds she'd gone from worried to *Is there even a bad guy here?*

Hopefully their show was enough, he could be watching by now. Jaz reached back and unclasped her bra.

Ryan's hands stretched out across her back, feeling every square inch, his lips never leaving her skin. She reached down, unbuttoning his shorts and felt them slip to the ground. Ryan gently pushed her back into the van onto the made bed. Jaz totally liked where this was going. He bent over to kiss her stomach as he stepped out of his shorts, then he crawled inside with her.

She lay on her back, her bra barely in place. Ryan paused as he leaned over her as if uncertain, but his eyes were drinking her in and she loved the way it made her feel. Reaching up she pulled him towards her; she needed to kiss him now before she burst. This time when she kissed him there was no resistance. With open mouths, they tasted and explored. Jaz sucked at his lip and gripped his shoulders as the rising tsunami of passion felt like it was about to come crashing in and destroy everything in its path, even her heart. Her chest was pounding, her body throbbing, her skin crying out to be touched.

Ryan broke away from their kiss and move to her ear.

The side door was wide open still, hopefully showing enough of was happening to send the bad guy on his way. So far so good.

'Have you spotted him?' he whispered.

Oh, was I meant to be watching out, she thought. Totally not possible right now. 'No, have you?'

'I caught movement.' Then a bit louder he said, 'I'll just get the light.' Climbing out of the van in his trunks, he turned off the light and put a plate over the top of the cooked sausages. Jaz quickly pulled off her leggings. She had to even the playing field.

Ryan took his time outside, which meant he was looking for the man, but this time so was Jaz. On the pretence of watching Ryan, she searched the shadows. There was nothing but ... hang on, yes, there was a small red glow from the end of a burning cigarette. Sniffing the air, she could also smell a hint of smoke.

'Now, where were we,' said Ryan jumping in and sliding the door almost shut.

Jaz squealed and laughed, playing it up. It was dark inside, which meant they could look out the small gap, which was what Ryan was doing now. She'd much rather go back to the kissing even though her lips tingled from his stubble.

'We might have to wait a while,' he whispered, meaning they were still being watched.

Jaz leaned on her elbow. Her bra slipped off and she threw it aside. Ryan probably couldn't see much as he lay in the dark but Jaz leaned over him, running her fingers up his chest. Her body shivered as her hard nipples pushed against his skin. The sensation nearly left her breathless. Her father's medallion was warm from the heat of their skin pressed together, the gold a conductor.

'Jaz,' Ryan warned. 'We can stop now,' he whispered.

Not content, she rolled on top of him. He was strong and hard underneath her and she couldn't help but move against him.

'Jaz,' he growled. His hands latched on to her arms tightly, almost to the point of pain.

But she ignored him, and lowering her head she kissed his chest, working her way down.

He cursed loudly. 'Oh my God, woman.' His voice was raw and animal-like. 'Will you stop,' he whispered.

'Why?' she replied. 'Aren't you having fun?' As if to prove her point she rubbed against him; it did nothing to ease the burning itch. She wanted more.

Ryan's hands slapped to her waist to stop her rocking, only to find her tiny G-string. Another roll of insanities flew from his mouth. He grunted and rolled her off him then lay there panting.

She put her head closer to his, moving her lips millimetres from his ear. 'Please,' she whispered. 'Just one night, that's all I ask.'

'Even that is too much,' he replied, sounding as if he'd just completed a marathon.

'Why? Are you really that scared of the Agency? Surely one night isn't going to matter.'

'It will to me. If I go down that road, Jaz, I can't come back. And that scares me.' His words were raw and honest. 'I care for you too much as it is and I'm worried this might ruin me, ruin us.'

'It won't.' Right then she would have said anything to get him to make love to her. How could sleeping together ruin what they had; surely it would only make it stronger? Unless that was the problem. 'Please, for me.' Jaz bent over and kissed his chest a few times then when he sighed she found his lips. Soft, gentle kisses.

His hand snaked along her skin, and stopped on her lower back. 'If you're sure. You won't be able to take this back,' he said tenderly.

'I've never been so sure of anything in my life.'

She felt Ryan relax in her arms, the things holding him back momentarily forgotten. He bent down and expertly kissed her soft mounds, working his lips across her skin until she was shaking with anticipation.

He held her with such tenderness that one would never think he had such strength to kill. By now it was just the two of them inside the Wicked mini-van. The rest of the world was forgotten.

She lay snuggled in his arms afterwards, waiting for her breathing to return to normal, feeling the rise and fall of his chest. It was everything she'd dreamed of and more. To be with the man she loved, there was nothing else worth comparing it too.

'I should get dressed and do a check,' he whispered. 'I want to get a look at what vehicles they have.'

He slid open the door so he could reach for his shirt and shorts.

When he was dressed he moved to leave the bed but she grabbed his hand. Nothing was said but the feelings inside her were thick and plenty. Ryan bent over and kissed her.

'I'll be back in fifteen minutes. If not, come looking.' He gave her hand a squeeze and then got out, taking a torch and grabbing a couple of sausages and pieces of bread on his way.

Jaz got dressed and sat by the table eating with the light still off. She wasn't game to put it on, worried it made her an easy target. She heard the movement before she saw anything, her mouth freezing mid chew so she could listen further.

'It's only me,' said Ryan as he came and sat beside her. He put the torch on the table. 'He's gone. I saw where he was standing, saw the cigarette he left. He went back the way he came, along the beach. We're far enough away from them that they don't see us as a risk.'

'That's good. When he spotted me, I just thought the worst.'

'They don't want to do anything that would cause this place to become a media circus, especially killing us. So, leaving us be would have been the safest bet. There are two utes with canopies down the other road. Set up like fishing utes. I counted five sitting around the camp light.'

'Anything at the beach yet?'

'No. I'll give it another half-hour and then check.'

Jaz nodded, pulling a piece from her bread. 'You want another sausage?' she asked. It seemed better than discussing what had happened earlier.

'I think I might.' He made himself another sausage in bread with sauce by the light from the moon, which when it came out from behind the clouds coated everything in silver.

They sat in silence for fifteen minutes or so, until all the sausages were gone and Jaz had put her jumper back on. She lifted it up over her nose to keep warm and was struck by how much her skin smelled like Ryan. Oh how she could live off it, like oxygen. If only she could stayed wrapped in his arms all night. Would they get to sleep again?

'You cold? Here, I brought a few extras.' He fished out a beanie and a black hoodie.

She put both of them on, again immersed in his scent.

'Thanks. And thanks for before. You don't know how much that meant to me.' She gave him a smile as he pulled on another jumper and some track pants.

'Yeah, sure,' he said strangely, as if someone had their hands around his throat. 'Wanna come to the beach?'

'Sure.'

So, maybe it was a little awkward. Jaz was unsure how to act. Flashes of what they'd done kept repeating through her mind, making her crave his touch again and feeling like a Ryan addict. Even just sitting beside him was hard work. She wanted to be connected to him, holding his hand or just leaning against his arm.

Had he known this would be the hardest part? The aftermath? Jaz would love to know what he was thinking. Did he regret it, had it changed the way he saw her now, had she got under his skin, could he love her? She'd take on the guys with the guns before she could work up the courage to ask Ryan these questions, for fear of his answers. What if it wasn't what she hoped?

Together they made a slow and careful trek to the beach, using a different path from before, this one was more a wide arc bringing them out thirty metres further up the beach. They remained quiet, lying down near the small bushes on the dunes.

Ryan had the binoculars and he tapped her shoulder. He signalled to her that he could see two drums in the water. It was still windy but lying in the sand kept them away from most of it, just the odd bit of sand got in her eyes.

When there was no sign of anyone on the beach or surrounds, Ryan leaned over and whispered, 'Why don't you go back and get some sleep. I'll come and do a shift change with you in a few hours.'

She mouthed, 'Okay.'

They worked through the night like this, so she didn't end up getting another chance to snuggle up to Ryan. But she kept herself awake on the dunes by reliving every single moment. She couldn't have asked for a more perfect first time, maybe minus the bad guys and the drugs. The Wicked van was fine, kind of cosy and different. Seeing one on the road now would only bring this moment back, but that wouldn't be a bad thing.

Jaz found the early morning stretch the hardest, it was so cold she'd dug her hands into the sand to keep them warm. It was time to swap shifts with Ryan but before she would wake him he'd dropped down beside her. She couldn't help the involuntarily smile that came with seeing him. Warmth radiated within her from his nearness.

'Morning. Last drum turned up yet?' he asked.

Even though he'd just woken up, he looked wide awake and ready to go. His lips were so close. Would he be offended if she kissed him?

'Yep, just saw them drive up the beach to collect it. It's a fair way north,' she said handing over the binoculars.

He looked for the ute. 'Good. I'll just go check and see if the other ute has left yet in case they don't travel together. Go back to camp and get ready, we might need to head out early, get in front of them.' He got up and disappeared into the bush behind.

At camp Ryan had already packed away the table and chairs. Jaz changed into fresh clothes, jeans and a blue T-shirt, sprayed on some deodorant and then checked everything else was in order. Ryan's shirt from yesterday was lying on top of his bag, and Jaz reached for it, wanting to see if it still smelled like him, but then she stopped herself.

'Ready,' said Ryan behind her.

Thank God, that was a lucky gut instinct. 'Yep. What's the go?'

'Red ute has just left, so we'll go now and sit in between them. Jump in.'

Leaving behind their camping spot, Ryan reversed the Wicked van out on the main track. There was no dust from the ute in front but Jaz used the binoculars and could see it up ahead.

Keeping a good distance, they followed it to Geraldton. It didn't stop — obviously keen to get back to Perth with its expensive cargo.

The trip home was quiet. Maybe they didn't know what to talk about after being together, or maybe it was because this mission was getting to the hardest part.

'I'm going to get some sleep. Wake me up when it's my turn to drive.' And with that, Jaz was out like a light.

She woke hours later with her stomach rumbling and her mouth dry. 'Where are we?' she asked, stretching.

'Just on the outskirts of Perth.'

'You didn't wake me!'

'You looked too peaceful.' He was smiling to himself. 'Quite entertaining too.'

'What? What did I do? Did I talk?' Crap, she'd had many dreams.

'You mutter and groan. Sometimes you were twitching as if punching someone,' he said.

'It was probably you.'

That made him laugh.

While tying her hair up, she searched for the ute. It was two cars in front.

'We're just going to make a car swap up here at this service station. The van will stand out too much now.'

Jaz didn't know the guy who was waiting for them with a silver commodore but Ryan shook his hand like they were good mates. Mates who had saved each other's back once or twice. They didn't stay long enough to introduce Jaz, it was an instant car swap.

'Ethan will take the van back to his place and we'll swap back after we're done,' he added. He put his foot down, trying to catch up to the ute. When it was in view, he slowed down to stay a few cars behind.

They followed it all the way through the city down to an industrial area in Canning Vale. It was harder to follow the ute without being seen. Ryan crept along slowly, pulling over if anyone came up behind him so they could pass. The ute turned down a street full of big sheds and drove into one that had a concrete wall and big metal gates on either side. One way in and one way out. They looked like storage units.

Ryan pulled into the car park for a wholesale direct place called Red Apple that sold furniture, homewares and tiles. They had about ten cars parked out the front, so one more car slotted in nicely.

'There's no way we can get in there,' said Ryan, using the binoculars to see inside further. 'It's a key entry. They must have a few storage units to hold the stuff, probably under a false name. But I'll get Pax to check it out.'

'Anna could probably get into their system and get a list of names who have hired a unit. We might be able to find something that connects Salvatore.'

Ryan agreed. Five minutes later the second ute arrived, entering the same way as the last. 'I'll go for a little walk, get a better look.' He reached for the packet of cigarettes, got out of the car and walked up the street before crossing over. He walked with his phone out, then paused by the metal gates as if he'd got a phone call. She could see him talking to himself but knew he'd be using this to see inside. He put his phone away and then leaned against the concrete wall just this side of the gate. The wall was over twice his height, so no way he could scale it, nor the gate.

What was he waiting for, she wondered. Quickly she pulled out her own phone and sent a text to Anna.

Hey, back from out trip. Loved it. That part wasn't an exaggeration. *Just in Canning Vale, nearly home. xx*

Ryan lit a cigarette as he leaned against the wall, pretending to look at his phone.

After a few minutes he walked off. She saw one of the utes drive out of a unit and out through the exit. Ryan motioned for her to start the car. Jaz jumped across and drove out of the parking lot, pausing to pick him up.

'Follow that ute,' he said getting in. 'I could hear them, the walls made their voices carry just enough to catch a few things. Sounds like the others are staying there to sort out the shipment but this guy is taking some now, someone's waiting for it.'

'Right.' Her pulse picked up. Things were getting interesting. Plus she was now driving and she didn't want to get caught. She put into practice Ryan's techniques that she'd observed, catching up to the ute but not getting too close.

'That's funny,' said Ryan. Jaz glanced his way. 'They're going to Jandakot Airport.'

A few seconds later a sign flashed past stating just that. It was getting harder to follow the ute as there was no traffic heading into the airport. Jaz dropped back further, Ryan using the binoculars to see which way they were turning.

'Stop here, Jaz,' he said. 'They've gone into that building up ahead. Looks like a plane hangar. The blue sign out the front says "Industry Aviation" and I bet it belongs to Salvatore.'

While Ryan searched it out from afar, Jaz googled the name on her phone. 'Yep, ten points to you,' she said. 'Owned by De Luca Industries.'

She picked up her phone, Anna had replied.

Great. Can't wait to catch up.

Jaz sent another one.

Stopped by Jandakot Airport for a look at Sal's planes. He's got a new blue sign up out the front. Looks great.

She knew her friends would get that, eventually.

'Let's go for a little walk, shall we?' Ryan got his gun out of the glove box and handed Jaz hers. They were the only things they'd taken with them in the car swap.

They tucked their guns in their jeans and covered them with their shirts. Ryan held out his hand. 'Make it look like we're going for a stroll.'

She didn't need telling twice. Her hand slotted into his like it belonged there. It took a lot of effort not to smile and skip along like a person completely in love.

'Nice day, isn't it?'

'Better if I'd had some breakfast,' she said. Her stomach groaned on cue.

Ryan laughed and looked so casual, as if they were enjoying a wander.

They walked past the big hangar, taking in as much detail as they could, then got to the end of the road and turned back. This time Ryan headed towards the building, which had a small entry office. 'What's say we ask someone for help.'

'What? Go in there?'

'Why not?' he said. 'We'd see more if we can get inside. We'll wing it.'

The small door wasn't locked, so they stepped inside. Just as the door buzzer sounded a man had walked in from the back entry, and he had a gun with a silencer on the end in his hand and blood across his shirt. Not what either of them were expecting.

Ryan and Jaz froze.

'Who are you?' the man with the gun asked as he tried to hide it behind his back.

But their eyes were on the blood splatter pattern across his shirt.

'Um … we were just looking for Pete Tolland. Is he here?' said Ryan.

The man frowned. You could see he was thinking about what to do. 'No one here by that name.'

She knew Ryan didn't want them to turn around and leave: one, because the guy might spot the guns hidden on them; and two, what would he do if their backs were turned?

'Okay, no worries, we'll ah … try the next building,' said Ryan as he shielded Jaz with his arm and stepped towards the door.

The man in the bloody shirt raised his gun and pointed it at them. 'I don't think so.'

CHAPTER 25

THE HANDGUN REMAINED pointed at them, going from Ryan to Jaz. Now what?

It was a stand-off. Nobody moved or spoke.

'Hey, Jeff, what's taking so long,' yelled another man.

Jeff, the guy with the gun, didn't move or reply. Jaz could see he was still uncertain what he should do.

'There you are,' said the guy who'd called out before. 'What're you doing?' He stepped into the office from the shed area. He had a silver ring through his eyebrow and a black circle in his earlobe. Then he turned and saw Jaz and Ryan. 'What the fuck?' His hand automatically went to his hip where a gun was tucked into his pants. 'Jeff. What're you doing?'

'They saw me, with the gun and my shirt,' Jeff tried to whisper. 'I didn't know what to do. Do we …?'

Jaz shivered. She knew damn well what Jeff was implying.

'Fuck man, the boss will be pissed.' Earring guy looked out the small front window. 'Who are you two?' he demanded.

'We were just looking for a friend who works around here. We didn't mean to bother anyone. We didn't see anything,' said Ryan putting his hands up. 'We just want to leave.'

'Don't hurt us, please,' begged Jaz. She hoped the look of an innocent girl might be enough to let them go.

'Fuck.' Earring man rubbed his head with both his hands. 'Take them out back. Boss hates loose ends.' Drawing his gun he trained it on Jaz.

'Sorry folks, you picked the wrong building today.' He motioned with his gun for them to head out back.

Jaz glanced at Ryan who nodded and reached for her protectively. They had to act the part of scared people, which Jaz was, she just didn't want to cry about it.

She put her hand behind Ryan's back, looking like she was clinging onto him when in fact she'd pulled out her phone. Burying her head into Ryan's side, she could just see her screen and sent Anna one simple message.

SOS

She knew they would track her phone to here. Then she slipped the phone into Ryan's back pocket just as the second man walked out behind them. She arched her back so her shirt hung loose over the gun, hiding it. They were herded through the back door into a massive hangar that had two charter planes inside. One looked as if it was being prepared for a flight, with two guys in overalls checking it over. Jaz swallowed hard when she noticed the splatter of blood in the far corner by a generator. Black plastic had obviously been on the floor and was now wrapped around a long body shape. Except the plastic hadn't caught all of it, red drops like paint blown through a straw splattered the cream cement. A similar pattern was on Jeff's shirt. Jaz's stomach rolled as she wondered who was lying in that plastic and what had they done to deserve being shot. A man nearby was about to pick up the body when he saw them enter.

All up Jaz counted five men. Two working on the plane, who didn't seem to have guns, the guy by the body who had a pistol in his pants and then the two idiots behind Ryan and herself.

As the rest of the men in the hangar spotted them, they all came to a standstill.

'What's going on?' said a voice coming from the aeroplane. He came out, put down a package of some sort.

Make that six men.

Had the man on the plane been hiding drugs ready to take somewhere? He descended the steps. Jaz drew in a sharp breath just as Ryan's grip on her intensified. It was Salvatore. Salvatore De Luca. Drug runner. Killer. All-time bad man.

Would he remember Jaz from the casino? She hoped not. A red dress and make-up made for good camouflage. Surely her jeans and blue T-shirt, with her hair back in a ponytail, would distance her from the casino Jaz?

'I see we have guests. Jeff, please explain,' said Sal as he reached ground with his shiny black leather shoes. He wore black dress pants and a grey button-up shirt with lots of gold accessories. He oozed money and importance.

Jaz was struck again at how imposing he seemed, similar to how she felt when she first met Ryan, that they had hidden depth, held themselves strongly and commanded attention. Salvatore was a handsome man for his age, his hair full and dark, his skin even and unblemished. But it was his piercing black eyes that really scared her the most.

'Um they caught me off guard,' said Jeff pointing to his shirt and the gun. 'I didn't think it would be safe to let them go. We can't afford attention right now.'

'We promise not to mention anything,' begged Ryan. 'Let me and my girl go, please.'

Salvatore put his a finger to his lip as if he was deciding what wine to have with his dessert instead of how to deal with them. Jaz hoped it wasn't death. That black plastic was not her friend. She shivered and crossed her arms.

Salvatore nodded to the man in the back corner. Next thing he was dragging over the roll of black plastic.

'Oh shit,' mumbled Jaz. She was ready to go for her gun and slaughter as many as she could before she was buried in that plastic. She glanced at Ryan, waiting for his signal. She knew it would come. Ryan would not let them die here. He gave her the smallest signal, wait.

The plastic was rolled out in front of them. Maybe Salvatore was just trying to scare them.

'I'm sorry it has to be this way. You're just in the wrong place at the wrong time.' Salvatore's gaze settled on Jaz.

Was he wondering how old she was? Maybe he felt bad?

He grimaced, then sighed. 'I really am stuck between a rock and a hard place and I have no choice.' Salvatore pointed his finger towards the ground.

This must be a well-known signal with his mates because in the next second she felt a knee in the back of her leg.

'Kneel down,' said Jeff behind her.

She refused to move. Neither had Ryan.

Jeff cracked Ryan over the head with the gun, he fell to his knees while shaking his head.

'No!' screamed Jaz. She turned to spit or punch at Jeff, or maybe both, but he grabbed her shoulder, clamping down and pushing her forward. Jaz landed on the plastic, her knees hitting the hard floor and her hands slapping so hard her medallion swung forward and hit her in the face. All she could think about was her gun. Was it still hidden? She couldn't bear to lose it, she only just got it. It was a birthday present for crying out loud. And it was engraved!

One of them grabbed her hair and pulled her back into a kneeling position. Jaz grunted from the pain and reached up to her head. Ryan was beside her, blood running from his temple. 'Are you okay?' she whispered.

He nodded.

Salvatore stepped onto the black plastic, it rustled underfoot. Jaz looked up at him, hoping the fear in her eyes might make him change his mind. 'Please, no,' she begged. But he moved closer and that's when Jaz realised he wasn't looking at her. He was looking at the medallion.

Salvatore reached for it. 'Wait,' he said to his men. 'Maybe I'll spare your life yet. Do you believe in God?' He was clearly taken with her medallion.

Beside her Jaz felt Ryan tap against her skin. *Now.*

He pulled out his gun and went straight for Salvatore, who'd made the mistake of getting too close. Salvatore jerked back, ripping Jaz's medallion from her neck.

'Put your guns down,' yelled Ryan. 'Or I'll kill him.'

Jaz shot up, about to pull her gun from her waist but she felt the hard press of metal against her head. 'Don't move, missy,' came the voice of earring man.

'Who *are* you?' said Jeff, completely surprised.

'Let him go or I put a bullet in your girlfriend's head,' said earring man.

Jaz could see Ryan wondering what to do. Salvatore seemed unruffled as he stood there.

'Let's calm down,' he said to his men. Salvatore then looked down at the medallion in his hand.

Maybe he'd had guns pointed to his head before because he seemed really blasé about it, as if Ryan wasn't even there.

But Jaz could feel the gun at her head. It caused her knees to knock together slightly. Grimacing, she pulled herself together. She had to remain calm too; panicking would only get her killed.

Salvatore turned over the circle of gold, reading the inscription on the back.

'Where did you get this?' he demanded suddenly. He leaned towards Jaz, causing Ryan to dig the gun in harder but to no effect. Salvatore's black eyes looked almost frantic. He held up her necklace. 'Where did you get this!' he yelled. 'It's mine, where did you find it?'

'Get back!' yelled Ryan, as he dragged Salvatore away from her.

Salvatore didn't fight him, he looked too confused. Jaz was still trying to process what he'd said. *It's mine.*

Before Jaz had time to process any of this, Ryan winked at her. *Go.* Instantly she spun and dropped, aiming a punch at earring man's groin. As he fell she grabbed his head and snapped it against her knee. Then she reached for the weapon in his hand, bending his wrist back in the process until he cried out and released it. With one last kick she knocked him out. Quickly she drew out her gun so she had a weapon in each hand. She aimed one at the man who'd rolled out the plastic and aimed the other at Jeff.

'Don't move.'

'Shit,' said Jeff. 'Who the fuck *are* you?'

Jaz gave him a small smile. While they had semi control of the situation, Jaz edged over to the body in the bag. 'Who was that?' she asked Jeff.

'Dalton. Tony thought he was a cop, now Tony's missing. As I said, we don't like loose ends.'

'I don't like loose ends either,' said Jaz. Panic flashed across Jeff's eyes.

Ryan cried out and went down. Jaz realised he'd been shot by a gun with a silencer. Using earring guy's gun, which also had a silencer, she aimed towards the direction of the faint sound by the tail of the plane and fired. She shot both men in the overalls and spun to face Jeff but he'd gone behind the generator. Salvatore had also run for cover.

'Are you okay?' said Jaz, running to Ryan. Blood was pouring from his shoulder, staining his shirt red.

'I'll live for now. Let's get out of here.'

Jaz helped him up and they ran towards the office. She glanced back with her gun raised, only to see the man who'd laid out the plastic. He fired his gun, Jaz felt the bullet pass closely.

'No!' yelled Salvatore, coming out of his hiding spot. His hands were up as he yelled at his man.

As they went through the door Jaz saw the confusion on Salvatore's man, his gun still aimed but not firing. The last thing she saw was her father's necklace hanging from Salvatore's hands. Damn. She wanted it back.

'Jaz, get the door,' said Ryan snapping her into action.

No sooner had they got outside than they ran into Taylor and Anna running towards them.

'What are you guys doing here?' said Ryan.

'Saving your arse, by the looks,' said Taylor. He took Ryan's gun, and trained it on the door of the plane hangar while Anna took the two Jaz had and did the same, giving them cover while Jaz helped Ryan to Pax's little red car.

'Is Pax here?' asked Jaz.

'No, we just borrowed his car. Mustang is a bit too memorable,' said Tay. His eyes remained on the door as he stepped back to the car. As soon as Jaz and Ryan were in, Tay and Anna jumped in the car, Jaz in the back with Ryan and Tay driving with Anna in the front.

'Let's get the fuck out of here,' said Tay as he revved the car and drove off. The whole time Anna had been watching the building, watching for Salvatore's men to come running, but none did. No one tried to shoot the car or even get the number plates. Maybe they didn't want to cause a scene, bring attention to Sal's building?

The scent of sickly metallic blood filled the small car and Jaz checked Ryan's colour. He wasn't too pale, yet.

Jaz ripped off her shirt and held it against the bullet hole in Ryan's shoulder before she fished out the car keys from her pocket and threw them to Anna. 'Can you follow us in our car? It's the Commodore parked up ahead.'

Tay stopped so Anna could get out. She left the guns in Pax's car.

'Where to?' said Jaz as she leaned against Ryan, trying to stop the flow of blood. His eyes dropped over her black bra and a smiled tugged on the corners of his mouth. 'You can't be in that much pain,' she whispered.

He looked back up into her eyes. 'You're taking my mind off it. Was that intentional?' he said. Tay hit a bump in the road, causing Ryan to grimace.

'Sorry mate,' called out Tay. 'Where to? Your place?'

'Yep. Jaz, can you call Tilly?'

Jaz used Taylor's phone and dialled the number Ryan called out.

'Hello?' Tilly's voice was unsure of the unknown number.

'Tilly, your pet bird has broken its wing. You better come quick.' Jaz repeated what Ryan said to say.

'Oh no. I'll be right there.'

That was all he said before hanging up. 'He's on his way.'

Ryan nodded. 'Tilly's good with bullets.'

Jaz threw Tay's phone in the front and shifted on the seat so she had a better press on his wound. She hoped it wasn't anything major. There was a lot of blood, the smell of it filling the small car and making her feel like she was sucking on metal pieces.

'Is he going to be all right? What happened in there?' asked Tay from the front.

'For the moment, I think so. Salvatore got away,' said Jaz. But she was too focused on Ryan to say any more. She stroked his face, the stubble prickling her fingers.

He reached up and covered her hand. 'Don't look so worried. I'll be fine. It's just a bullet.'

Only Ryan would see it like that.

'What about you?' he asked at a whisper. 'Did Salvatore say what I thought he said?'

Jaz closed her eyes for a moment, trying to see Salvatore in her mind.

'I don't know what that was all about, Ryan.' Or the part where Salvatore let her go. Why would he do that? Was that medallion really his? Maybe he was mistaken? It was all a bit weird. Jaz was just thankful that they'd come out of that place alive. Part of her had been worried that the black plastic was going to be her final resting place. Jaz shivered at the thought.

Ryan squeezed her hand.

'It'll all be okay, Jaz. Don't worry.' He kissed her hand and then rested his head on the back of the seat.

Even with Ryan's blood all over her hands and bits of it smeared across her chest, she knew he'd survive this. With all the scars on his body, this was just a scratch. Another day in the playground. She leaned over and kissed him. 'I know. After all, we have the phoenix on our side.'

Jaz kept her pressure on his wound as Ryan smiled and his dark iron-stone eyes sparkled flecks of life. One little bullet wouldn't knock down this soldier.

He winked at her. 'That we do, Jaz. My own little phoenix.'

Next in the MTG Agency series

THE CRESCENDO

From one of Australia's Queens of Romance comes the debut in a brand new YA series about secrets, strengths, and what lies beneath the surface.

Jaz finds her life turned upside down by a shocking revelation, the death of a friend and the news that the love of her life has gone MIA on his huge undercover mission. All this, while sitting exams and finishing school. With the help of her friends she will risk her own life to save Ryan, even if it means walking on the devil's side and dealing with the bad guys she's been trying to take down.